Linda Gillard lives and writes on the Isle of Skye, off the north-west coast of Scotland. She is a former actress, teacher and freelance journalist.

Her novel *Star Gazing* was shortlisted for the Robin Jenkins Literary Award and the Romantic Novel of the Year 2009.

For more information log on to www.lindagillard.co.uk

D0311025

Also by Linda Gillard

Emotional Geology
A Lifetime Burning

Star Gazing

Linda Gillard

piatkus

PIATKUS

First published in Great Britain in 2008 by Piatkus Books
This paperback edition published in 2008 by Piatkus Books
Reprinted 2009, 2010

A CIP catalogue record for this book
is available from the British Library.

ISBN 978-0-7499-3897-0

Typeset by Phoenix Photosetting, Chatham, Kent
www.phoenixphotosetting.co.uk
Printed and bound by Clays Ltd, Bungay, Suffolk

Papers used by Piatkus are natural, renewable and
recyclable products sourced from well-managed forests and certified
in accordance with the rules of the Forest Stewardship Council.

 Mixed Sources
Product group from well-managed
forests and other controlled sources
FSC www.fsc.org Cert no. SGS-COC-004081
© 1996 Forest Stewardship Council

Piatkus
An imprint of
Little, Brown Book Group
100 Victoria Embankment
London EC4Y 0DY

An Hachette UK Company
www.hachette.co.uk

www.piatkus.co.uk

For my father
Charles Frederick Gillard
(1925–2005)

As a man is, so he sees.
William Blake

ACKNOWLEDGEMENTS

I would like to thank the following people for their help and support in writing this book:

Tina Betts, Liz Broomfield, Dr Lyn Cresswell, Adrienne Dines, Margaret Gillard, Amy Glover, Philip Glover, Ralph Glover, Nicky Grantham, Gillian Green, Linda Henderson and Erica Munro.

Winter 2006

Chapter One

Marianne

This is not a ghost story. Not really. But it was Christmas and I did feel as if I'd seen a ghost. Or rather *heard* a ghost. Except that you don't hear ghosts, do you? Clanking chains, hideous moans perhaps, but on the whole people see ghosts, or so I understand. It's an experience I've been spared.

But I thought I'd heard one.

The woman takes care getting out of the taxi, reaches inside and removes a briefcase and carrier bag. She sets them carefully on the kerb and fumbles in a capacious handbag for her purse.

As the taxi pulls away she turns to face the grey Georgian terrace, elegantly anonymous, typical of many in Edinburgh. Dressed in a full-length woollen coat and dashing velvet hat, the woman extends a booted toe and places it, deliberately, on a manhole cover. She bends and picks up her bags, straightens, pauses for a moment, then without looking to left or right, she strides across the pavement towards the steps leading up to a front door. A keen-eared observer might hear her counting under her breath.

Before she has taken four paces there is a hiss of braking wheels and the sound of a bicycle skidding on pavement, followed by an angry adolescent shout.

'*Jesus*! Didn't you see me coming? Are you blind or what?'

Shaken, the woman turns to face the cyclist. As she adjusts

her hat, knocked askew, her hands are unsteady but her voice is firm. 'Yes. As a matter of fact, I am.'

Marianne

That's right, I'm blind.

I'll just give you a moment or two to adjust your prejudices.

But, I hear you ask, shouldn't I have been escorted by a Golden Labrador? Or waving a white stick? At the very least, shouldn't I have been wearing enormous dark glasses, as favoured by Roy Orbison and Ray Charles?

I know, I know – it really was my own stupid fault for wandering about looking *normal*. (Well, I'm told I do. How would I know?)

'I *am* blind and *you* have no right to be cycling on the pavement. If you have a bell, might I suggest you try using it in future?'

But the cyclist is already gone. She bends to pick up the bag she dropped, feels the shifting of broken glass, hears the steady drip of liquid onto the pavement. With sinking heart she mounts the steps and delves into her handbag again for her door key. The loss of the Burgundy is a disaster – how will they cook *boeuf bourguignonne* without it? And the meringue nests will be as shattered as her nerves. Encountering the cold metal of her phone, she wonders whether to ring her sister with a last-minute shopping-list.

The door key falls from her chilled fingers. She gasps, straining her ears to locate the direction of the small sound it makes as it hits the ground. She bends, sweeps the stone with bare hands, cursing the cyclist, Christmas and most particularly her blindness. Something wet and weightless lands on the back of her hands.

Snow ...

She feels the prickle of tears, blinks rapidly and sweeps the doorstep again, then plunges her hand into the evergreen foliage of a potted plant, shaking it, listening for the clink of a falling key.

Silence.

She is considering what comfort might be derived from

sitting on the steps and bursting into tears when she hears footsteps approach, then come to a halt. She registers a habitual flutter of apprehension. The footsteps are male.

'Can I help?' A man's voice, not local, nor one that she knows. Or ...?

'I've dropped my door key and I can't find it. I'm blind.'

She hears the sound of change jingling in pockets as he mounts the steps quickly. After a moment he says, 'It's fallen onto the basement stair ... Here you are.' He takes her chilled hand, places the key in her palm and murmurs, '*Che gelida manina* ...'

'Yes, I've lost my gloves too. Must have dropped them somewhere.'

'No, they're dangling from your coat pocket.'

'Are they?' She feels for the gloves. 'Thank you. And thank you for finding my key.'

'No bother. I hate to tell you this, but your shopping seems to be bleeding.'

'It's red wine. I dropped it. It's been one of those days.' She opens her handbag and pushes the gloves inside. 'Do you like opera? Or do you just break out in Italian every so often?'

'I'm a sucker for Puccini.'

She considers. 'Musically very appealing, but ideologically unsound, I always think. Women as passive victims of glamorous men. Rather repellent in the twenty-first century.'

'I hadn't really thought about it like that.'

'You wouldn't. You're a man.'

'A chromosomal accident. I'm sorry.'

She laughs. 'No, *I'm* sorry. For being so rude. Forgive me – I was rather shaken, losing my key. Cross with myself and taking it out on you. Hardly fair. I keep my key on a chain that I put round my wrist so I *can't* drop it, but I was in a hurry and I didn't bother ... Are you from Skye?'

He pauses a moment before answering. 'Aye. Well, I was brought up there. I was born on Harris. But my parents hankered after bright lights and the big city. So they moved to Portree.' She laughs again. 'I take it you know Portree?'

'Only by reputation. I knew a Skye man ... A *Sgiathanach*.'

'*Sgiathanaich* are loyal. We tend to go back.'

5

'Do you?'

'Aye, when I can. It's a great place. As long as you don't crave excitement.'

'Your parents were disappointed then?'

'Och no, they died happy in their beds.' She senses a smile. 'Of culture shock.'

'Well, there are worse ways to die.'

'Aye. A lot worse.'

'Thanks for your help.'

'No bother. Will you manage with the broken glass?'

'Oh, yes, my sister will deal with it, after she's given me a thorough scolding for being so damned independent. I'll just leave the bag on the doorstep. The food's ruined anyway.'

'Well, if you're sure there's nothing more I can do?'

'Thanks, I'll be fine now.'

She hears his feet on the steps again. He calls up, his voice more distant now. 'I'll run into you at the opera, maybe? I presume *Turandot* meets your stringent feminist criteria?'

'Ah, now *she's* a girl after my own heart. Chews men up and spits them out. And if they can't guess the riddles – off with their head!'

'But the prince confounds her. With his name.'

'Yes. Puccini's misogyny always triumphs in the end.'

'You're getting cold. Away indoors. And wipe your feet – you're standing in a pool of red wine.'

'It was very nearly a pool of tears.'

'I'll see you around, maybe.'

'Well, you might see *me*, but I definitely won't see you. Goodbye.'

Marianne

Has it ever struck you how language favours the sighted? (Of course not, because you can see.) I don't just have a problem seeing, I have a problem *talking*, trying to find words and phrases appropriate to my experience. Just listen to how people go on: *Oh, I see what you mean ... Now look here ... The way I see it ... Reading between the lines ... I didn't see that coming! ... It depends on your point of view ...*

6

You get the picture?
I, of course, don't.

People often ask me why I go to the opera when I can't see the singers act, I can't see the set or costumes and I can't see any lighting effects. Why don't I just stay home and listen to a CD – surely it's the same? I ask them if they think it's the same looking at a reproduction of Van Gogh's *Starry Night* as standing in front of the actual painting? (I wouldn't know, of course, but I do know people who have stood before that canvas and wept.)

I tell sceptics and doubters that I go to the opera because opera pours a vision of a wider world into my ears in a way that no other art form that I can access does. Sculpture and textiles, on the rare occasion I'm permitted to touch them, excite me. Plays, novels and poems move, entertain and educate me, but they don't rock me to my foundations and make me *see*. I can read Tolstoy's account of the French retreat from Moscow, either in Braille or as an audio-book, but I have never seen a city. Or snow. I've never seen a man, let alone an army. Tolstoy uses a visual language that I can read, haltingly. It's not my mother tongue.

But music I can 'read' much more easily. In fact, I don't need to read it at all. When I hear music it goes directly to my heart, it pierces my soul and stirs me with nameless emotions, countless ideas and aural pictures. Nowhere am I more conscious of this than at the opera. At times I am so shaken by what I hear, by what I feel, I wonder if my constitution could actually cope with the addition of a visual component.

I lied to the man on my doorstep about my dislike of Puccini's victim-heroines, or rather I told him a half-truth. What I cannot bear is their *pain*, and when their suffering seems random, point-less – as Tosca's, Mimi's and Butterfly's does – I think what I feel, at some deep level, is angry. And I don't want to feel angry, especially not in the opera house.

I have far too much to be angry about.

Anger is a place I don't go, a colour I never wear.

I have two wardrobes in my large bedroom. One of them contains black clothes and the other contains cream and ivory. (These

7

adjectives are labels that my elder sister Louisa has allocated for me. For all I know she could be dressing me in sky-blue pink, as our mother used to say, a colour no more difficult for me to imagine than black or ivory.)

Wearing coloured clothes would be too complicated for me. If I wish to look smart for work or for my limited social life, and if I wish to be independent, I have to have clothes that will match or blend. Louisa and I thought this through carefully. She rejected navy blue because there are apparently many different types of navy. (She also said she couldn't bear to look at me in navy since this was the colour we wore for years as school uniform.) Louisa said black and cream would co-ordinate if I got confused and put an item of clothing away in the wrong wardrobe.

Light-coloured clothes are hazardous of course. They show stains and dirt. Eating when you're blind is fraught with difficulties, so I spend a fortune on dry-cleaning. I rely on Lou to tell me when it needs to be done, but at least I don't ever have to stand in front of a mirror agonising over what to wear. It's either a cream day or a black day. Occasionally Lou prevails upon me to wear a brightly coloured scarf or pashmina to ring the changes. She says my eyes are an attractive opal blue and certain colours bring it out.

I hope the colour is more attractive than the word. 'Opal' is an ugly-sounding word, like all words for which there is no rhyme, such as 'pint' and 'orange'. Perhaps they aren't ugly sounds, merely unique, and therefore odd. When you cannot see what words describe, you tend to focus on the words themselves. Words are a form of music and I suppose I hear them differently from the sighted. Louisa describes my opal eyes in breathless tones, as if she is paying me a huge compliment based, I gather, on a comparison with the precious stone, which she tells me is quite spectacular. I just hear an ugly, faintly ridiculous word.

I don't wear colours.

I don't do anger.

Nor, I'm afraid, love. Not any more.

A monochrome existence, the sighted might say, but even that implies the presence of one colour. *You* might use the word 'colourless', but what colour do you then see? People seem to describe dull things as 'colourless' when – apparently – they are grey or brown.

When we were young I asked Louisa if anything was *literally* colourless. She thought for a while and said 'glass'. Then she said 'rain'. I asked her if all water was colourless and she said, no, not from a distance. The sea or a lake is coloured because it reflects the sky, but she said individual drops of water were colourless; rain, as it fell through the air, was colourless.

It's a paradox. Things that look colourless to you are my artist's palette. Rain is the only thing apart from my sense of touch that gives me any sense of three dimensions. Water falling from the sky defines shape, size and quality by the sounds it makes when it lands.

Water colourless? Not for me.

Harvey was dead. Long dead. I hardly even thought about him any more, perhaps because I'd never had any visual memories of him – no photographs, no wedding video to watch to keep the memories alive, no children to remind me of him. To me Harvey was just a body and a voice. A very faint one now, but then he was always soft-spoken, perhaps to compensate for the fact that some people believe blindness affects the ears as well as the eyes, so they raise their voice when speaking to you. Harvey did-n't do that. He knew how sensitive my hearing was, how I saw with my ears.

But Harvey died.

I didn't see *that* coming either.

I ran into him again. Not Harvey, the man from Skye. At the theatre. The opera, in fact. During the interval of *Die Walküre* Louisa bought us both drinks, settled me at a table and went off to join the queue in the Ladies. She left me stewing in a soup of sound, the kind of aural overload that I find distressing: the quack of elderly ladies; the clatter of teaspoons and the chink of sturdy cups; the murmur of male voices breathing urgently into their mobiles; English women sounding like neighing horses; Scotsmen scouring the ear with aural Brillo pads. I'd already taken a hammering from Wagner and was thinking of abandoning the two G&Ts and joining Louisa in the

Ladies when a male voice asked me if a chair was taken. I recognised him immediately. I was about to reply but by then he'd recognised me and was sitting down, asking me what I thought of the singing.

His voice was so similar. Like toffee. Smooth and pitched low. But this voice didn't have the drop of vanilla, the hint of a drawl that Harvey had inherited from his Canadian mother. This voice was more like a good dark chocolate, the kind that's succulent, almost fruity, but with a hint of bitterness. He hit his Highland consonants with the same satisfying 'click' that good chocolate makes when you snap it into pieces. (The blind are as fetishistic about voices as the sighted are about appearances, so allow me, if you will, to describe this man's voice as chocolate. *Serious* chocolate. Green & Black's, not Cadbury's.)

When I'd met him on my doorstep I knew immediately it wasn't Harvey's voice. In any case, Harvey was dead. (I may be blind but I'm not stupid.) When I heard that voice for the second time, I knew at once who it was, but again I remembered ... So I was already thinking about Harvey when he told me his name.

'Harvey.'

'I beg your pardon?'

'My name's Harvey. Keir Harvey.'

'Did you say Hardy?'

'*Harvey*. Keir Hardie was the founder of the Labour Party.'

'I'm aware of that. He's also dead.'

'Aye, but his spirit lives on.'

'In you?'

'Not that I'm aware. It could have taken up residence without my knowing, I suppose.'

'Do you have socialist leanings?'

'Practically toppling over.'

'Well, that might account for it. If you were possessed, I mean.'

'Do I strike you as possessed?'

'No ... Self-possessed, perhaps.'

'That's an odd expression. I mean, who else would own you?'

'Well, in your case, possibly Keir Hardie. Perhaps you should change your name.'

'It's *Harvey*. Like the rabbit.'

'What rabbit?'

'In the film. With James Stewart.'

'What film?'

'*Harvey*.'

'I've never seen it.'

'Have you ever seen any film?'

'No. I've been blind since birth.'

'Aye, well, you missed a good one there. Harvey is a six-foot rabbit that only James Stewart can see, which could have something to do with him being always out on the bevvy. But the rabbit is remarkably good company, for all he's invisible.'

'You didn't apologise.'

'What for?'

'When I told you I've been blind since birth, you didn't say, "I'm sorry" in a tragic voice. People usually do.'

'Well, it wasn't my fault, so I don't really see why I should apologise. Is it obligatory?'

'I think it's said more as an expression of compassion. Fellow feeling.'

'Embarassment, more like.'

'Yes, very probably. And you're not embarrassed.'

'Not by your inability to see. I'm deeply embarrassed that you mistook me for a dead socialist.'

'It could have been worse. I might have taken you for a six-foot rabbit.'

'How d'you know I'm not?'

The middle-aged woman who bustles through the crowded bar is small but determined. She adjusts a beaded pashmina draped round her plump shoulders and, with a well-aimed nudge of her elbow, squeezes her way through the press of suits and evening gowns to a low table where a woman sits nursing a gin and tonic, staring into space. The family resemblance is striking. Both women are fair, even-featured, blue-eyed. The extravagant blondeness of the woman on her feet owes much to the skills of her hairdresser. The fair hair of her seated sister, Marianne, is ashen, in places grey, drawn back into a simple chignon suggesting the pale, poised severity of a ballerina. Despite her greying hair she is evidently younger than the sister who now bears down on her, round face shining despite recent ministrations with a powder compact.

'Sorry I was so long, darling.' She bends, picks up a glass and takes a large swig. 'Oh, God – the ice has melted!' She puts the glass down again. 'There was an interminable queue in the Ladies and then I was accosted by a fan. She wanted to know when *Eldest Night and Chaos* was coming out. So I gave her a bookmark – I had some in my handbag. She was thrilled.'

Marianne doesn't look up but sighs. 'Really, Lou, the imbecility of your titles beggars belief.'

'That's Milton, I'll have you know.'

'I'm aware it's Milton. You, my dear, are not. Now be quiet a moment and let me introduce you to Mr Harvey.' She indicates a chair on her right with a wave of her hand. 'This is the kind man who retrieved my door key for me – when I lost it at Christmas, do you remember? Mr Harvey, this is my sister, Louisa Potter who, in another guise, is a famous author. Of very silly books.'

Louisa laughs nervously. 'Marianne, darling, there's nobody there! The chair's empty.'

'Is it?' Marianne's large eyes register no emotion but her head inclines slightly towards the adjacent chair as if she is listening. 'Well, he was here a moment ago. He was talking to me just before you arrived. How very odd!'

Louisa sinks into the empty chair beside her sister and thinks about kicking off her high-heeled shoes. She considers the worse discomfort of trying to get them back on again after the interval and decides to suffer. 'Did you have a nice chat? With your mystery man?'

'Yes, thanks.'

'I wonder why he slipped off like that without saying anything? Very bad-mannered.' Louisa swirls the remains of her ice cubes around in her glass. 'Perhaps he spotted someone he knew. Or maybe he was paged. A medical emergency. He might have been a surgeon.'

'For goodness sake, Lou, do you have to turn everything into a melodrama?'

'Well, *you* said it was odd, disappearing like that. I was trying to account for it.'

'He wasn't a surgeon anyway.'

'Oh? What does he do?'

'I've no idea, but he's not a surgeon. We shook hands. His was rough and decidedly workmanlike. I'd say he works outdoors.'

'Now who's inventing mysteries?'

'I'm not inventing, I'm *deducing*. From the evidence of my senses.'

'Damn, that's the bell for Act Two.' Louisa takes another mouthful of watery gin and struggles to her aching feet. 'Listen out for his voice. He might be sitting near us.'

'He won't be talking. He's here on his own.'

'Well, now I *am* intrigued. A man who works outdoors with his hands and goes to the opera *alone* ... I presume he's not elderly?'

'The handshake wasn't.'

'Young, then?'

'No, not young. Well, he didn't *sound* young. I can't always tell with voices.'

'Was he chatting you up?'

'No, of course not! Lou, you really are impossible.'

'Not impossible – just an incurable romantic and a diehard optimist.'

'A nauseating combination, if I may say so.'

'Thank you, sweetie. Love you too.'

As Marianne rises from her chair and reaches for her cane, Louisa turns the pages of her programme. 'How many more acts of this musical torture do we have to endure?'

'Two. Add philistinism to your long list of failings.'

'I know Wagner was supposed to be an orchestral genius – you've told me often enough – but I just feel sorry for the poor singers, rambling on and on in search of a tune. Give me Puccini any day.'

'You and Mr Harvey both.' Marianne extends her arm in the direction of her sister's voice. Louisa searches her inscrutable face, then takes her arm and links it affectionately with her own as they join the chattering throng moving slowly towards the auditorium. 'I'd really like to meet this man. A solitary, male opera-goer with labourer's hands, who loves Puccini. Fascinating! If you put him in a book no one would believe you.'

'I wasn't aware that credibility was a criterion in fiction these days. Especially not yours.'

'I write fantasy, darling,' Louisa replies amiably, patting her sister's hand. 'Anything goes. You don't have to believe it. You just *consume* it. Like chocolate.'

Chapter Two

Louisa

I feel I should explain. About my sister. Marianne.

What you need to understand about Marianne is that, despite the fact that she's blind – perhaps because she's blind – she's always had a very vivid imagination. So certain allowances have to be made, were always made: by our parents, doctors, teachers and so on. It was always understood that Marianne lived life in her head – well, what else could she do, poor thing? She was blind – and the boundaries between fantasy and reality were a little hazy for her at times.

She developed a philosophical bent at university. She used to say that, as sisters, we had more in common than genes. We both lived in imaginary worlds of our own creating. The only difference was, mine made me a lot of money. (That was a dig, of course. I didn't mind. Marianne's been through a lot. As I said, you have to make allowances and I do.)

It occurs to me, you don't know who I am, do you? So sorry – let me introduce myself! My name is Louisa Potter, but you'll know me as Waverley Ross. That's my nom de plume. What's in a name? An awful lot, apparently. My publishers didn't think Louisa Potter sounded either Scottish or sexy and I had to agree. As an English pupil in a Scottish school I was known as 'Potty Lou' and dreamed of marriage so I could change my prosaic surname to something glamorous like Traquair or Urquhart. A husband never materialised, so I settled for a nom de plume.

It's all part of the marketing. No matter how good a writer you are, without a good marketing strategy you're dead in the water. So I was advised by those in the know to become 'Waverley Ross'. Sounds Scottish, doesn't it? And strong. It's supposed to sound sexy as well, although I always think of Edinburgh railway station when I hear the word 'Waverley', but I gather my hordes of American fans, bless them, conjure up swirling mists and Sir Walter Scott.

I'm an author – a very successful one – of vampire romance. Upmarket vampire romance, I hasten to add. It's a big genre and one needs to be aware of the nuances. There's an awful lot of tat out there. Sick tat too. I don't write that. I write Scottish Gothic vampire romance. (Hence my nom de plume.) I did a history degree in Edinburgh, fell in love with the city and nineteenth-century Scottish literature, and my writing career grew out of my passions.

All my books are set in Edinburgh. They're pretty formulaic, I admit, but that's what people like. You know where you are with a Waverley Ross. In Edinburgh, doing battle with the powers of darkness, righting wrongs, fending off over-sexed vampires of both genders and all sexual proclivities.

I do quite a lot of sex but nothing distasteful. (In my books, I mean.) No rape and definitely no S&M. My books are very traditional – just love stories really – but the men have to be supernatural because frankly, a good hero is hard to come by these days. It's difficult finding an excuse to create a tall, dark and handsome hero who dresses in flamboyant clothes and behaves in an unpredictable but masterful way. (And, believe me, that is what women want. Well, it's what they want in fiction. My gay following too. They're all soppy romantics at heart.)

I began my writing career writing Regency romances (don't knock it – so did Joanna Trollope) but they didn't sell and I wasn't getting anywhere. Then it occurred to me that everyone was fed up to the back teeth with political correctness. The last thing women wanted to read about was men behaving like something out of Jane Austen. I realised what we actually wanted was bad boys. But not real bad boys. Vampires. Sexy vampires who were – to a man – tall, dark and handsome. (I do throw in the occasional blond, just to ring the changes. I don't think you can do anything with redheads but my assistant, Garth, says I should be more open-minded.)

Being supernatural, my vampires have extraordinary powers and physical attributes, plus an uncanny facility for shedding their clothes at key dramatic moments. To be honest, this last trait is a bit difficult to make convincing because, as any Scot will tell you, it's extremely cold and damp in Auld Reekie, but my thesis (this actually came to me when I had my first hot flush) is that vampires are hot-blooded creatures, immune to cold, hunger, thirst and pain. (But not, of course, sexual frustration.)

Anyway, I digress. My books (see www.waverleyross.com) have enabled me to live with my sister in a certain degree of luxury in a desirable part of Edinburgh. Marianne may scoff at my work – she refers to my characters as my 'imaginary friends' – but she's happy enough to enjoy what my labours buy. I don't begrudge her a penny. She's all the family I have, she's excellent company (if you have a thick skin) and she keeps the flat ticking over when I'm away on promotional tours. She works part-time answering the phone for a blind charity, but she doesn't need to. She does it to assert her independence. I understand that. I'm sure I'd feel exactly the same in her position.

So we rub along together quite nicely, a couple of old spinsters becoming increasingly eccentric with the passing of the years. I said to Marianne the other day, 'I'm over fifty – I need to slow down,' and she said, 'I'm nearly fifty – I need to speed up.' She was exaggerating, of course. At forty-five Marianne is six years younger than me. It seemed a big gap when we were children but I think that was a lot to do with her blindness. I'd already started school when she was born, so Marianne was always something of a solitary child, isolated by her age and her handicap. That's probably why she developed such a vivid imagination. She had imaginary friends too! Hers never made her any money but I'm sure, in their way, they were a great comfort to her.

Heaven knows, there have been times when poor Marianne has needed comfort.

Marianne

One of my favourite walks in all seasons is Edinburgh's Royal

17

Botanic Garden, known fondly to all as the Botanics. I can find my way there on my own. I've memorised the route as a sequence of numbers – the paces I take before turning a corner or crossing a road. There are landmarks that I navigate by – a manhole cover, a postbox, a pedestrian crossing. I usually take my cane because people leave things on the pavement that I don't expect to be there: rubbish bins, bicycles and the like. But these unexpected obstacles aside, I can walk confidently to the Botanics, enjoying the scents and sounds along my route, anticipating the blissful moment when I can walk through the gates and leave the traffic behind.

I love the garden in all seasons. I especially love it when it rains. I like to shelter under the trees when they're in full leaf and listen to the patter of rain as it forms a kind of sound-sculpture for me, defining the size and shape of a tree, giving me an aural sense of scale, of distance. I have no concept of landscape and only a vague understanding of what distance must look like. I experience distance mainly as the difference between loud and soft, but sound quality isn't always related to distance. A man's voice might be very soft, but he could be lying beside you. Volume is not a true guide.

Music gives me some inkling of landscape. The sheer scale of orchestral music, the volume and the detail, can put me in touch with something much bigger than myself, take me beyond my personal boundaries, the world that I experience with my fingertips or my cane. Music tells me there is a wider world and what it might be like.

I know it exists, of course. I listen to the news; I did geography at school; I read books about faraway places just like any other armchair traveller, and Louisa and I have visited some of them. But for me the Earth is a conceit, something I'm told exists but cannot see – like Pluto or Neptune for you. Astronomers deduced that Neptune must exist long before they devised telescopes powerful enough to view it. They thought it must be there because something was affecting the orbits of the other planets. There was a gap in the galaxy where a planet ought to be and they trusted that there was. It was an act of faith: faith in mathematics and physics.

There is a gap in my life where the Earth ought to be. I have to take its existence on trust. I cannot see or feel the Earth, I am merely informed by my senses of the minutiae of its being. It's much the same for you, but sight allows you to appreciate what others see, through a camera lens, through telescopes, from space-ships. Thanks to this second-hand sight, your world is much, much bigger than mine can ever be.

But when I listen to an orchestra play a symphony, I have a sense of what it might be like to contemplate a mountain range, a fast-flowing river, the skyline of a city. Music helps me see. So does rain. Rain helps me see things that my fingers can't encompass, like a tree or a glasshouse. That's where you'll find me when it rains. In the Botanics. In one of the glasshouses, or sheltering under one of my favourite trees.

But I dislike winter. Not for all the usual reasons – dreary weather, short days. What are those to me? I don't like winter because there are no leaves left on the trees, no leaves to make music with the rain. My trees fall silent. Once a blanket of snow has fallen, my whole world becomes muffled, indistinct. (You would say *blurred* – how I imagine the world looks to the myopic.) There are no dead leaves crackling underfoot, few birds sing and I'm deprived of many of my markers, like manhole covers, some-times even the kerb. My walk to the Botanics becomes a perilous undertaking.

I hate the silent world of winter because it makes me *feel* blind. I can experience the cold and wetness of snow, but I can never have a sense of a wintry landscape except as an almost silent world, bereft of the usual sounds that are its distinguishing features. In the depths of winter I suffer from depression, brought on by a kind of aural blankness. Those of you who suffer from Seasonal Affective Disorder will have some idea what I mean. You miss light, I miss sound. My little world with its modest horizons is transformed temporarily into one I don't recognise, and every single winter this comes as a dreadful shock.

Louisa says this is more or less what it's like for the sighted. The known world is transformed overnight, obscured by snow, and therein lies the thrill: you get out of bed one morning, look out the window and your world has turned white. I don't need to look. I

19

can *hear* what has happened. The silence of snow is claustrophobic for me. Unsettling. I lose the familiar sounds that I associate with feeling safe and confident. Without those sounds I'm disorientated. I have to re-navigate, re-negotiate my life.

I have no understanding of colour, so I don't know what colour white is. But if silence were a colour, I think it would be white.

I knew I was being watched. To begin with I sensed it, but dismissed the feeling, then I became certain. It's a feeling I have at the back of my head, a feeling that makes my hair stand on end and my shoulders hunch, as if I'm bracing myself for fight or flight. I suppose it must be a remnant of an animal instinct that lies dormant in one of the areas of the brain for which scientists have so far found no use. I don't know whether this sense is likely to be more developed in the blind or whether we are just more paranoid. (The latter seems more likely, especially if you are a woman.)

One of the reasons I don't use my cane as much as I should is because I don't like to advertise to the world that I'm blind. I'm vulnerable enough on the streets as a woman without letting criminals and perverts of all denominations know that I'm easy prey. I try to look and behave as if I'm sighted. What I actually look, I suspect, is drunk. I trip and stumble, touch railings and walls, as if I'm unsteady on my feet, but it probably draws the attention less than a white stick.

But despite my precautions, my attempts at invisibility, my dressing in black, my intention of blending in with the leafless skeletons of trees, someone had noticed me.

And was watching.

Seated on a wooden bench Marianne turns her head slowly in the direction of the approaching footsteps. She thinks of getting to her feet and walking briskly in the opposite direction but wonders if an element of chase might be exactly what the stalker would like – if indeed there is a stalker. In any case she finds it difficult to walk quickly, even with her cane. Instead she reaches into her bag for her personal alarm, registering briefly that if she uses it, she'll empty the garden of birds, animals and possibly startled, law-abiding humans.

A cold gust of wind lifts a wisp of hair and blows it across her face. *Hamamelis*. Witch hazel ... And something else, another scent. But it's wrong. Out of season. A memory surfaces and seconds later she places it.

'Is that you, Mr Harvey?'

Silence and stillness.

Then, 'I thought you were supposed to be *blind*? Are you working some kind of benefit fraud?'

'I *am* blind.'

'And a seer? Or just a mind-reader?'

'What, might I ask, are *you*? A stalker? You've been watching me, haven't you?'

'Only because I was trying to work out if it *was* you, then whether you'd mind being disturbed. You seemed deep in thought.'

'I was listening.'

'To the birds?'

'To the trees.'

He sits beside her. 'How did you know it was me?'

'Smell. I was down-wind of you.'

'*Smell*? I showered this morning. Very thoroughly.'

'I didn't mean a bad smell. It's probably your cologne.'

'I don't wear any.'

'Shampoo, then. Or maybe it's just your natural smell. My nose is very sensitive. I recognise people by voice and smell. I'm pretty good at it, but it's not a lot of help with judging character. It's harder for the blind, meeting new people. You have to be ... cautious. You never know what you're getting.'

'It's always a blind date.'

'Exactly. You *aren't* a six-foot rabbit, are you?'

'No.'

'Well, that's a relief.'

'I'm six foot two.'

'And furry?'

'Only in the usual places.'

'I could hear you were tall.'

She hears a sound pitched somewhere between laughter and astonishment. '*How*?'

21

'Where your voice comes from. You must get bored looking at the tops of people's heads.'

'Not as bored as they must get looking up my nostrils.'

'Something else I'm spared. So just how furry are you?'

'Not very. Ears normal length too. Well, for a rabbit ... What did you smell? I'm fascinated.'

'Oh, hawthorn blossom, I think.'

'You're kidding me?'

'No. It's a good masculine smell. Sharp. Exotic, in an understated way.' She lifts her head and he watches her profile as her delicate nostrils flare, like an animal scenting danger. 'I think it's you, not the shampoo. I can smell a soapy, chemical scent on top of the hawthorn. What were you photographing? Not me, I hope.'

'How did you –? Och, you heard the shutter! I was photographing trees.'

'Why?'

'I compare what I see this year with what I saw this time last year. I make notes, keep a record. I'm tracking climate change.'

'Is that your job?'

'No, just an interest of mine.'

'Do you live in Edinburgh?'

'No. But I sometimes work here. And Aberdeen. Sometimes abroad.'

'Where's home?'

'Wherever I happen to be.'

'I get the impression you don't like personal questions.'

'Do you?'

'Not particularly.'

'Another thing we have in common.'

'Apart from a love of opera, you mean?'

'Aye, and a love of trees.'

'How do you know I love trees?'

'Folk who sit here on a cold winter's day must love trees. There's little else to look –' He pauses. 'Ah.'

'You fell into the trap. Don't worry. You lasted longer than most before making your *faux pas*.'

'So was I wrong? About you and trees?'

22

'No. I do love trees.'

'Even though you can't see them?'

'I can *hear* them. You can hear the bare branches tapping against each other in the breeze. Listen! ... It sounds like me, feeling my way along the pavement with my cane. I listen to trees. And I feel them.'

'Do you?'

'Yes. I lay my hands on them. Feel the texture of their bark and leaves, try to gauge their girth.'

'You touch wood.'

'Yes, I touch wood. Primitive, isn't it? But very satisfying. Are you superstitious, Mr Harvey?'

'Keir. Aye, I suppose so. I'm from the islands. A healthy respect for the supernatural goes with the territory.'

'Do you believe in an afterlife?'

'No.'

'Neither do I. I sometimes wish I did, but I don't. I think this is it, don't you? We get one crack at life and have to make the best of it.'

After a moment he says, 'You lost someone.'

It's not a question and she is thrown momentarily. 'What makes you say that?'

'Folk talk like that when they've been through the fire. Death concentrates the mind.'

'Yes, it certainly does. That's about all that can be said for it.'

The conversation languishes and she shivers. He looks down at her ungloved hands. 'You're not married?'

'I was. Many years ago.'

'Divorced?'

'Widowed.'

'I'm sorry. You must have been quite young.'

'Twenty-seven. My husband was only thirty-three.'

'What happened?'

'I don't talk about it.'

They are silent for a long time, then the peace of the garden is shattered by an ambulance siren approaching, then receding. She hears him change his position on the bench, then clear his throat.

23

'Would you prefer to be on your own? I was gate-crashing anyway and I seem to have effectively killed the conversation.'

'Oh, you're still there, are you? I thought you might have vanished again, like you did at the opera. You know, I blithely introduced you to my sister, then felt a complete fool.'

'I'm sorry. I saw someone. Someone who shouldn't have been there. Someone I really didn't want to see ... But that's no excuse. My behaviour was very rude. Civility is not exactly my strong suit. As you may have noticed. Would you like me to vanish now?'

'No. I mean, if you *want* to leave –'

'I don't.'

'Then stay. I'm enjoying your company – though you might think I have a funny way of showing it. I sit here for hours on my own while my sister writes. If you can call what she does writing. I think monkeys on typewriters might come up with similar stuff. *Blind* monkeys. But it pays the bills, so I mustn't sneer. What do you do?'

'I'm a geophysicist. I work in oil and gas exploration.'

Standing abruptly, she says, 'You know, it's really too cold to sit here. We'll catch our deaths. I need a coffee. Better still, a hot chocolate.' She puts a hand up to her eyes, masking them, but not before he has seen tears.

'Are you OK? What did I say? I've upset you.'

'No, it wasn't you, I just wasn't expecting ...' She turns away, her head bowed.

He senses the muscles bunched in her shoulders, knows she would run if she could. Extending an arm he gently lifts the chilled fingers of one of her hands. He places them between his palms and she feels warmth radiating from his rough skin, restoring the circulation. 'Come on, let's get some coffee. Will you take my arm?'

She looks up but doesn't face him. 'My husband was an oil man too ... He died. In 1988. The sixth of July.'

She hears the faint whistle of breath between his teeth. 'Piper Alpha?'

'Yes.'

'Marianne, I'm sorry.'

24

'That's why I don't talk about being widowed. What, in God's name, is there to say? Maybe I'll talk about it one day, when I've come to terms with it. Give me another fifty years or so and I might be able to take a more philosophical view. But for now, I'm still angry. Incandescently angry.'

Marianne

It was – still is – the world's worst-ever offshore disaster. The flames could be seen for sixty miles.

One hundred and sixty-five oil workers died in an inferno when the Piper Alpha oil rig exploded. The sixty-one men who survived did so by leaping hundreds of feet into the sea, despite serious injuries and the rubber in their survival suits melting in the heat. Two heroic crewmen died attempting to rescue workers from the sea by boat. The bodies of thirty men – including my husband – were never recovered.

It was, apparently, an accident waiting to happen. The Cullen inquiry concluded that the management had been grossly deficient. The platform was in poor condition. There had been cutbacks in maintenance. Major refurbishment was taking place without production being interrupted. The day shift neglected to talk to the night shift and when the night shift activated equipment that had been partly decommissioned by the day shift, all hell was let loose. Literally.

It was a corporate massacre, but no one was ever prosecuted.

There's a memorial in Hazlehead Park in Aberdeen. It's surrounded by a rose garden. The names of the 167 victims are engraved on a granite plinth. I can read Harvey's name with my fingers, but I can't see it, of course. I can't see the rest of the memorial, can't even feel it. The three bronze figures of oilmen in working gear and survival suits are mounted above head height. To give visitors a good view, I suppose.

I'm told the memorial – designed by a woman – is very moving. The three figures face north, east and west and their symbolic gestures and details of their appearance are a sort of coded statement about the oil industry, life, death, the universe and everything.

Sorry if I sound cynical. Bitter, even.

I am.

I spend some time every July sitting in the re-named, specially dedicated North Sea Rose Garden, facing a memorial I cannot see. (The roses smell nice.) Then I take a taxi to the seafront and sit on a bench facing out to sea in the direction of the marker buoy, 120 miles north-east of Aberdeen, which marks my husband's grave.

They tell me there's a light so the marker buoy is visible day and night, especially from Piper Bravo, the new platform that was built just 600 metres away from the site of Piper Alpha.

I can't see the marker. I can't see the sea. But I face them both every summer, believing they are there, believing that it matters *I* am there, trying to believe that somehow Harvey knows I'm there.

God, I *hate* July.

'I think outside Scotland people have practically forgotten. Well, it's not the sort of thing you want to remember, is it?' In the café Marianne sips hot chocolate, warming her hands on the mug. Keir hasn't spoken for some time, but she's heard him exhale, sensed him sink into the chair beside her, oppressed by her story. 'I didn't just lose my husband … I was pregnant.'

'Are you sure you want –'

'Oh, yes. The only people I ever talk to about it are people I don't know and will probably never meet again. You're performing a sort of service – if you can bear to listen.'

'Aye.' He touches her hand briefly, as if to reassure her of his physical presence. 'If you can bear to talk, I can bear to listen.'

'I was three months pregnant when Harvey died.'

'*Harvey*? Oh, Christ, I'm really sorry –'

'Don't worry about it. I like rabbits. The idea of them anyway. And I think I like you … First of all people told me the pregnancy was a blessing – I'd have something to remember him by. Then when I lost the baby, people said that was a blessing too. I could marry again, unencumbered. I used to wonder if I was on the receiving end of more than the usual amount of crass insensitivity, simply because I was blind. Some people do actually speak more slowly when they realise you're

26

blind. That's one of the reasons I go to such lengths to disguise my disability. To avoid being patronised.' She sighs and takes a mouthful of chocolate. 'Oh, let's change the subject. I'd rather talk about your furry ears. Do you have any other anatomical abnormalities?' He is silent. 'Keir, are you still there? I'd hate to think I've been unburdening myself to thin air.'

'I'm still here. Would you like me to describe myself to you?'

'Would you tell the truth?'

'I'd try. But I can't say I ever give my appearance a great deal of thought.'

'How refreshing. Something else we have in common.'

She hears him shift in his chair. 'I'm forty-two. Tall. A big guy, I suppose. Big bones and a fair bit of muscle. My hair's dark. Very short.'

'Eyes?'

'Two.'

'Both in working order, presumably?'

'Aye. One's blue and one's green.'

'*Really*?'

'Aye. They're different colours. Most folk don't notice. Or they notice there's something odd about my eyes, but can't work out what it is.'

'How extraordinary. Go on.'

'What more is there to say?'

'Well, would you say you're attractive?'

'Dogs seem to like me. And old ladies.'

'You're dodging the question.'

'How would I know?'

'Oh, come on! Men always know if women find them attractive.'

'I'm not sure that I do. Do *you*?'

'Do I what?'

'Find me attractive?'

'I can't see you.'

'You can't see anyone. It's a level playing field. Voice and smell, I believe you said.'

'And touch. But that comes later.'

27

'It needn't. You could read me with your hands and answer your own question.'

She is still for a moment, in apparent contemplation of her empty mug, then she turns towards him. Raising her hand towards his face, she finds it, then spreads her fingers, tracing the lines and planes of his brow, cheeks, nose and – lingering a moment – his mouth. She places both hands at the sides of his head and smiles as she feels short, spiky hair, sleek like an animal's coat. Leaning back in her seat she extends a palm until it meets his chest, registering a soft woollen jumper and hard shirt buttons beneath. She moves her hand across, feeling the undulation of muscle, until she finds his upper arm which she follows downwards, arriving at a large hand resting loosely on his thigh. She sketches his hand with her fingertips then moves them to his thigh where she lets them rest for a moment, exerting just the smallest pressure. Withdrawing her hand, she leans back.

'Thank you.'

'Well. That was ... stirring.'

'It was also very informative. I think you sold yourself a bit short in the physique department. Not so much a rabbit – more of a bear.'

'So did you answer your own question?'

'If the colour of your hair were a smell, what would it be?'

'Impressive diversionary tactic. A smell for a colour? That's a tough one. It's a rich brown. Goes a bit red in the summer.'

'Useless. I need smells.'

'Walnuts. Walnuts when you crack them open at Christmas.'

'And your eyes?'

'Which one? The blue or the green?'

'The blue.'

He is silent for a moment, then says, 'Juniper.'

'And the green?'

'The smell of ... autumn leaves. Decaying. That November smell. Smoky.'

'Lovely! You're good at this game – I can *see* you now. You aren't a rabbit at all. Or even a bear.' She extends a hand again and places her palm on his chest, leaving it there. 'You're a tree.'

Chapter Three

Louisa

I have to confess I didn't really notice any change in Marianne. I was very busy with the final stages of one book and the birth pangs of another. My GP says I should spend less time on creation and more on recreation. My publishers, on the other hand, seem quite happy for me to work myself to death, death being actually quite good for business as it stimulates interest in your backlist.

It had struck me that Marianne seemed more cheerful. She perhaps took more care with her appearance, even asking me to advise her about accessories. I should have twigged, I suppose, but she never mentioned anyone and I never saw her with anyone. It's not as if she ever brought anyone home and introduced us. (Admittedly she did try.)

Marianne had been single for so long that, frankly, I didn't ever think of her in relation to men. Not that she's unattractive, more uninterested. Her eyes are a little disconcerting of course, but they're large and an unusual blue. Her blonde hair is going grey now, but she has a reasonable figure, I suppose because she eats very little and walks a lot. I tend to sit at the PC, nibbling, so the less said about my figure, the better. I thought about hiring one of those hunky personal trainers but the truth is, I don't really have time to exercise and when I do stop work, I'm exhausted. I just want to put my feet up with a large G&T. And possibly a personal trainer.

Marianne eats sensibly, walks for miles and never misses an opportunity to tell me I'm a heart attack waiting to happen. I take no notice. I know it's just her rather warped way of saying she worries about me.

Perhaps I should have worried more about her. If I'd been less preoccupied with my own affairs I might have realised she'd found a new interest in life and I might have guessed what it was. But the irony was (I say irony because Marianne is, of course, blind), it appeared she was being courted by The Invisible Man.

Marianne

He said he supposed we'd run into each other again. I said I hoped so. It was one of those awkward conversations where no one actually issues an invitation. Well, what sort of invitation would seem appropriate? I'd told him half my life-story; he'd told me nothing of his, but he'd let me run my hands over him, as if he'd wanted to be known. I'd felt his lips, his eyelashes, even the muscles in his thigh, but I didn't know where he lived and clearly he didn't want me to know.

I asked for his mobile number but he said he was about to go away. I said, 'Anywhere nice?' He said, 'The Arctic Circle.' He didn't ask for my number. We stood on the pavement outside the Botanics, sheltering under my umbrella, the enforced intimacy at odds with the stilted conversation. Eventually I said, 'Well, you know where I live,' and he said, 'Aye, I do.'

I assumed I'd never see him again.

Two weeks later, when I'd almost forgotten about the conversation in the café (almost, but not quite), I received a padded envelope containing a cassette. Louisa sorts the post and she'd left mine on the hall table, as usual. I tore open the envelope, felt for a covering letter, but couldn't find one. Lou had gone out to the hairdresser's so I couldn't ask her to read the label on the tape. I took it into my bedroom, dropped it into the cassette player and pressed 'Play'.

After a few seconds I heard a wind howling. It was eerie: a constant whine, almost musical in the way it swooped up and down in pitch. Suddenly a man's voice was raised above it, almost shouting.

30

'Hello, Marianne. This is a postcard from Keir. I'm in Hammerfest, Norway, seven hundred miles inside the Arctic Circle, and it's bloody cold. Makes Edinburgh seem balmy. Hammerfest is the northernmost town in the world. They used to hunt polar bear but now the ice is receding, everyone's looking for Black Gold – including me. It's another Klondyke up here. Plenty of fights and not enough women to go round. Lots of reindeer though ... Guess what? I'm the tallest tree.'

There was a click followed by the sound of raucous singing and inebriated male laughter. The song came to a ragged, unmusical climax and was warmly applauded by the performers themselves. There was another click, followed by Keir's voice once again, sounding stern.

'PS. Do *not* attempt to get that rousing little ditty translated from the original Norwegian. I made some preliminary enquiries as to the subject matter and believe me, you're better off not knowing.' He paused, then added, 'Och, it was kind of catchy though, wasn't it? ... Cheers, Marianne.'

I don't know when I've been more touched or thrilled by a gift.

Not since Harvey used to send me taped love letters.

I carried the tape around in my handbag for a week. I don't know why, I just liked the thought of it being there, a piece of the Arctic living in my handbag, like Narnia inside the wardrobe. But then I had my bag snatched outside Jenners. (Needless to say, I was using my cane.)

I think I was possibly more upset about losing the cassette than the contents of my handbag. I hadn't made a copy or even played it to Louisa. I didn't think she'd really see the joke and I wasn't sure how I was going to explain the remark about the tree. But if I'm honest I have to admit I enjoyed the extraordinary luxury of a secret, something I didn't have to share with Lou, something I didn't have to experience *through* her.

At least, I think that's why I didn't tell her. Of course, it might have been because I didn't trust myself to keep girlish excitement out of my voice, or because I feared I might blush. Whichever way you look at it, it amounts to the same thing: I didn't want to share Keir.

*

I received a second postcard-cassette. It purported to be the sound of a glacier calving, dropping icebergs into the sea: creaks and groans, then a noise like a rifle shot, followed by a tremendous roar. It sounded like the execution and death throes of some Arctic leviathan.

Keir appeared to be on board ship. I could hear waves and a ship's hooter. He said very little other than to explain what was happening. At the end of the message he said, sounding quite impersonal, 'I'll be back in Edinburgh on the thirtieth. If you want to hear any travellers' tales, I'll be in the Botanics café at twelve on the thirty-first. Fortunately you'll be spared the holiday snaps.'

And that was it. Not even 'Cheers, Marianne' this time.

If I'd known what flight he was on, I might have gone to meet it, though I'm not sure how you meet someone at an airport if you're blind. Stand around looking conspicuous, I suppose. But there was no way of letting him know I'd be there. In any case, it would have been a ridiculous thing to do. For all I knew, he'd be met by a girlfriend or work colleagues. I chastised myself for thinking like a lovesick teenager and dropped the tape into the waste paper bin.

Later that day I went to retrieve it, but our cleaning lady had been and she'd emptied all the bins. I was livid – livid with the cleaner and livid with myself. Livid that I'd thrown the tape away, livid that I'd tried to retrieve it, but mostly livid that I was livid.

I recited the date and time of the proposed assignation, like a mantra, until I felt calm again.

Louisa

Marianne came home one day, all smiles, and said she'd invited someone to dinner: a Mr Harvey. She was irritated when I didn't know who she meant. She explained and I had to point out that I hadn't actually met Mr Harvey at the theatre – he'd disappeared before I arrived.

She said it didn't matter, she was sure we'd get on. I told her I didn't want to play gooseberry and offered to go out for the evening but she said it was 'nothing like that' and that I should invite a friend to make it a foursome. So I invited Garth.

Garth is a Goth. Yes, I know, the alliteration is wretched, but his poor mother wasn't to know. (In case you don't know about Goths, they dress in black satin with silver chains, wear black eyeliner and white foundation. And that's just the boys.) When Marianne first met Garth, she enquired where the noise of rattling chains was coming from, but apart from that, she had no problem with him, which might not have been the case if she'd been able to see him.

Garth is a sweet boy, one of my most devoted fans, and he maintains my website. He looks like one of the living dead but actually he has a very practical side. (Did you know that, according to a survey, Goths have more GCSEs than any other cult?) Garth is thorough and pays scrupulous attention to detail. He's doing a PhD on the history of witchcraft in Scotland but he also helps me with research. Despite what my critics say – foremost among them, Marianne – I don't just churn out books. A lot of work goes into them and a good deal of historical research. We can't all be Shakespeare, but we can be accurate. It's just a question of doing the necessary research. Or rather Garth doing the necessary research. I don't really have time – too busy on the creative side. It's a completely different part of the brain and I don't think you can just shuttle back and forth from one to the other without suffering some sort of cerebral jetlag.

We took a lot of trouble over the menu for Mr Harvey. Marianne would have everything just so, but that wasn't unusual. I didn't set any particular store by that. I was looking forward to a delicious meal and had starved myself in anticipation, so I wasn't best pleased when he was late. Garth always looked malnourished and I couldn't tell whether his subdued manner was a result of hunger or boredom.

When Mr Harvey was thirty minutes late, Marianne went to the kitchen and turned the oven down very low. (There are blobs of nail polish on the controls, in case you were wondering.) Garth and I had been putting away the gin but the mood still wasn't very convivial. I was hungry, Marianne was tense and Garth's small-talk was limited. He and I were comparing Robert de Niro's Frankenstein with Boris Karloff's when Marianne suddenly got to her feet and said, 'Sod it. Let's eat.' And so we did. Garth and I

33

tucked in but Marianne just picked at salad and wouldn't even touch the Orange Meringue Bombe. She looked worn out, poor thing.

After dinner she picked up the phone for the third time to check it was working. I could have killed that man. There was no excuse for not ringing unless he was lying in some casualty ward. I don't know why, but I started to wonder ... Perhaps because she seemed so upset but, at the same time, she didn't seem all that surprised. It was almost as if she'd known he wouldn't show, as if that's what she'd expected. But perhaps I was imagining things. (That is, after all, my job.)

As soon as Garth left, Marianne started loading the dishwasher. I could tell from the clatter in the kitchen that she was angry. I know I shouldn't have said it, but I'd had quite a lot to drink by then and I was tired, not to mention genuinely concerned about our dinner service. (The design is discontinued.)

She was scraping plates noisily into the bin when I said, 'Marianne, do you think it's possible you could have been overdoing things lately?'

She stopped scraping and said, rather sharply I thought, 'What do I do that could possibly be overdone? What are you getting at, Lou?'

'Nothing! I just wondered if you might have been ... mistaken?'

She turned abruptly. I should have seen the warning signs. 'Mistaken? About what?'

'About this man. Mr Harvey.'

'His name's Keir. What do you mean?'

'Well, I mean it must be very difficult having only your hearing to go by. And everybody knows ears can play tricks on you.'

'Are you suggesting I imagined him?'

'No, of course not!'

'Then what are you saying?'

'Just that it seems very odd. Not turning up. Not even phoning.'

'It's not odd, it's bloody rude.' She bent over the dishwasher and rammed a handful of dirty cutlery into the basket.

'I dare say there's a reason,' I said, trying to be conciliatory. 'Maybe he lost your telephone number. Or had an accident.

There could be all sorts of reasons why he isn't here. Why don't you give him a ring?'

'I don't have his mobile number.'

'Well, ring him at home. He might have left a message on his answerphone.'

'I don't have the number. I don't even know where he lives. Anyway, he's not the kind to leave messages on answerphones. He doesn't do explanations.'

'Marianne, forgive me for speaking so bluntly, but what evidence is there that this man actually exists?'

'You think I've made him up?'

'Not deliberately, no. But I think it's possible that your mind is playing tricks on you. It's probably all my fault for leaving you so much to your own devices, but with the deadline for Blood Will Have Blood *looming, things have been just insane.'*

'Is that what you think I am? Insane?'

'No, of course not, my dear!'

'Don't you "my dear" me!'

'Marianne, calm down! Naturally you're upset. Nobody likes being stood up.'

'Oh, so you admit he exists, then? Or do you think I've been stood up by a ghost? By a figment of my own imagination?'

'I don't know what to think! All I'm saying is, it doesn't add up.'

'He sent me a postcard!'

'Did he? Oh, that was nice … How did you know it was from him?'

'It was a tape. A message on a cassette.'

'Where from?'

'The Arctic.'

'The Arctic? Oh, for goodness' sake! Show me!'

She started putting crockery onto the dishwasher rack, shoving it in any-old-how. *'I can't. It was stolen.'*

'Somebody stole a tape?'

'It was in my handbag when it was snatched.'

'Well, it's hardly evidence then, is it?'

'Who's on trial here – him or me?'

'Nobody! I'm just trying to establish beyond a shadow of doubt that Keith exists.'

'Keir! His name's Keir Harvey, he's nothing to do with the Labour Party and before you ask, no, he is not a rabbit!'

I laid my hand on her arm. She was shaking. 'Marianne, I really think you should go and sit down. Take one of my tablets, they'll make you feel much calmer –'

She yanked her arm away and yelled, 'I'm perfectly calm!'

And that's when she broke the sauceboat. It hit the worktop. Chocolate sauce went all over the kitchen and Marianne's cream silk trousers. I was so cross.

'Oh, now look what you've done!'

'How can I, you stupid woman? I'm blind!'

She stalked out of the kitchen, colliding with a chair. I heard her bedroom door slam, then the sound of crying, but I thought it would be best for me to clear up first. I knew she wasn't crying about her silk trousers or even the sauceboat, but I didn't think there was anything useful I could say about the elusive Mr Harvey.

Poor Marianne. She'd even given him the same name.

Chapter Four

Marianne

There had been men. A few. I was widowed at twenty-seven and, for a blind woman, I was not unattractive, or so I was told. In my thirties I went through an interesting period of trying to find a life partner in an abortive attempt to escape from the smothering symbiotic relationship I'd developed living with my sister. I'd gone to stay with Louisa when Harvey died and so she was around for the miscarriage. By the time we'd got over that, we thought it would be a good idea to pool our financial resources and buy somewhere in Edinburgh. I was keen to make a new start. I certainly didn't want to retain my flat in Aberdeen. Even now the sound of an Aberdonian accent has me fighting off a panic attack. The yearly pilgrimage to Hazlehead Park is all I can manage.

My period of modest promiscuity probably had more to do with finding a father for a child than finding myself another husband or even just a lover. I failed on all counts and entered my forties older, wiser, childless and celibate. And, it has to be said, slightly relieved. Blind motherhood would always have been a tough option, but I didn't even get beyond the vetting process. Blind sexual relationships are even more fraught with difficulty than the sighted variety, especially for women.

Perhaps I should explain. The sort of men you attract if you're blind fall into one of three categories:

A. *The Romantics*. These are men who think there's something spiritual, beautiful, quintessentially *feminine* about being blind (for which read helpless). Blindness brings out the Galahad in this type. They charge about being helpful on a heroic scale. Woe betide you if you don't wish to be rescued and set upon a pedestal.

B. *The Sexually Insecure*. These men believe that if you're blind (i.e. defective), you'll be grateful for any interest shown in you, even if it comes from a short, fat, malodorous clod so unappealing, a sighted woman would cross the road to avoid him. (In some ancient cultures blind girls were sent to work in brothels, presumably to service clients so deformed or otherwise loathsome that your average working girl would take one look and go on strike. Alternatively, blind girls may have been encouraged to follow this career path for a different reason. See C below.)

C. *The Perverts*. There are, unfortunately, a number of men who are turned on by the idea of a blind woman. Whether it's the Peeping Tom factor or the reputation the blind have for sensory over-compensation, I've never hung around long enough to find out.

What all these men have in common is, they expect a blind woman to be *grateful* for their attentions. (Perhaps I'm being unfair. Isn't that what most men expect of women?) That's what renders me a second-class citizen. Not being blind. Blindness is just a series of practical problems for which one eventually finds a solution. I don't consider myself handicapped, except by others' views of me. What constrains me, angers me, demeans me, are other people's expectations, in particular the universal expectation that I should be grateful for their help, for their concessions, for inclusion in their sighted world, to which I don't really belong.

Keir hadn't treated me like that. He didn't seem to be Type A, B or C. (Definitely not A or B and if he was a closet C then he'd blown his chance of a fantasy scenario.) Keir had been different. He was offhand, almost rude. He made no concessions to my blindness. It was almost as if 'sight, lack of' wasn't an issue, simply a distinguishing characteristic, like his height. The only person who'd ever treated me like that was Harvey and he learned how to do it over a period of years, the few years we had before he was killed.

38

So I was caught off-guard. I was vulnerable. (When is one not, when one is blind?) I was almost forty-six, nearer fifty than forty – an uncomfortable realisation. I'd assumed my sexual organs and appetite had long atrophied through lack of use and was surprised, a little embarrassed, even dismayed to find that this wasn't so, although to say I felt a sexual attraction to Keir would have been overstating the case.

All right, it *wouldn't*. Who am I kidding? I have only voice, touch and smell to go on and he'd passed with flying colours in all those departments. In addition, he seemed not only an interesting person, but a nice one. I *liked* his rudeness. It was stimulating. Refreshing. And it was never a result of a lack of consideration or imagination, as was so often the case in my dealings with sighted people. Keir's blunt manner, his off-the-wall take on things, seemed to be the result of his seeing fairly clearly (for a sighted person) what life was actually like for me. So add empathy to his list of virtues.

I suppose it's no wonder my sister thought I'd made him up. So did I at times. Like when he didn't show up for dinner. I couldn't forgive Keir for not turning up, for not ringing me the day after, or the day after that. I couldn't forgive him for disappointing me, for creating his own category – there's a first time for everything – of *Dilettante*, a combination of A, B and C, without the staying power of any of them.

No doubt I'd had a lucky escape, for which I should be grateful. (You see? Gratitude is unavoidable, however hard you try.) But I wasn't grateful. I was hurt. Humiliated. I was angry.

I was still angry a week later when I decided to go for a walk in the Botanics. I stood at the sitting room window listening for rain. I couldn't hear any but decided to take the umbrella anyway. I slammed the door of the flat and set off down the wide staircase, rehearsing exactly what I'd say to Mr Keir Harvey if he had the misfortune to bump into me. But of course he wouldn't. He'd see me coming and walk the other way.

My anger flared again as I walked across the tiled hall, footsteps echoing, and opened the heavy front door. I stepped over the threshold, turning, and walked into a wall of flesh and bone. I shrieked and stepped backwards, tripping over the door-sill. Hands caught me by the elbows and pulled me upright again. A voice, *his* voice, was saying, 'It's me. Sorry, Marianne. It's Keir.'

A wave of relief overwhelmed me: I wasn't about to be mugged or murdered. But I didn't want to feel relieved. Not *grateful*. Lord, anything but that.

I opened and closed my mouth, trying to find words to express the cocktail of emotions provoked by the sudden shock of Keir's presence, his voice, his hands on me. I'd intended, if I ever met him again, to be frigidly polite, dismissive. But what came out was anger.

'You've got a bloody nerve – just turning up on my doorstep! Why didn't you ring?'

'I didn't have your number.'

'Rubbish! I heard you put it on your mobile.'

'My phone got smashed. So did I.'

'You were *drunk*?'

'No. There was an accident. On the rig. I fell.'

'Oh, really?'

He lifts her hand and carries it to his forehead where she feels scabbed flesh quilted with stitches. She recoils.

'Good grief! I'm sorry. Are you all right?'

'I am now. I *was* concussed, otherwise you'd have had flowers and a grovelling apology.'

'Oh, don't worry about that. As long as you're all right.'

'Oh, aye. Limping a bit. One of the other guys is not so good though.'

'Do you want to come in?'

'You were on your way out.'

'Only for a walk. What were you doing lurking on my doorstep? Were you about to ring my bell?'

'Well, I haven't been walking up and down singing, "On the street where you live", if that's what you mean. Sorry I alarmed you. When I heard the door opening I stepped back, but not far enough.'

'Come upstairs and I'll make us some coffee. You can tell me about the accident.'

'There's nothing to tell. Accidents happen all the time, especially on rigs. I'll live.'

'I sincerely hope so,' Marianne replies as she closes the door behind him.

She calms herself with the ritual of making coffee, at ease in the familiar surroundings of her own kitchen. Carrying a loaded tray into the sitting room, she asks, 'Where are you sitting?'

'I'm not. I'm standing, so you don't trip over my big feet. Here, let me take the tray.'

She sits in an armchair opposite the sofa and hears the asthmatic wheeze of cushions as he sits down facing her. Reaching for a mug of coffee, she says, 'Help yourself to milk and sugar.'

'Thanks.'

'Why didn't they send you home?'

'They wanted to keep me in. For observation.'

'No, I mean when you were discharged, why didn't you go home? I presume you do have one?'

'I owed you an apology. I don't make a habit of standing women up. Especially not blind ones.'

'You mean you came back to Edinburgh just to say sorry?'

'I couldn't get hold of your number –'

'We're ex-directory. You could have sent a card.'

'Aye, but you couldn't have read it, so I thought I'd better come in person to explain. Besides, I wanted to see you again.'

'Why?'

She hears him sigh. 'You don't make things easy, do you? Look, I know I'm supposed to suggest we have dinner, then go through the waiting-for-phone-calls routine, meet the family and pets –'

'Did I ever tell you about Garth?'

'Who's Garth?'

'My sister's pet Goth.'

'Is that a breed of dog?'

'Never mind. You were saying?'

'I was saying, I wondered if we could just cut all the crap and skip to the part where you say "No".'

'Keir, what on earth are you talking about?'

41

'I've got leave. Sick leave as a result of the accident. So I'm going home for a wee while.'

'And where exactly *is* home?'

'Skye.'

'That's a long way from here.'

'Aye. So I was wondering ... Would you'd like to come?'

'To Skye? You mean come and stay with you?'

'Aye.' She makes no reply and he continues, 'There'd be separate sleeping accommodation – you need have no worries on that score. I'm not importing you for lewd purposes.'

'Well, you needn't say it as if that was the last thing on your mind. You make me feel like the antidote to desire.'

He sighs again. 'I'm sorry, that did sound pretty crass, didn't it? I thought you might be … concerned.'

'For my virtue, you mean? What use is virtue to me? Anyway, I'm a widow, if you remember. Not somebody's maiden aunt.'

'Now who's talking about herself as if she's the antidote to desire?'

'Oh, I'm scarcely a woman in the eyes of the world. I don't see, so I don't shop. I don't have children. I don't even have a man. In the eyes of the world, I'm just *blind*.'

'In the eyes of the world, maybe. Not mine.'

She hears him swallow coffee, then place his mug on the table.

'So, you're inviting me for a sort of holiday?'

'Aye.'

'I'm not much of a one for scenery.'

'I realise that.'

'And I get awfully crabby when I'm off my home turf.'

'You can be pretty crabby *on* it.'

'So why are you asking me?'

'I want to show you Skye. And I use the word advisedly.'

'I get the guest room?'

'No, you get my bed. There's only two rooms.'

'But you're optional?'

'Entirely. As is the full Scottish breakfast. There's no electricity but the house is warm and dry. Cosy. From an aesthetic point of view, it's a bit primitive, but you'll not be into interior design in a big way, I should imagine.'

'And this is your *home*?'

'Aye.'

She is silent, her head bowed, apparently deep in thought.

He clears his throat and says wearily, 'This is the point where you say, "No, I couldn't possibly."'

She lifts her head. 'Why would I say that?'

'I don't know. You can't get leave from work, maybe?'

'But I can.'

'You don't like to leave your sister on her own?'

'At the moment I'd like nothing better.'

'You don't actually *know* me?'

'That's very true. There have been times when I've even doubted your existence.'

'Don't apologise. God has the same problem.'

'And works in equally mysterious ways, his wonders to perform.'

'I'm not promising wonders. The weather will be terrible. You'll be holed up, listening to the wind and rain. But if it ever stops you'll be climbing hills and watching stars.'

'I can't watch stars.'

'Maybe not, but I can tell you about them.'

'You're going to teach me about the stars?'

'Aye.'

She puts her coffee mug down and her voice falters. 'How … how did you *know*?'

'Know what?'

'That I've always wanted to know – since I was a tiny child – what twinkling looks like? I mean, what twinkling is *like*.'

Keir thinks for a moment, then says, 'It's a kind of pulse. A gentle throbbing of light. Not like a headache. A beautiful, magical throbbing … I had a girlfriend once who tried to explain the mysteries of female sexual arousal to me and she said, "You know he's the one for you if the sight of him makes your genitals twinkle." '

Marianne is silent, then asks, 'Were you the one for her?'

'I think so.'

43

'But she wasn't the one for you.'

'Afraid not, for all she was a poet.'

The sound of distant traffic has altered. Marianne can tell from the swish of wheels that it's started to rain. 'I should have gone for my walk. I like walking in the rain.'

'Will you come with me, Marianne?'

'To listen to the stars?'

'Aye.'

'Try stopping me.'

Louisa

Well, he wasn't what I expected. But then I'd been expecting nothing, so anything at all would have been a pleasant surprise. And what I got was a very pleasant surprise.

He came to the flat to collect Marianne and her luggage before they set off for Skye. He was tall, well over six feet. I had to crane my neck to look up at him, which I always think is a rather pleasing sensation when you're with a man. He looked younger than Marianne. I don't know why I'd thought he'd be older, or indeed any age at all since I'd assumed he didn't exist. I suppose I'd thought Marianne would have fantasised about somebody older than herself, if you see what I mean.

He was dark, with short brown hair, a bit reddish. Conker brown. Shiny like a conker too. His hair was cropped close to the head giving him something of an ascetic look, like a monk, but his eyes were lively and humorous. Crinkly. Otherwise his face was unlined, but I'd have guessed his age as early forties, no more. There was something disquieting about those eyes. I got the impression they didn't miss much.

He had stitches in his forehead and some technicolour bruising on his face, making him look a bit like Frankenstein's monster, but it was nevertheless a handsome face with a straight nose and a generous, slightly crooked mouth, which seemed to go with his ironic turns of phrase.

He was broad in the shoulder and very tall. Oh, I think I already said that, didn't I? It's just that it really struck you, the size of him, as he stood there looking so solid and masculine in our fussy sitting room. He looked quite out of place in his walking boots, jeans and fleece jacket, like a lumberjack at a vicarage tea party. But there could be no doubt about the corporeal existence of Mr Harvey as he stood on our hearthrug, larger than life. My little sister had done well for herself.

It crossed my mind – with a pang of disappointment – that he might be gay. Marianne has always had an affinity with gay men. She likes their bitchy humour and the fact that there's no sexual game-playing. She's always said gays make better and more loyal friends than women. So I did wonder.

But he didn't look gay. I know you can't tell, but I thought the way he looked at Marianne, watched her when she spoke, the way he helped her on with her coat, all suggested he was thoroughly heterosexual, so much so that I caught myself thinking, 'Gosh, I hope Marianne doesn't fall in a big way and get hurt.' Then he did something – something quite small – which made me think again.

Marianne was buttoning up her coat, talking to me, getting ready to leave. She had her back turned towards Keir. Over her shoulder I saw him look at her, then hesitate. He lifted his great big hands and – so gently, as if he was handling something precious or fragile – he slipped his fingers under her long, loose hair where it was caught inside her coat collar. He gently pulled it free, gathering it up in his hands, then he let go, watching it cascade over her shoulders and, as he did so, he smiled. Not at me, nor at Marianne. He just smiled.

That was when I had second thoughts. Marianne didn't turn towards him, she just tossed her head and shook out her hair. I looked at the pair of them and thought, 'Oh, Lord – I hope he doesn't fall in a big way and get hurt.'

I kissed Marianne goodbye. I was a bit tearful, I don't know why. She was only going away for a week. Keir handed me a small carrier bag and grinned, saying it was a gift for me. I looked inside and there were two gift-wrapped boxes. Probably chocolates, I thought. He enveloped my hand in one of his and said he would take very good care of Marianne. I didn't doubt that for one moment.

After they'd gone I felt quite flat. I couldn't settle to work. I tried to console myself with the thought that poor Marianne was about to spend a week on Skye feeling cold and damp, perhaps strug-gling with the indignities of a chemical toilet. Rather her than me! (Although perhaps the nights wouldn't be so very cold and damp.) Far from feeling apprehensive about her eccentric holiday, with her even more eccentric companion, what I actually felt was jealous.

That realisation made me feel even more disgruntled, so at lunchtime I switched off the PC, poured myself a large G&T and settled down to watch guilt-free daytime TV, without Marianne's acerbic comments to inhibit my channel-hopping. I was about to tune in to a re-run of Buffy the Vampire Slayer *when I remem-bered Keir's presents. The thought of some quality chocs cheered me up. Sure enough, one box contained Belgian choco-lates. The other turned out to be a DVD.*

I don't suppose I need to tell you what it was.

Harvey.

It was awfully good. (So were the chocs.)

Chapter Five

Marianne

I hardly ever think about sex. I don't particularly miss it. But I think about men. Men other than Harvey, I mean. (I try very hard not to think about Harvey. His life was so completely subsumed by the manner of his death that thinking about him means – will always mean – thinking about how he died.) But I think about other men. Sometimes. Men and maleness. I think I miss the *difference* of men.

I can hardly remember what sex feels like and you can't really fantasise about something you've forgotten. Virgins can fantasise about sex because they might be right, it *might* be like that. But when you've forgotten how it feels to make love and try to remember, you know it wasn't quite like that, it must have been better than that, surely? And you realise the memory has gone. You know the only thing that could remind you what it was like would be making love with a man.

But that wasn't going to happen. I was quite clear about that. I was quite clear because there was absolutely no question of my asking Louisa to shop for condoms. Nor was I prepared to stand at the counter in Boots, at the mercy of a gormless shop assistant who might compound my embarrassment by enquiring if I preferred ribbed or flavoured.

Whether the lack of sexual opportunity was a disappointment, I didn't bother to ask myself (though I suppose the fact that the shopping difficulty had occurred to me tells its own story). I confess I might have envisaged – very briefly – some romantic scenario

47

worthy of Louisa at her worst. I was, after all, about to be whisked away to an island in the far north by a man I hardly knew and who was (Louisa assured me) quite attractive. I was prepared to believe her. Keir was taller than me, younger than me and nicer than me. Louisa would have said it doesn't get a lot better than that, not when you're middle-aged and single. Certainly not if you're middle-aged, single and blind. Nevertheless, there would be no sex. Unless, of course, Keir, in true Boy Scout fashion, came prepared.

He struck me as the sort of man who might be ready for anything.

Keir installs Marianne in a waiting black cab, loads their luggage and announces 'Waverley' to the driver. As he eases his bulky frame between Marianne and their cases she says, 'We're going by *train*?'

'Aye.'

'It's an awfully long way.'

'That's why we're going by train. My Land Rover's parked at Inverness anyway. D'you not like trains?'

'I've hardly ever used them. They're pretty awkward if you're blind. And impossible if you're travelling alone. A train journey will be something of a novelty for me.'

'Aye, that's what I thought. Long car journeys must be high on your list of all-time boring activities, I should imagine.'

'Depends on the CD collection of the driver. If it's Louisa you have to suffer some pretty ropey tenors. I can only assume their looks must compensate for their voices. Do we have to change trains?'

'No, we go all the way to Inverness, have lunch, then pick up the Land Rover, head west to Kyle, then drive over the bridge to Skye.'

'You know, I'm not sure I approve of islands being connected to the mainland by bridges. Seems perverse to me.'

'You might think differently if you lived there. Isolation can be a mixed blessing. And the bridge has brought us many benefits.'

'Such as?'

'Pine martens.'

'*Pine martens*? They're animals, aren't they?'

'Aye. Mammals. The size of a cat.'

'They walked across the bridge?'

'Aye ... Carrying their wee suitcases.'

At Waverley, Keir pays the taxi driver, shoulders his rucksack and picks up Marianne's case. Offering her an arm, he escorts her across the concourse to the platform.

'You walk very confidently without your cane.'

'I fall over very confidently too. I've got one in my bag but I don't use it if I can help it. But then I don't often venture out of familiar territory.'

'So I'm taking you outside your comfort zone?'

'Oh, yes. In more ways than one ... Are you laughing at me?'

'No, I'm not.'

'But you were grinning?'

'Aye, as it happens, I was. How did you know?'

'An educated guess.'

'Based on what evidence?'

'The silence ... And your arm relaxed suddenly.'

'I feel like Doctor Watson tagging along with Sherlock Holmes. I can see I'm going to have trouble keeping up with you.'

'Not as much trouble as I'm having keeping up with *you*,' she replies. 'Do you think you could possibly slow down? You do have the advantage in leg length.'

'Sorry. We're about to get on the train. Wait here while I stow the luggage, then I'll find our seats and come and fetch you.'

'Do you want the window seat?'

'So I can admire the view?'

'No, so you don't have folk thumping you with their luggage.'

'Oh ... Sorry. Forgive the sarcasm. I'm feeling rather nervous. The unfamiliarity.'

'No problem. Will I take your coat? I'll put it in the rack overhead.'

'Thanks.' Marianne hands him her coat and settles into her seat.

'The seats opposite aren't reserved so you can stretch out your legs for now.'

'They *are* stretched out.'

'Sorry. I forget other folk aren't as obsessed as I am with legroom. Another reason I prefer the aisle seat.' He sits down beside her and Marianne is thrown momentarily by the unexpected body contact in their narrow seats.

'When do we get to Inverness?'

'Midday or thereabouts. Then we'll have lunch and drive to Skye.'

'You're really excited about showing me your island, aren't you?'

'Is it that obvious?'

'Yes. Even to me.'

'It's not mine, anyway. I'm merely a custodian. A caretaker.'

'You're not there much of the time.'

'No, but when I am, I take care of things.'

'What sort of things?'

'All creatures great and small ... Och, that's not strictly true. They take care of themselves well enough. I just make sure the right conditions prevail. I'm not really a caretaker. More a maintenance man. Part-time,' he adds.

'What sort of things do you do?'

Keir is thoughtful, then says, 'Keep the twenty-first century at bay.'

'Hmm ... Sounds like a full-time job to me.'

As the train slows down Marianne turns to Keir and asks, 'Are we coming into a station?'

'Aye. Perth.'

'Gateway to the Highlands.' She smiles. 'I love to hear Scots say Perth. *Pairth.* So much more musical than *Purth,* which sounds like a verbal belch ... Oh, do I hear the rattle of a tea trolley? I could use a coffee. How about you?'

Keir looks round his seat, along the carriage. 'She won't be here for a wee while. I'll get them when she passes.'

'Are you waiting for a call?'

'How did you *know*?'

'You keep checking your phone. I hear you pick it up off the table, then you put it down again.'

'I'm not exactly waiting. It's a call I hope I don't get.'

Marianne waits for him to say more. When he doesn't, she asks, 'Do you have many visitors? On Skye?'

'Me personally? Or did you mean tourists?'

'You personally.'

'No. You're the first.'

'*Really*? Have you not been there long?'

'Years.'

'So why no visitors?'

'I like being alone. Usually,' he adds.

'There, and I thought this was going to be a holiday. I now feel weighed down by responsibility.'

'Because you're my first visitor?'

'Yes. I don't like the idea of being a human guinea pig.'

'More of a pioneer.'

'Are you taking me because I'm blind? As some kind of good deed? I have a suspicion you suffer from an over-developed Boy-Scout complex.'

'I'm taking you because you're the first person I've met who I think might appreciate my world the way I do.'

'Which is?'

'With your whole mind and body, not just your eyes.'

She frowns. 'I'm not sure I understand.'

'Well, *seeing* seems to me a pretty narrow way of appreciating the world. Superficial.'

'What do you mean?'

Keir turns his head and looks at her profile outlined against the window. Something about the set of her head tells him she is alert, listening hard, but not for the first time he's thrown by the lack of eye-contact. Instead he focuses on her ear, small, neat and convoluted, holding back her heavy ash blonde hair. A thin tendril has escaped and lies against her cheek, swaying with the movement of the train.

Keir talks softly into Marianne's ear. 'Sound penetrates your

51

body. So does smell. You heard that rattling trolley and reacted to it. You smelled the coffee and you experienced a craving. Touch affects your body too, obviously. These seats are too narrow for a guy like me. You can feel the pressure of my body against yours, can't you?'

'Yes, I can.'

'If you didn't know me that would feel like an invasion of your personal space. Och, maybe it does anyway.'

'No, it doesn't. It's rather reassuring, actually. I know you're there.'

'But sight leaves the body untouched. There's no physical penetration of the eye.'

Marianne purses her lips. 'Light rays on the retina?'

'OK, but you're not aware of them. When you see something – I mean when sighted folk see – it's out there, *beyond* the self. It isn't in your eye the way a sound is in your ear, or a smell is in your nose. It's detached from the self.'

'Fascinating! Of course, I'll have to take your word for it.'

Keir looks away and surveys the other passengers: reading, dozing, sending text messages as Perth recedes and the train moves out into the countryside again. 'It's not you with the limited perception, Marianne. Folk who can see just don't seem to *look*.'

She smiles. 'So you *are* taking me because I'm blind.'

He leans towards her and the pressure of his shoulder against hers increases. Instinctively, Marianne shrinks back against the window. Keir pulls away and she registers a fleeting disappointment. 'If you could see them, would you still touch trees?'

'I don't know. I like to think I would.'

'Aye, it's natural human behaviour! Think of the way we clamber on rocks and climb trees when we're kids.'

'I didn't.'

'But you probably wanted to.'

'Yes, I did.'

'Everybody does! We want to feel our bodies in touch with the Earth, with other living things – with pets, trees, the sea ... It's how we are as kids. Then we forget. We ... disconnect.' He turns away again. Leaning back in his seat he murmurs, 'That's when the trouble starts.'

'Trouble?'

'Some people think conservation is about saving animal species. Especially the cuddly ones. They don't realise we're also trying to prevent the human race from committing suicide.' He pauses for a moment and then says with careful emphasis, 'We're links in a chain. The chain only works when we're all linked together.'

'People and animals, you mean?'

'*Everything.*'

As the percussive tea trolley approaches Marianne says, 'You know, I have a feeling this trip is going to be an education ... '

Marianne

Keir's voice was his own now. I'd heard it often enough and for long enough to become acquainted with its distinct timbre. The Highland understatement was there but also the Highland energy, a combination that at times made me wonder if he might be suppressing laughter or apoplexy. There was something pent up, reined in by his careful precision of speech. I realised now that the pitch and accent were Harvey's but the vocal mannerisms weren't. The vocabulary wasn't. The silences weren't.

Keir had become his own man but my enjoyment of his company, his conversation, his attentiveness, even the proximity of his body next to mine in the railway carriage, all this was coloured by memories I was reluctant to revisit. The pleasure of various kinds that I felt in his presence was marred by fear of various kinds. To my utter dismay, I knew the fear uppermost in my mind – already – was that of loss. But how could I fear to lose what I didn't even possess?

Perhaps it was just habit. It's hard to describe the loneliness of being an oil wife, the hatefulness of it. Life is never normal. It's lived at two extremes. You are miserable or euphoric. When your husband's offshore you wish your life away waiting for him to come home. That's on good days. On bad days, you worry. You are *consumed* by worry. You are haunted by premonitions of danger, injury, even death. I had no premonition of the Piper Alpha tragedy but afterwards some people said they did. The fact is, dread becomes so much a habit, it would be difficult to recognise a presentiment of anything untoward. If your husband can't get off an oil platform for three days because of appalling weather, you tend to dwell on the fact that all that stands between him and annihilation is a monstrous Meccano-like construction clinging to the seabed. You trust it's safe. He trusts it's safe. Everyone trusts. We have to. How to live otherwise?

When your man is home, it's Christmas, whatever the season. Special food, special wine, sex, catching up on news, shopping, more sex. (Do oil couples have sex more often on average because of the enforced celibacy, I wonder? Do oil wives try harder, competing subconsciously with the porn that we know is available and suspect our husbands watch, even though they assure us they don't?)

Because of my blindness there were special hardships. I could never comfort myself with photographs. When Harvey was abroad, I couldn't anticipate long love letters to be read and re-read in private, in the bath, in bed. I had to content myself with phone calls until a friend, finding me in tears one day after speaking to him, suggested I tape our calls to play back at leisure. It was a short step from there to Harvey buying a dictaphone and sending me taped letters and journals, self-conscious at first, but eventually entertaining and briefly romantic in their closing moments as he signed off. (Try getting a male Highlander to talk about his feelings. You'll need the conversational equivalent of the culinary device that removes snails from their shell.)

I dated and labelled all the tapes in Braille as I received them. When he died I put them away with his clothes, his books (which I would never read) and his CDs (which I would never play). After a year I was able to get rid of the clothes, with Louisa's help. She was very good, very practical. The removal was surgical in its swiftness and precision and I was anaesthetised by exhaustion after a year of grief – first for Harvey, then for the baby. Selling up in Aberdeen, getting rid of Harvey's stuff, telling people about the miscarriage, Louisa saw me through all of it with a large box of Kleenex and a constant supply of gin and tonic. She was tactful but brisk. It was necessary. I was only twenty-seven. I needed to begin again.

The tapes now live in a beautiful oblong mahogany box. I know it's beautiful. I can feel. The box is Indian and ornately carved. I used to enjoy running my fingers over the patterns on the lid and on the sides, trying to read them. After Harvey's death the box became the repository for his tapes and the photos of us he used to have on display. When he was alive I'd kept the tapes on a bookshelf with my CDs and audio-books but after the worst was over, I took them off the shelf and put them in the wooden box he'd given me, for which I'd never found any practical use.

After I'd placed the tapes inside, shut the box and put it away, I felt as if I'd put them in a coffin, buried Harvey's voice. It's perhaps an indication of my dire mental state at the time that I derived a kind of comfort from this mock-burial. Perhaps this too was necessary. There had been no funeral. His body had never been recovered, had never been laid to rest in a coffin. I don't doubt that my subconscious selected an appropriate last resting place for his voice: a beautiful wooden coffin, made in India, a place we'd said we'd visit one day for a second honeymoon, one day, when life wasn't quite so mad.

I can't listen to the tapes. I tried once or twice many years ago and it all but destroyed me. Now I don't dare. To hear Harvey's voice is for him to live again. With the passing of time, ink and photographs fade. A letter becomes worn along the creases and eventually falls to bits, but the tapes are ageless, immortal, the voice unchanging, unbearable. It's as if he's in the room.

To listen to those tapes is to summon up Harvey's ghost. But he was a ghost even while he was alive. Each time he went away, it was a kind of death. He ceased to exist for me. He became an exercise in imagination, at best a disembodied voice. My husband existed for me only when I could hear him, touch him, hold him in my arms. When I couldn't do that, I took his existence on trust. I had to. The joy of his homecomings was intensified by a sense that he'd come back to life, had justified my faith in his existence. Each time he came home safely, it felt like a small miracle. No, a *big* miracle.

After Harvey died, I used to jump whenever the phone rang and my heart would pound with hope. It was months before I stopped praying it would be Harvey, my husband resurrected, his voice telling me he was on his way home, there'd been a terrible mistake ... When Keir first spoke to me, I thought for a moment the miracle had occurred again, that Harvey had come home. The sensation passed quickly, but I was shaken. Memories were stirred – some good, mostly bad.

Now Keir sounds like himself. I know his voice and delight in it. But when he's not there, when I have only the memory of his voice, when I cannot feel (as I do now) the pressure of his body adjacent to mine, a small, fearful and familiar voice asks if he exists. If Keir doesn't speak, doesn't touch me, he becomes a ghost, like Harvey. Something I must will into existence as an act of faith. My faith.

Keir's shoulder is at the level of my ear now. I sense the slight rise and fall as he breathes. Perhaps he's asleep ... No, his arm moves as he turns the page of a magazine. If I angle my head slightly, I know my hair must fall onto his shoulder. My scalp senses the contact. It seems the most comfortable and natural thing in the world to incline my head further, to rest it on his shoulder and close my eyes.

He says nothing but becomes very still. I enjoy what is for me a rare luxury: Keir is silent but I know he is there. I don't have to believe it. I *know*.

After lunch in Inverness, Keir escorts Marianne from the restaurant to the car park. Cold gusts of wind scythe the air and she turns up the collar of her coat, her teeth chattering as she waits for him to load their luggage.

'Have you travelled in a Land Rover before?'

'No. Louisa and I tend to get the bus to Jenners.'

He opens the passenger door. 'There's a step up. Quite high. Then there's a handle ... here.' He takes one of her hands and places it on the inside of the door. 'But the really useful one is here. Lean in.' He places a hand between her shoulder blades and presses gently, indicating the direction she should bend, then places her other hand above the dashboard. 'You can haul yourself in using that bar. When the road gets a bit bumpy – as it will when we're on Skye – you can steady yourself using that. But otherwise I think you'll find it a pretty comfortable ride.'

'I can't wait.' She lifts her foot and pedals in mid-air, searching for the step.

'May I?' Keir bends, circles her ankle with his fingers and lifts her foot up to the step. 'There you go. It's higher than is convenient for a woman, even one as fit as yourself.' He closes the door behind her and reappears at the other.

'All right, Sherlock – how do you know I'm fit?'

'Muscle tone. And you don't get out of breath keeping up with me, for all you complain.' He climbs in and fastens his safety belt. 'You must walk a lot.'

'I do. And I swim.'

'Gym too?'

'Sometimes. Louisa and I go together. It's part of her eternal and entirely unsuccessful weight-loss plan.'

'That's where I've seen you before. I thought when we first met I knew you from somewhere.'

'Me too.'

'My voice?' He sounds surprised.

'Yes. You sounded – you sound a bit like my husband. Like Harvey.'

The name hangs in the air between them for a moment, then Keir says softly, 'The accent, I suppose.'

'Yes. When we met, for a minute I thought –' She breaks off. Tactfully, Keir turns the ignition key and puts the Land Rover into reverse.

Two hours later, they stretch their legs at Kyle of Lochalsh on the north-west coast, in sight of Skye. Marianne's spirits lift at the smell of the sea and the sound of squabbling gulls. As they set off again Keir says, 'In a minute or two, when we start to climb, we'll be going over the bridge to Skye. Beneath us will be a wee island, *Eilean Bàn*, a wildlife reserve. Gavin Maxwell ended his days there.'

'The otter man?'

'Aye.'

'He'd approve of his home becoming a wildlife reserve.'

'He'd maybe not be so keen on the bridge being built on top of it. *Eilean Bàn* holds the bridge up.'

'I suppose the building work drove the otters away?'

'Aye. But they came back.'

'With their suitcases, no doubt. I wonder if Maxwell's spirit patrols the island?'

'I thought you didn't believe in ghosts?'

'I don't. But just because *I* don't believe in them doesn't mean to say they don't exist. People used to believe the world was flat, but it wasn't.'

'That's a neat way of hedging your bets.'

Marianne sits up, alert and smiling. 'We're going downhill now, aren't we? I can feel it.'

'Aye. You've arrived. Welcome to the Misty Isle, Marianne. Welcome to Skye.'

They have been driving for a few minutes and Keir is describing a view of the islands of Scalpay, Raasay and the mainland beyond when his phone rings. He looks down at the display briefly. Swinging the wheel, he pulls over to the side of the road and answers the phone.

'Annie? Any news?' He listens while a woman talks. Marianne hears his breathing change, then the sound of a woman sobbing at the other end of the phone. Keir utters a single word on a despairing out-breath: 'When?'

Marianne reaches for the door-handle and starts to get out of the car. Keir's hand shoots out to restrain her. 'It's OK,' he whispers. He speaks into the phone again. 'Annie? Are you there? The signal's not so good. Can you hear me? ... Is your mother with you? ... Aye, that's good, that's good ... You'll let me know then? About the funeral? ... No, I'm on Skye just now. But I'll be there ... Och no, I'm fine – a few bruises, is all ... Look, Annie, if there's anything – Aye, I know. But if you need me for *anything*, anything at all ... Aye, you too, pet ...'

Keir hangs up and tosses his phone onto the shelf above the dashboard, startling Marianne. He opens his door, jumps down, strides across the road and stands, shoulders hunched, his hands plunged deep into his jacket pockets, staring grim-faced out to sea. It begins to rain and he turns his already wet face to the sky.

'Keir?'

He looks back and sees Marianne standing beside the Land Rover, calling out, facing in the wrong direction. She gropes her way to the edge of the road and stumbles into a shallow ditch. Reaching out, her palms meet bare, vertical rock and she flinches at the film of icy water trickling down over the steeply angled planes of stone. She wipes her hands on her jeans and calls again, the wind whipping her voice away. 'Keir? Where are you?'

He jogs back across the road to her side and takes her arm, guiding her out of the ditch. 'Sorry, I just wanted – I needed a bit of space. I knew this was coming. I mean, it was ... not unexpected.'

'Was it the man who was in the accident with you?'

'Aye. Did I tell you about that?'

'Yes. Well, you mentioned another man had been injured. Allowing for your habitual understatement, I guessed things didn't look too hopeful.'

'No. He died this morning. Never regained consciousness. That was his wife.'

'Poor woman.'

'Aye.'

'He was a friend of yours?'

'Aye. An old pal. We go way back.'

Marianne waits for Keir to elaborate, then realises his silence speaks of the inarticulate depths of male friendship. 'If you want to turn round and go back,' she says gently, 'that's fine by me.'

'Och no, that's the last thing I want to do.'

'You're sure? I really don't mind.'

'What I need to do now is get home, light the stove, crack open a good bottle and brood – at *length* – on the transience of life and the whims of the Grim Reaper. Do you drink whisky, Marianne?'

'Yes.'

'Then we'll raise a glass to Mac tonight and we'll start the holiday tomorrow. It's what he would have wanted. Ach ...' Keir bows his head and says, his voice suddenly harsh with anger, 'He was full of life, that guy! And one hell of a shinty player. You should have seen him! And I'm not going to apologise for that one.'

Marianne lifts her hand up to his face. She finds it and lays her fingers on his cold, damp cheek, registering the slant of bone beneath. 'You mustn't feel guilty, you know. For surviving. Harvey's workmates did. Men who should have been working a shift that night, but weren't, for one reason or another. There's nothing you could have done.'

'I'm not so sure. But thanks anyway.' He opens the passenger door. 'Hop in and we'll be on our way.' He takes her arm but she doesn't move.

'You know, I sometimes wish we would all treat each other as if we were about to die. Say all the things that should be said. And *not* say the things that shouldn't. It would be different, wouldn't it, if we could see death coming.'

'If you *could* see it coming, what would you do differently?'

They stand facing each other, buffeted by the wind. Marianne sways and Keir puts out a hand to steady her. She shivers violently, then says, 'I wouldn't have told Harvey I was pregnant.'

'Why not?'

'It was just one more thing for him to worry about. He wasn't particularly pleased. The pregnancy wasn't planned and he didn't think I would cope. If he had time to think before he was incinerated, his last thoughts might have been, "I'm leaving a wife behind. And she's pregnant. And blind." '

'Maybe it was a comfort to him to know life would go on. Without him.'

'Maybe. Did Mac have kids?'

'Three.'

'Oh, God.'

'They'll be taken care of. Annie's family will see her through it. So will Mac's. It will be very hard, but she'll cope.'

Marianne leans into the Land Rover and grips the bar ready to heave herself in, then says, 'You think you won't cope. But you do.' Keir looks down at her hands, the knuckles white, the flesh mottled with cold. 'Somehow you just do.'

'Aye. You look death in the eye and re-negotiate terms ... Come on, into the wagon with you. We've a way to go yet.'

Marianne

I remember the last conversation I had with my husband. I remember his very last words. It wasn't a conversation, it was a row. We parted in anger. We didn't even kiss each other goodbye.

But you cope. Somehow, you cope.

Chapter Six

'This is as far as the wheels take us.'

Keir switches off the ignition and peers through the windscreen at the torrent of rain hammering the bonnet of the Land Rover. 'The rest of our journey's on foot and we've two choices. There's a narrow winding path that leads down to the house. You'd manage that, but it would take a while and you'll get soaked. Or ...' He pauses.

'Or?'

'Or I can carry you down the steps.'

'*Carry* me? Don't be ridiculous! I can walk down. I'll just be slow.'

'I use the term "steps" in its loosest sense. I've set a series of flat rocks into the hillside at intervals. They'll be muddy and treacherous and the distance between them suits my legs not yours. If you want to tackle them you'll have to go down backwards. Scrambling. A piggyback might be more dignified. And much safer.'

'Thanks for the offer, but I'll walk down the path.'

'OK.'

As they get out of the Land Rover the wind whips the door out of Marianne's hand. She climbs down, then cries out, '*Sod it!*'

Keir calls from the back of the vehicle where he is opening the door for their luggage. 'What's wrong?'

'I just stepped into a hole full of water and flooded my shoes.' She feels her way to the back of the car where Keir is strapping on his rucksack. 'I don't suppose you have such a thing as an umbrella?'

He laughs. 'In this wind?'

She hears him haul her suitcase out of the car and says hurriedly, 'I can carry my case. It's really not that heavy.'

'I suggest you just concentrate on coping with new and uneven terrain and leave the luggage to me.'

She sinks down onto the floor of the Land Rover, taking shelter from the worst of the rain. 'Keir, I wish you'd stop behaving like something out of Jane Austen.'

'Why?'

'Because it makes me *feel* like something out of Jane Austen.'

'And that's bad?'

'Yes.'

'Because you've spent your whole life trying not to feel helpless.'

'Yes,' she replies, lifting her chin. 'I have.'

He is silent for a moment and regards her tired, wet face, framed by hair hanging in sodden rats' tails. He shoves the case back into the car and she feels the Land Rover sink as he sits beside her. 'And just supposing I've spent my whole life wanting to be a hero?'

She puts her head on one side like a bird, as if listening more intently. 'Have you?'

'Aye ... Some. '

Marianne says nothing. As the rain drums more heavily on the roof of the car she kicks her feet together in an attempt to stir her circulation. Her shoes make a dispiriting squelching sound. She groans and says, 'I'm probably heavier than I look.'

'And I'm probably stronger than I look.' He unbuckles the rucksack, flings it back into the Land Rover along with the suitcase and slams the door. Turning to Marianne, he takes her arm and says, 'Come over here. There's a rock in front of you, a wee bit lower than your knees.' He takes hold of both her hands. 'Step up onto it.' She climbs on to the slippery, uneven stone and he lets go. 'OK, I'm standing in front of you now with my back towards you.'

She extends her hands and finds his shoulders level with her chest. 'Oh Lord – I haven't done anything like this since primary school. I'm frightened of strangling you.'

'You won't. Hop on.' With a whoop, Marianne flings herself at his back and he hooks his arms behind her knees. 'Hold tight now.'

She wraps her arms more firmly round his neck and Keir descends crab-like, stepping sideways. As she lurches from side to side, Marianne giggles. 'This is rather fun, actually.' Her mouth close to his ear, she says, 'I think we should come to some arrangement. Schedule the heroics, I mean.'

'Yours or mine?'

'Both.'

'Sounds like a good idea.'

'So it's your shift until we get indoors.'

'And then?'

'Then I'll wow you with my sightless cooking. Juggling with Sabatier knives, plate-spinning, turning water into wine. It's quite a performance.'

'Och well, that's good. With no electricity, we'll have to make our own entertainment.'

He stands still, breathing heavily.

'Am I getting heavy? Do you want a rest?'

'No, I was stopping to admire the view in the last of the light. When you clear the tree canopy and you first see the house. It's a ritual moment. That's when I know I'm home. Can you hear running water? That's the burn.'

'Yes. And what sounds like ... a waterfall?'

'Aye, the water falls, then the burn circles the house and carries on down to meet the sea about a quarter of a mile away.'

'Must be handy for chilling wine in the summer.'

'Aye. You can shower under the waterfall as well. Not to be recommended at this time of year, except for card-carrying masochists. Hold tight. We're nearly there.'

The noise of the stream recedes. The ground begins to level out and Keir walks more quickly, then stops. He releases her legs and Marianne slides down his back to the ground again. Opening an unlocked door, he leads her out of the rain into a structure that she can tell straight away has a corrugated iron roof.

'Oh, listen to the rain! It sounds like the Edinburgh Tattoo.'

'This is what Americans would call the mudroom.' She hears the turn of a key. Taking her arm, Keir leads her inside the house. 'Stand there and drip while I light the stove.'

As she unlaces her shoes, Marianne hears him move away, then the clank of a metal door, a scrabble for matches and the sound of wood and paper catching light.

'That was quick!'

'I always lay the fire before I leave. Come and sit down.' Keir relieves her of her wet coat and she kicks off her shoes. He leads her to an armchair by the stove. 'I'll go back up and get the luggage. You'll be OK for a few minutes?'

'Yes, of course. I shall sit and inhale wood smoke. Glorious.'

'If carcinogenic.'

'Oh, who cares? Life is terminal.'

'Aye, right enough.'

Her face falls and her fingers fly to her mouth. 'Oh, that was really tactless of me considering the news you had today. I was forgetting in all the excitement. I'm so sorry, Keir.'

'Don't be. I never thought Mac would make it. I've had more than a week to grieve already. You hope, but ... Well, you'll know yourself, accidents on rigs – bad ones – go with the territory. There's a lot of bloody waste ... *Are* you excited, Marianne?'

'About this trip? You bet I am. This is a real adventure for me. Pure Enid Blyton – a much maligned author, in my opinion. I hope you've got in a good supply of cocoa,' she says, rubbing her hands together to warm them. 'I feel a midnight feast coming on ... Keir, you've gone quiet again. Are you laughing at me?'

'No, I'm just tired. And relieved.'

'What about?'

'That you're pleased to be here. That you haven't complained about the rain. Or the cold. Or the undignified mode of transport.'

'You or the Land Rover?'

'Me.'

'I wouldn't have missed that for the world. You can't afford to stand on your dignity if you're blind, you know. It doesn't do. I can just about cope with feeling beholden, but I warn you now, I don't really do grateful. You'll just have to take that as read.'

'I think you'll find I'm pretty good at reading between the lines.'

'Then you'll know how relieved *I* am.'

'Relieved?'

'That it was poor Mac and not you.' He doesn't reply and she adds brightly, extending her hands towards the stove, 'It's definitely warming up now. Wood-burners are marvellous, aren't they? I expect they create a lot of dirt but that's not something I ever worry about. What the eye doesn't see ...'

He opens the front door. 'I'm away up the hill now to get the luggage. Speak kindly to the stove – it needs encouragement.'

'Don't we all. Take care on those steps.'

'I always do. We're a long way from a hospital. A long way from anywhere.'

'What a thrilling thought,' she replies, peeling off dripping socks.

'How do you take your whisky?'

'As it comes, thanks.'

Keir places a glass in her hand and says, 'Now you get the tour. It won't take long. This place is tiny but it's as well to point out some hazards. Which, as it happens, is what I do for a living.'

'What is?'

'Hazard prediction. Identifying conditions that could be hazardous to drilling operations.'

'How on earth do you do that?'

'"How on Earth" ...' He smiles and raises his glass. 'I like that. 3D seismic technology is how. And I have a wee crystal ball that comes in handy ... We're in the kitchen now and it has an old Rayburn. When it's alight you'll be aware of the heat, so that's not a hazard. The table and chairs are over here against

67

the wall, out of the way, and everything is stored on shelves or cupboards, so there's nothing to trip you, apart from the rug which is threadbare in places. I'll maybe roll that up so you've an even surface to walk on.'

'Really, there's no need. I have a very good memory. Once I've moved around a bit, I'll remember the layout. Mobility isn't a problem for me except when people *move* things. Guests always seem impressed when I cook for them – even just make a cup of tea – as if it's some wonderful feat, but really it isn't, not if everything is where you left it. *You* could make tea with your eyes closed if you knew where everything was. The feat, if feat it is, is one of memory.'

'And I suppose your memory develops without sight for back-up? Now I come to think of it, when folk try hard to remember something they often shut their eyes. Using some kind of inner eye to visualise, I suppose ... OK, there's a back door on the far wall. Outside there's a rough sort of garden and a pond, so mind your footing if you go out there. There are paths – I'll show you round tomorrow. So, if we retrace our steps to the entrance to the kitchen – on your left you have the front door where we came in. On your right, a door leading to the bathroom, which is very small, just a loo and a shower. If you step across the hall now – Marianne, are you *counting*?'

'Yes. And memorising. I navigate by a sequence of numbers, you see. The number of paces between things.' Keir makes no comment. 'What's the matter? You've gone quiet again.'

'I was just thinking. It must be difficult. Being a blind child. If your safety depends on feats of memory, sequences of numbers, it must be hard to be spontaneous, to play, to be a *child*.'

'You fall over a lot and you're permanently covered in scabs and bruises, but you just get on with it. I was at boarding school with a lot of other blind children. We were all in the same boat,' she adds briskly. 'Where are we now?'

'In the sitting room. To your right is the open-tread staircase that leads up to the sleeping area. That's a platform over the sitting room and it's partly open, but there's a safety rail, about waist height. I'll show you in a minute. In here we have my

68

desk by the window and there's an armchair beside the stove – both of which you're already familiar with. On the far wall is the sofa where I'll sleep.'

'Is it a sofa bed?'

'No, but it's big and comfy. It lets down at the ends so I can stretch out.'

'I could have slept on that. It might even have been safer for me than negotiating the stairs.'

'Aye, I wondered about that. It's up to you, but if you sleep down here you've no privacy. There's no door. There's no curtains either and the bathroom isn't big enough to get dressed in. I thought you'd prefer to be in the bedroom. But it's up to you.'

'You've obviously given this a lot of thought. Perhaps I would be better off upstairs.'

'Aye, and you'll be warmer too at night. Shall we try negotiating the stair now? Will you follow me up? There's a handrail on your left. There's ten steps and they're open-tread, mind.'

Marianne follows him up the staircase. He draws her into the middle of the room, then positions himself at the head of the stairs. 'I'm standing in front of the stair now so you can't fall. You'll only be able to stand upright in the centre of the room, which is where you are now. Put your hands up and you'll feel the sloping ceiling. There's a double bed – not made up yet – and a small table and a chair under the window, which is in the roof and has no curtain. There's a chest of drawers beside the bed. I'm clearing the top now so you can put your things on it. On the wall facing the bed there's shelves and baskets containing clothes and assorted junk. And that's it. Not much to it. There's more of interest outside than in. One other thing I should mention – there's no electricity so the lighting is oil lamps.'

'Keir, I don't need any light!'

'I know, but the oil lamps will be another hazard. You'll need to know where they are and if they're alight. That's another reason I thought you might be better off up here. Less to worry about.'

'I imagine I'll feel the heat from the lamps if they're alight. And I'll smell them.'

'Aye, that's what I thought. I'm sure it won't be a problem. Less of a problem in fact than cables trailing round the room. How's your glass?'

'Empty.'

'A shocking dereliction of duty on the part of the host. Will you come down and have another or will I bring it up to you while you unpack? Do you need a hand with anything?'

'No, just find me a space to put my clothes – a drawer or basket or something. I didn't bring much.'

She hears him pull open a drawer, scrape the contents out and dump them elsewhere. 'Top drawer beside the bed is now empty. Do you want some hangers?'

'No, but if there was a hook for my dressing gown it would make it easier to find.'

'No problem. There's a picture hanging on a cup-hook here, at the side of the bed. If I remove the picture ...' He lifts her hand and presses her fingers to the wall. 'There. Can you feel? Hang your dressing gown on that.'

'What is it a picture of?'

'Why d'you ask?'

'Well, you've given me a tour of your home without telling me anything about it. Nothing about the pictures, the books, the mementos. You've shown me the skeleton. I wondered what the flesh and blood man was like.'

'What d'you want to know?'

'Tell me about your books. What's the oldest one you own?'

Without hesitating, Keir replies, '*The Observer Book of Birds*. Given me by my granny for my seventh birthday '

'Your newest book?'

'Well, now.' He exhales. 'The newest would be ... aye, *The Revenge of Gaia*. James Lovelock.'

'Science fiction?'

'Sadly, no. It's about global warming. A horror story. Now are you having another whisky or no? I'm quite happy to drink alone.'

'What's your *favourite* book? If you were about to be thrown into a prison cell – solitary confinement, say – what would you grab?'

70

'Och, this is fun ... *Walden.* Henry David Thoreau. Or – no, perhaps a volume of poetry.'

'By?'

'Norman MacCaig.'

'Which one?'

He exhales. 'Can I phone a friend?'

'Which one, Keir?'

'The *Collected Poems.* That would get me through a long stretch.'

'Thank you! Now I know something about you.'

'That you didn't before?'

'Before, I only knew what you chose to tell me. My picture of you is more complete now. What was the picture you took down, by the way?'

'My family. An old photo of us visiting this house. In the 70s.'

'So you're how old?'

'Eleven or twelve, I suppose.'

'Who else is in the photo?'

'My granny. My parents. My brother and sister. And my dog.'

'Your parents who came here from Harris and died happy in their beds?'

'Aye. You've a good memory.'

'You made quite an impression.'

'Did I?'

Ignoring the query, she says, 'But this wasn't your home, surely? It's too small.'

'It was my grandparents'. We often came to visit. My mother was from Skye originally. She married a Harris man – a schoolteacher – but she always wanted to come back.'

'So you've been very happy here, I should imagine. For a long time, man and boy?'

'Aye. My grandparents gave the house to my mother who wanted to sell it as a building plot. But I wanted to keep the house as it was, so I bought it from my parents.'

'Is it the house or the land that means so much to you?'

'The land.'

71

'What are you doing with it?'

'I'll tell you tomorrow when I show you round. Let's go and eat. D'you fancy an omelette?'

'Fine. But there's no hurry. I'm not starving.'

'Are you coming down for that whisky?'

'In a minute. I just want to unpack a few things. Take my glass and go on down and I'll see if I can find my way around on my own.'

'Supper in half an hour, then?'

'Sounds good to me.'

Marianne hears his feet descending the wooden stairs; an aimless, cheerful whistle; the chink of bottleneck on glass. She unpacks her underwear into the empty drawer, hangs her dressing gown on the cup-hook and stows her wet shoes neatly under the bed. Having deposited her toiletries bag on the end of the bed, she paces the room a couple of times, counting, and decides the safest way to locate the stairs is to count from the window, walking in a straight line to the top of the staircase.

She extracts a heavy object from her case: a bottle swathed in tissue. Cradling it in one arm she reaches out, searching for the window. She turns about-face and counts five paces to the head of the stairs and feels for the rail. Descending carefully, counting all the while, she finds herself on level ground and breathes more easily.

'Keir? Are you in the kitchen?'

'Sitting room. I'm behind the stair. Wait! Stay there till I've moved my boots. I left them lying in the middle of the floor.'

She extends her arm in the direction of his voice. 'A contribution to the store cupboard.'

He takes the bottle from her hand and unwraps it. 'Champagne?'

'Yes. Wildly inappropriate, I know, but I'm rather limited in what I can choose as gifts for people. I thought you might find something to celebrate. The arrival of some migrating bird, perhaps?'

'Or the departure of the midges. Och no, we must drink this before you go.'

'Well, that *was* the general idea. You never know – cocoa

72

might begin to pall after a while. I'm off in search of the kitchen. I'll leave you to get on.'

As she turns away, Keir shouts, 'Mind the stair!', grabs her arm and pulls her to one side. Marianne loses her footing but he keeps her upright with an arm round her waist and a firm grip under her forearm. 'You were going to walk head-on into the staircase. You're underneath it and you'd have cracked your head. Sorry if I startled you.'

'No ... I'm all right. Thanks.' Righting herself, she lays a hand against his chest and, with a small shock, encounters crisp, curling hair, then bare skin. Pulling away quickly, she stutters, 'Sorry – were you ...? Oh, God, Keir – you aren't naked, are you?'

Laughing, he replies, 'No, but I was getting changed.'

'Oh. I'm sorry, I didn't mean to barge in. I should have knocked.'

'There's no door.'

Still flustered, she says, 'We're going to need some sort of system, aren't we? There's no door upstairs either.'

'I've already thought of that. Come to the foot of the stair.' He takes her elbow and leads her a few paces. 'Have you got your bearings?'

'I think so.' She points. 'Front door ... Kitchen ... Sitting room?'

'Aye, that's right. Over here, just before you go into the kitchen, I've hung a wind chime.' A random but not unpleasant series of notes sounds above Marianne's head. As they die away Keir resumes, 'We'll use it like a doorbell. I'll jangle it if I'm coming up and you can do the same if you want to let me know you're around. But obviously privacy is less of an issue for me.'

'Because you're a man, you mean?'

'No, because you're blind. I can *see* where you are. What you're doing.'

'Oh. Yes, of course ... You should go and get dressed. It's chilly away from the stove. Thanks for the wind chime. A brilliant idea. I shall enjoy using it.'

'It will also let you know when I'm coming in and out of the

73

house. As soon as the front door opens it will ring and let you know.'

'But in a much gentler way than a doorbell.'

'Aye.'

'Really, there is no end to your thoughtfulness. Thank you.'

'It's not just for your benefit. Sudden loud noises seem intrusive here. I don't like them. And they startle the birds. I try to keep things natural – or at least musical.'

'No opera, then?'

'Only on the iPod and in the car. No electricity here. I've got a battery-operated radio if you crave music or news.'

'No, I'm very happy lost in the *Brigadoon* time-warp, thanks. The kitchen's just here, isn't it?'

'Aye, straight ahead. Marianne ...' He touches her elbow. 'I'm sorry if I alarmed you. When I caught hold of you. But it would have been an almighty crack on the head.'

'Oh, take no notice of me – I was just a bit thrown, that's all. And feeling vulnerable, I suppose. Men try some funny things on once they know you're blind.'

'You're kidding me?'

'No, unfortunately.'

'Bastards!'

'Oh, I've had some unpleasant experiences in my time. But, don't worry – that wasn't one of them.'

Marianne

On the contrary. But I withdrew in confusion, like something out of Jane Austen.

I suppose I might have handled it better if it hadn't been so long since I'd handled a man. It's at times like these that I miss having working eyes, eyes which I gather can signal your feelings, eyes that can invite, repel, permit, forbid, regardless of the words one is obliged to utter for form's sake. How, without expressive eyes, could I have kept a door open, signalled to Keir that he could perhaps enter if he wished?

By touching him again. Which is what I wanted to do, but didn't. When the wind chime jangled I wanted to fling my arms round his neck. If he'd been fully clothed, perhaps I would have.

But instead I said 'Thanks' and kept my hands to myself, because I didn't know what holding him would have meant – to him or me – other than that I just wanted to hold him. And life isn't that simple. Not mine, anyway.

(So much for treating people as if we all have a year to live. What a load of sentimental codswallop I talk.)

I felt my way back upstairs, counting, and sat on the bed. Below me I could hear Keir moving around, unzipping pockets in his rucksack (or, imagination working overtime now, was it his jeans?) and putting things away in drawers and cupboards. The clank of the stove door, followed by a dull thud and a whiff of wood smoke told me he'd thrown another log on the fire.

I felt for the toilet bag I'd left on the bed and took out my hair-brush. I brushed my hair vigorously, showing no mercy to tangles, until my hair crackled with static. I vented my irritation with myself and my blindness, with the game I wanted to play but couldn't, because I hadn't been dealt a full hand.

When my hair was smooth and hung straight and heavy to my shoulders, I pushed it behind my ears and gathered it up into a ponytail, reaching into the bag for a band to secure it. No-nonsense hair for my no-nonsense life.

Penance observed, I sat composed on the edge of the bed, hands folded demurely in my lap, mentally undressing Keir. I comforted myself with the thought that, although difficulties and confusion might arise with the two of us confined in such a small space, my thoughts at least were my own.

Which, given the direction they were running in, was just as well.

Chapter Seven

After supper Keir writes a letter of condolence to Mac's mother while Marianne – at her insistence – makes up her bed above the sitting room. She retires early, exhausted with the effort of negotiating and memorising new territory. Lying in bed she hears Keir wash up and get ready for bed; the stove door opening and shutting; the slither of a sleeping bag as he shakes it out; the creak of the sofa as it takes his weight.

Marianne lies on her back trying to catch sounds from beyond the interior of the house. The wind has dropped now and at first she thinks there is silence outdoors, a silence so absolute as to be almost palpable. Then beyond the hiss of the stove and the grumble of falling logs she hears a chuckling noise, a musical gurgle which she realises is the burn running along beside the house, tumbling over rocks and stones as it hurtles down to the sea. The sound is both constant and constantly changing. Marianne lies in bed, enthralled. She longs to share her excitement with the man who had the vision to bring her here, but suspects he's already asleep.

Re-tuning her ears to the room below, she identifies the rustle of pages turning. Too noisy for a book. A magazine, presumably. She wonders what sort of magazine. A professional journal? The latest developments in exploration geophysics? Or a wildlife magazine? That seemed more likely. Keir appeared to compartmentalise his highly organised life and Marianne thought his life as an oil man would not be allowed to impinge on his alternative life here on Skye. Domestic schizophrenia was something her marriage had had to accommodate and she understood the necessity of inhabiting only one world at a time.

Keir clears his throat softly and turns a page.

'Keir? Are you awake?'

'Aye. What's the matter?'

'Nothing. I just wondered what you were reading?'

'The RSPB magazine.'

'Thought so.'

'Let me guess now – that would be the way I whistle as I turn the pages?'

'If it had been *Playboy*, you'd have been turning them more quickly. Less text. What are we doing tomorrow?'

'That depends how wet you're prepared to get.'

'I like rain. If I'm out, I prefer rain to sunshine.'

'Well, you've come to the right place. I'll give you the tour in the morning, then I thought we'd take a picnic and maybe have lunch in the tree-house.'

'Tree-house?' She sits up.

As he hears the rustle of the duvet, Keir calls out, 'Mind your head!'

'Is there really a tree-house?'

'Aye.'

'Did you build it?'

'My grandfather built the original. I've modified it.'

'A *tree-house*!' She laughs.

'Don't mock.'

'I'm not mocking, I'm delighted! Delighted at the thought of my tree-man living in a tree-house.'

'Have you ever been in one?'

'Now, I ask you – is it likely? Of course I haven't! How do you get up there?'

'A rope ladder.'

'Oh ...' He hears a small sound, an exclamation half-swallowed, something that could be delight or disappointment, he's not sure.

'Marianne? You OK?'

'Perfectly. Just having trouble containing my excitement. A

78

tree-house ... I'm going to be up in the treetops! Will I be able to get up there, do you think? A rope ladder will be tricky.'

'Not if I hold it steady at the bottom.'

'That means I'd have to go up first.'

'We'll get you up there if I have to give you a fireman's lift.'

'Permission granted to employ whatever undignified mode of transport deemed necessary. This is *so* exciting! You know, you shouldn't have told me. You can't possibly expect me to go to sleep now.'

'And it doesn't look as if I'm going to get any either.'

'Sorry – am I keeping you from "Playmate of the Month"?'

'No. Booming bitterns. Get to sleep. You've got a strenuous day tomorrow. And it's your turn to cook.'

Marianne lies down again, curls up in her duvet and murmurs, 'All this ... and cocoa too.' The last thing she remembers hearing is the sound of Keir chuckling. Or perhaps it was the burn.

He is woken by a dream. Mac on the rig. The moment when Keir sees the accident waiting to happen. Mac laughing and shouting in a high wind, pointing, not seeing, not hearing the Samson post behind him, the badly welded steel upright as it comes adrift, sways a moment, then falls. Keir dives full length, aiming his body at Mac who flies across the platform. As the two men hit the ground, Keir wakes.

The wood-burner has gone out but he lies in his sleeping bag sweating, his big limbs aching from the confinement of the train, the Land Rover, the sofa. He arches his back and stretches his legs. Putting a hand to his stitches, he remembers hitting the ground and splitting his forehead, lying face down, staring at a patch of blood-coloured rust on the deck, watching his blood pool beside it, then hearing Mac fall, but not being able to move, finally not being able to see ...

In the end it had been a glancing blow, but still fatal. Keir's dive made sure Mac wasn't killed outright, but that was all. His heroics simply prolonged the agony for the family. Annie had a week to sit by her unconscious husband, planning how to break it to the bairns; a week in which hope must have ebbed away

79

like Mac's life, leaving a vacuum that would never be filled except with grief and rage.

Keir recalls Marianne sleeping above him. He listens for her breathing. Nothing. Then the sound of her turning over, the groan of a board above his head. He sits up and looks out the window at the night sky. No stars. A moon almost obscured by cloud. He shivers and rubs bare arms. It's cold, very cold. Snow tomorrow, probably.

Marianne stirs again and murmurs, a sound that catches Keir by surprise, a sound that reminds him of women he's slept beside; women awake who murmured as they lay beneath him. He smiles briefly in the dark, then shrugs back down into his sleeping bag.

'Keir?'

It's only a whisper and he's not convinced she's really awake until she repeats his name, no louder. 'Keir?'

'Aye?'

'You can put the light on if you want to read – it won't bother me.'

'No, I've been looking out the window. And now I'm just lying here, thinking.'

'About Mac?'

He hesitates, then says, 'Aye.'

'Do you want to talk about it?'

He thinks perhaps he *would* like to talk about it, thinks what a relief it might be, just to stare into the darkness and unburden himself, vent his anger, say what he saw, what he sees, to a faceless, understanding female. Instead he says, 'I'd rather talk about the stars.'

'Oh, yes, please do! What time is it anyway?'

He reaches for his watch. 'About one.'

'Oh dear. I didn't realise it was the middle of the night. What can you see? Are the stars twinkling? You said there are no curtains. Is the room full of moonlight? What is moonlight like? People do go *on* about it.'

'Moonlight? It's eerie. Like cold, still water . . . You know when there's a mist in Edinburgh and the air is full of vapour? You feel like you're breathing water. The air's clammy and it seeps into your clothes, into your bones. That's a bit like moon-light. Cold. And mysterious . . . It can look very beautiful. Or sinister.'

'Tell me about the stars.'

'Are you cold up there? The stove's out now. It's always a bit temperamental on the first night. Wait and I'll light it again.' He unzips his sleeping bag and kneels in front of the wood-burner, feeling on the hearth for a box of matches and a candle. He lights it, opens the stove door, then rakes over the ashes and a few glowing embers. He pushes in screws of paper, some kindling, then as the wood catches light, a log.

'Mmm, wonderful smells!' Marianne calls down from upstairs. 'A candle? I can smell beeswax. You haven't lit the lamp?'

'No. Too much bother. And too bright. You need darkness to see stars,' he says, blowing out the candle. 'I used to hate the summer when I was a kid. Being eaten alive by midges and it never getting dark . . . You don't see stars unless it's dark and I used to miss them. Can you hear me?'

'Perfectly. The wooden floor reverberates with your voice. You sound very close in fact. Go on.'

'In summer I used to stand at my bedroom window – when I should have been in bed asleep – staring up at the sky, knowing that the stars were there, I just couldn't see them. So I used to plot their positions, work out where they'd be if I could see them.'

'Like the astronomers who predicted Neptune.'

'Aye! You know about that?'

'Oh yes. I collect stories about the redundancy of sight. Tell me what you can see now. And don't worry whether or not I understand. I'll just listen to it as story. No, as *music*. The music of the spheres.' She laughs softly. 'A space opera.'

Satisfied that the log has caught, Keir gets into his sleeping bag again and looks out the window. As the moon appears from behind a cloud he sees that snow has started to fall in big, slow flakes. It collects at the corners of the window frame and is beginning to drift on the sill. He turns away from the window, lies down on his back and aims his voice upward, towards

Marianne. He speaks in a soft, steady monotone, as much incantation as description.

'If you look east, one of the brightest stars you'll see is Arcturus. It has a yellow-orange glow. Most stars look cold. Icy. They'd sound like . . . flutes. No, piccolos. *Shrill*. Arcturus looks warmer. A cello maybe . . . It looks like the stove feels when it gives off just a bit of heat. Arcturus glows, but it doesn't burn or blaze like the sun. It's like the feeling you might have for an old friend . . . or an ex-lover, one who still means something to you. Steady. Passionless. On second thoughts, make that a viola . . . How am I doing?'

'This is utter *bliss*. I want you to make me a tape of this. To listen to when I'm back home. Tell me more.'

Keir rolls onto his side and props himself up on an elbow, looking at the stove. 'If you look west, you'll see Orion, the hunter. He's easy to spot. He's massive. My esteemed colleagues on the rigs would say he was built like a brick shithouse. His right arm's raised up in the air, wielding his club. His left arm is extended and holds a shield – some say a lion's skin. His shoulders are wide and a big, bright star called Betelgeuse sits on his shoulder. I couldn't get my mouth round it when I was a kid so I used to call it "Beetlejuice" . . . There's an even brighter star at Orion's foot: Rigel. Now Rigel really hits you between the eyes. It's fifty thousand times brighter than the sun, but it's fourteen hundred light years away. What I really like about Orion – och, this guy is so cool! – is, he has a fancy belt. He's big in the shoulder but kind of narrow in the waist and he has a belt made up of three bright stars. And hanging from this superb belt is another cluster of stars, quite close together, that dangle and form his sword. The middle star is really the Orion Nebula, which is a cloud of dust and gas, but it looks just like a star . . . Now if you look to the left of Orion, snapping at his heels you'll find the brightest star in the sky: Sirius, the Dog Star, Orion's hunting dog. Sirius is quite close, only eight light years away and it's forty times more luminous than the sun, so that's why it looks so bright. Think of . . . a clarinet, the way it dominates the other instruments of the orchestra. Sirius outshines all the

82

other stars and draws your eye. My grandfather had a sheep-dog like that . . . Star. That was his name. No good as a work-ing dog – unreliable and a show-off. So he gave him to me. Star was always at my heels, wanting attention. A complete pain in the arse, but I loved him and he loved me. I gave him a secret name. Sirius. And I used to pretend to be Orion the hunter, with a leather belt my big brother gave me and a stick for a sword . . . Once Sirius caught a hare. He killed it and brought it to me, dropped it at my feet, like an offering. I was completely choked.'

'Why?'

'At the foot of Orion there's another constellation. Lepus. The Hare. I thought this was proof that Sirius *knew*, knew what his secret name meant, knew who I was pretending to be.' Keir turns his head to look up at the window. He watches snowflakes swarming outside, then says softly, 'Are you still awake? You're very quiet.'

'I'm completely entranced, that's why.' He hears the rustle of bedclothes above him as she turns over. 'Thank you, Keir. That was all quite, quite wonderful.'

'You should try and sleep. I've an exhausting day planned for you tomorrow.'

'Oh, I'm far too excited to sleep. I shall lie awake now and watch the stars in my mind's eye.'

He doesn't reply, then after a moment begins to recite.

> *'Thou being of marvels,*
> *Shield me with might,*
> *Thou being of statutes*
> *And of stars . . .'*

'What's that?'

'A Gaelic prayer. More of a charm, half pagan as it is. A charm for sleep.'

'Is there more?'

'Aye, plenty . . . *Compass me this night,*
Both soul and body,
Compass me this night

83

And on every night.
Compass me aright
Between earth and sky,
Between the mystery of Thy laws
And mine eye of blindness.'

He hears the small sound of her sudden intake of her breath, but continues:

'Both that which mine eye sees
And that which it reads not:
Both that which is clear
And is not clear to my devotion . . .

Goodnight, Marianne.'

'Goodnight . . . And thank you, Keir.'

'Och, no bother.'

She hears the zip of his sleeping bag and a creak as the sofa settles beneath him. Lying still, hardly breathing, Marianne recalls a phrase from the charm: *Thou Being of Marvels . . .* She smiles and thinks of Keir, then to her dismay, finds she has begun to tremble, and not because of the wintry chill in the room.

Louisa

When she'd been gone for several days I received a postcard from Marianne. I presumed she must have dictated the message.

Dear Lou,

Sight-seeing is not an option but I'm nevertheless experiencing Skye. Everywhere we go I hear a beautiful, soothing texture of sounds. And so many different kinds of rain! It's never silent but always quiet enough to hear the smallest sound, like water trickling over rocks. I feel as if I've been given spectacles for my ears – my world of the senses is suddenly in sharp focus. I'm drunk on a cocktail of peat smoke, damp vegetation and the sea, washed down with the odd dram of very good whisky.

Having – as they say – a wonderful time.
Love,
M.
x
P.S. I asked Keir to choose a card for you.

It was one of those humorous postcards, completely black and captioned 'Night Skye'. At first I thought the joke was in pretty poor taste, but the more I thought about it, the more I thought it was just the sort of weird choice Marianne herself would have made. Keir also sent me a card and the two arrived together. His was pictorial, showing a spectacular view of mountains. The message was brief.

Hi Louisa
Marianne appears to be enjoying herself. No mishaps and she's coping very well off home territory. She even seems to like our terrible weather.
Best wishes,
Keir

It was sweet of them both to think of me sitting worrying at home and I did appreciate the reassurance, but of course neither of them had told me what I really wanted to know.

I showed both cards to Garth when he called round to fix a problem with my laptop. Despite (or perhaps because of) his public school education, Garth likes to affect the speech patterns of a cockney costermonger. He read both cards, handed them back to me and said with a grin, 'You reckon they're shaggin' then?'

Chapter Eight

Louisa

Life took an interesting turn while Marianne was away. (Perhaps life took an interesting turn because Marianne was away.)

Garth and I had been to an evening lecture on Mary Shelley (a much under-rated author, in my opinion) and we walked home, deep in discussion. As the February sleet turned to snow we took a short-cut up a side street, then through an alley. An ill-advised decision as it turned out, but I was accompanied by Garth and it wasn't very late, so my guard was down. We were debating whether Frankenstein *constituted a study of bad parenting as well as motherlessness when a man suddenly sprang up from behind a pile of rubbish bags. Shabby and desperate-looking, he emerged from the cover of the bags, like Magwitch among the tombstones, and lurched towards us.*

One is used to beggars, tramps and all sorts in Edinburgh, so although I was startled, I didn't panic immediately, not until I'd registered our surroundings: a badly lit side-street; the absence of people; the sound of traffic now distant. Clutching Garth's arm, I was aware he was rigid with tension, then that he was shaking.

He must have seen the knife before I did. It wasn't a very big knife, but there was something about the way the man held it that made me think he knew how to use it and would have no scruples about doing so. Magwitch said, 'Don't move!', a quite unnecessary instruction since Garth and I were rooted to the spot with terror. He lifted the knife, brandishing it in my face, but kept his eyes on Garth. 'Wallet and phone, pal. One at a time.'

Garth stammered, 'Leave 'er alone! You can 'ave 'em, mate.' He reached inside his long black overcoat and slowly handed over his mobile, then his wallet. Magwitch pocketed them both, still watching Garth, though his eyes flickered once in my direction. They were dead, dulled with drugs, hunger or cold – perhaps a mixture of all three.

He turned to me and snarled, 'Bag.' I thought at first this was just an insult, then realised he was asking for my handbag. I proffered it without hesitation. It was a large leather bag with a shoulder chain as well as handles, a bag big enough to contain all my writer's paraphernalia of notebooks, pens, index cards and so forth. I could see Magwitch thinking how conspicuous the bag would be, how heavy to carry as he ran. He gestured with the knife then barked, 'Open it. Gie's your purse.'

Now, there was a flaw in the design of that bag which was in any case never intended to carry all the kit I put in it. If you held the bag by one handle and released the catch, it tended to gape open and, if you weren't careful, the contents of the bag fell out.

I wasn't careful.

I let go of one of the handles, released the catch and the contents of my handbag fell at Magwitch's feet. Phone, purse, spectacles, powder compact, nail polish, fountain pen and key ring clattered to the ground. He seemed to be thrown by the noise and glanced over his shoulder, then back at me. If looks could kill, I'd have been a goner. He muttered, 'Stupid fucking bitch,' then did a little dance of indecision, shifting his weight from one ill-shod foot to the other. I prayed for him to turn and run. Instead he growled, 'Pick them up! Purse, then phone.'

I extended a hand towards Garth and clutched at his arm as I kneeled down among my scattered (in some cases shattered) belongings. Garth must have bent to help me because Magwitch grunted, then said, 'Don't move, laddie, or Ma's had it.'

Well, that was the last straw. I was already frightened and tearful, but this was the final insult. Now I was angry. Grasping my phone in one hand and my purse in the other, I got up from my knees into a crouching position. I stared at Magwitch's feet, aligned my body, took a deep breath and launched myself upwards, head-butting him in the groin.

He fell over backwards, screaming. I yelled 'Run!' and without waiting to see if Garth followed, ran as fast as I could towards light, noise and traffic, shedding my high-heeled shoes at the earliest opportunity. Only when I hit the busy thoroughfare of Lothian Road did I pause for breath. I was overjoyed to find Garth beside me, laughing and weeping, black eyeliner coursing down his whitened cheeks. We stood on a street corner, hugging and congratulating each other until Garth had the wit to hail a taxi. I hobbled over to the cab and gave the driver my address, then Garth pointed out that my keys were still lying in the alley. I explained that, since the time Marianne had lost her key, I'd left a spare with a neighbour.

When we arrived home, I told Garth that under no circumstances was I spending the night alone in the flat since Magwitch now had my keys, my address book and a motive for murder. Garth lived alone in a seedy area populated by Magwitches, so I wasn't the least surprised when he agreed to stay.

And that's *how it all started.*

Marianne

When I woke something was different. *Everything* was different. The sounds, the scents, the smell and feel of the duvet cover, the chill in the air, all of this was unfamiliar. As I surfaced from sleep my heart began to pound and I tried to work out where I was.

There was a smell of frying bacon. (Louisa never cooked breakfast, never *ate* breakfast, but succumbed as often as not to coffee and a Danish mid-morning.) There was the sound of someone trying to be quiet in a kitchen: loud, metallic noises followed by quieter sounds as memory and consideration kicked in. There were other smells: coffee, wood smoke, something herbal and soapy. Gradually my senses assembled the jigsaw: I was upstairs in Keir's house. He was below, in the kitchen, freshly showered, brewing coffee, cooking breakfast, tending the stove.

I lay still on my pillows, absorbing my surroundings. There was something else, something I couldn't put my finger on, something that was different from yesterday ... The burn. I couldn't hear the burn. It had been faint indoors but I'd fallen asleep to the sound of it murmuring. Now I couldn't hear it at all.

At the foot of the stairs the wind chime rang, then rang again, a little louder. I heard Keir's footsteps on the stairs, slow, deliberate.

'Marianne? Are you awake?'

She sits up in bed pulling the duvet around her, even though her body is well covered by fleece pyjamas. 'Yes. Are you in the room yet?'

'No, on the stair. I've made you some breakfast.' Keir ducks his head as he enters with a tray. 'Or are you one of those bloodless females who start the day with yoghurt and herbal tea?'

'I could murder a bacon roll.'

'Now that's what I like to hear. I've got a tray here and I'm putting it in front of you. There's coffee on your right and a bacon sandwich on your left. Sliced white so you can relish the full slum-dwelling experience. There's plenty more coffee, just give me a shout. I thought about bringing up the pot but I imagine a mug is easier.'

'Thank you. This is all just wonderful.'

He stands at the end of the bed and watches her bite into the sandwich; thinks how different she looks with her smooth, ashen hair disordered. 'It's nice and warm in the kitchen when you want to come down. I'll teach you how the shower works.'

'Thanks.' She waves the sandwich in the direction of his voice. 'This is delicious, by the way.' Swallowing, she says, 'Keir, there's something odd about the sounds outside. What is it?'

He smiles. 'Can you sense that? Is it quieter? Even with me banging around in the kitchen?'

'It seems quieter *outside*.'

'Aye.'

'I can't hear the burn.'

'No, you won't. It's sluggish now. With ice.'

She lifts her head as realisation dawns. 'Has it *snowed*?'

'Aye, it has. Inches of the stuff. Are you up for a snowball fight? You can blindfold me to make it fair. We'll do it like Jedi Knights in training. *Feel the force, Luke ...*'

Choking, she exclaims, 'Your jokes are in appalling taste!'

'Aye, but they make you laugh.'

'Only because I have a macabre sense of humour. Sit down. You don't have to hover like an old family retainer.'

Keir sits at the end of the bed and says, 'It must be bad enough being blind, but not being able to laugh about it – that would be terrible. Wouldn't it?' he adds, a note of uncertainty in his voice.

'You're right, it would. *I* don't mind, but Louisa would have forty thousand fits if she heard you. Her illusions would be completely shattered.'

'Louisa's illusions? What might they be?'

'Oh, I don't know exactly. I don't ask.' Marianne takes another bite of her sandwich. 'I think she perceives you as a tall, dark stranger, whisking me off for an adventure. Who knows what Louisa thinks? She scarcely lives in the real world.'

'And you do?'

She stops chewing and says, '*That* was a bit cutting.'

'No, I meant, d'you feel as if you're living in the *same* world? As me? As Louisa? Your world must extend only as far as you can reach with your stick. As far as you can hear, smell. Am I wrong?'

'No. It is a much smaller world.'

'But deeper. More intensely felt, I'd imagine. Or do you worry that you imagine too much? Or inaccurately?'

'Six foot rabbits, you mean?'

'Well, the feedback must be very limited where you can't touch.'

'Not as limited as you might think. I'm aware of your every movement sitting at the end of the bed. The mattress transmits it to the muscles of my legs. Even if I hadn't already read you with my hands, I'd know you were a big man because of the way the mattress is responding.'

'*In bed with an elephant* ... They say that's how Scotland felt after the Act of Union – like a mouse in bed with an elephant. However friendly the elephant, we'd not get a good night's sleep ... Does Louisa's world include a man?'

'No.' Marianne leans back on her pillows, licking her

fingers. 'I don't know why. I'm sure she'd like one. I don't know what she looks like, of course, let alone from a male point of view, but she's kind. And rich. And not nearly as stupid as she likes to make out. She cultivates the daffy blonde bit.'

'Why?'

'To redress the balance, I suppose. She probably thinks it reduces my sense of being handicapped, makes me feel more competent. Lou means well, but it can get a bit irritating.'

'The kindness? Or the daffiness?'

'Both. I suspect no man has taken her on because he thinks he'd have to take me on as well. Which isn't the case. I could live independently. Lots of blind people do. I managed at university and I managed when Harvey was offshore. It would just be more difficult for me, that's all. Can you pass me a tissue? I put some down somewhere, but I don't remember where.'

'There's some kitchen towel on the tray.'

Groping for the towel, Marianne continues, 'I'm curious. How does Louisa strike you? Speaking as a man, I mean?'

'Well, she's not my type. Never would have been, even when she was younger, but she's attractive if you like your women ... ample. And fluffy. And plenty men do. And you can tell she's interested, she hasn't given up. That's attractive to a man. The old antennae are still waving.'

'Really? Must be the HRT. Were they waving at you, then?'

'I think they might have been. I wasn't paying her that much attention.'

'You said in the Botanics you couldn't tell if women found you attractive.'

'I meant blind women. Has Louisa never married?'

'No. Nor has she lived the life of a nun. But nothing's lasted.'

'What about Garth the Goth?'

'*Garth*? He can't be more than twenty-five!'

'So? They say men are past their sexual peak at forty and women are just reaching theirs. Louisa might appreciate a bit of ... athleticism.'

'But what would a man Garth's age see in *Louisa*?'

'You'd be surprised. Kindness. Humour. An accommodating

and sensual woman, one who wasn't obsessed with cellulite and liposuction. And then there's always gratitude.'

'*Gratitude*?'

'Don't underestimate it. Men are just as insecure as women, maybe more so. We've far more to prove, to women and to ourselves. We lie awake at nights and fantasise about grateful women. Young women can be pretty damn scary. And not a lot of fun to go to bed with. Obsession with your appearance and your mobile phone can be a bit of a turn-off for a guy. Someone like Louisa might seem a more relaxing proposition to young Garth.'

Marianne considers her sister in this new light and says, 'Were *you* interested, then?'

'In Louisa? No, I was speaking hypothetically. You asked for a male opinion.'

'Have you had relationships with older women?'

'Aye, when I was younger. There was a career woman in Aberdeen who loved her job and didn't want to settle down with babies. I was young enough to feel flattered by the attention and callow enough not to mind being treated as a sex object. It was fun while it lasted.'

'You never married?'

'I've never looked for anything permanent. Which is probably why I've never found it.'

'Oil marriages don't tend to last, anyway.'

'It's a lousy deal for both partners. For the wife especially. Have there been many men since Harvey?'

She pauses before answering, then says carefully, 'A few.'

'Ah! We entered a conversational no-go zone. I didn't see the sign.'

'I'm sorry, Keir, but I suddenly feel very odd sitting here in my pyjamas talking about my sex life – and yours – with you sitting on the edge of the bed, not the *least* like an elephant. I don't know what's going on.'

'Nothing's going on. We're just talking. You told me Louisa saw me as some sort of ... *hero*. I wondered how you saw me.'

'I don't see you, do I?'

'You do, but not with your eyes. Don't worry, I'm not going

93

to try anything on. I find you too fascinating to risk frightening you away. And I'm too much of a hero – in my *own* eyes – to take advantage of you. But I thought it might be good to deal honestly with each other. Not least because I don't know how to read you. You don't give out all the usual signs. And you certainly don't say all the usual things. So I'm having to make it up as I go along.'

'So am I.'

'My, aren't we the spontaneous ones! Would you like more coffee?'

She laughs. 'You don't have to back off, you know.'

'I wasn't. I was offering you more coffee before asking my killer question.'

'Which is?'

He shifts his weight on the bed, then says, 'When you heard about Mac's death, you said you wished we treated folk as if we knew we were about to die. Say all we wanted to say.'

'It seems rather a foolish thing to have said now. I was thinking about Mac's poor wife. And Harvey.'

'Aye, I know. But I've been wondering ... What would you say to me if you knew you were going to die? Or *I* was going to die?'

'Oh, that's not fair!'

He shrugs. 'You don't have to answer.'

'But you know I will.'

'I hope you will.'

She is silent, then says, 'You *aren't* about to die, are you?'

'Not as far as I know. But it's an uncertain world.'

She plucks at the duvet, scowling. 'You're bloody impossible, Keir. You just don't play by the rules.'

'What rules?' he says softly. 'Shinty's my game. And let me tell you, shinty's not a game for jessies.'

'If we didn't have long ...' She scrapes her hair back behind her ears and sighs, exasperated. 'Oh, it's such a stupid question!'

'So don't answer.'

She sighs again. 'If we didn't have long, I'd ... I *think* I'd ask you to hold me ... I'd probably ask you to make love to me as well.' She covers her mouth with a hand and shakes her head. 'Oh, God, I can't believe I just said that! What on earth did you put in the coffee?'

He is silent for a moment, then says, 'But you're not asking now?'

She places her fingertips together in front of her lips, as if about to pray. 'No. I'm not asking now.'

'Then I'll get you that coffee.'

Relieved of his weight, the mattress tilts and Marianne feels momentarily giddy. As his footsteps retreat, she calls out, 'Keir?'

'Aye?'

'What would *you* say?'

He pauses at the top of the staircase, his head and shoulders bowed to accommodate the sloping ceiling. 'Much the same.'

He descends slowly but forgets to duck at the foot of the stairs. The wind chime jangles.

Marianne

I negotiated the stairs, the shower, then the stairs again. I got dressed and went downstairs, feeling more confident with each journey. I presented myself in the kitchen where Keir was washing up. I heard him stop scrubbing at a pan and after a moment he said, 'D'you always wear black?'

'No. Sometimes I wear cream. It makes life simpler. I don't have to think about colours clashing.'

'Would it matter if they did? It's not something I ever think about.'

I was thrown by the question and asked, randomly, 'What are you wearing?'

'Jeans and a polo neck. And a zip-up fleece. '

'What colours?'

'The polo neck's dark brown. Think ... double bass. And the fleece is greeny-blue ... Harp.'

'Greeny-blue? Like your eyes?'

'No, they're green *and* blue.'

'Now, that I would like to see.'

'Twinkling stars ... My eyes ... Anything else?'

95

'Snow.'

I hear the washing-up water splash, then drain away. Keir takes my arm. 'Come with me ...'

Keir leads her across the kitchen to the back door. As he opens it, Marianne feels a wave of cold, damp air envelope her, as it does when she opens the freezer at home. He shuts the door behind her and she shivers at the sudden change in temperature. Folding her arms across her chest for warmth, she says, 'Tell me what you see.'

'Snow.'

'And?'

'More snow. Sunlight shining on the snow.'

'What does it look like?'

'Dazzling. It hurts your eyes almost.'

'And if it were a sound?'

'A *sound*? Bloody hell, you don't ask a lot.'

'Come on, Keir, you're good at this, you know you are. Humour me.'

'If it were a sound ...' He gazes at the snow-covered land-scape. 'Aye, you know those strings at the beginning of *The Flying Dutchman* overture? The very opening chords?'

'Oh, yes. They're *piercing*!'

'That's what it looks like.'

'*Thank* you!' She turns away, smiling, and faces the white landscape, as if equipped now to assess the view.

Marianne

Keir said there were crocuses buried underfoot but daffodils in bud, standing bravely in the snow. He lifted my hand to rifle dangling catkins and I felt the long cold flowers trickle through my fingers. He cleared snow from a garden bench, spread something water-proof and we sat in the weak February sun. I turned my face up towards the warmth. Behind us there was the constant drip of melting snow falling from the roof; to one side, a furious flurry of bird activity in a hedge. We stopped talking to listen to a wren that was sheltering, Keir said, in a pile of dead and damaged wood he'd cut back after a gale and stored for fuel.

I'm told that the wren is a tiny bird, comparable with a mouse in size, and that it creeps about something like a mouse, but to listen to that assertive, even strident call, you'd think the bird was much more substantial – the size of a blackbird at least. Keir said it was a case of serious over-compensation, like short men who drove big, fast cars.

'What does that say about men who drive Land Rovers, then?'

'I used to drive a sensible car. Low fuel consumption. If not green, then green-ish. Then one night I had an altercation with a stag in Glen Shiel, on my way home. At about fifty miles per hour. The car was a complete write-off. So was the stag.'

'And you?'

'Nothing more than bruises and shattered nerves. After that, though, I'd a hankering to ride around in a Sherman tank. The Landy was a compromise. It's practical and it makes me feel safe. I figure I take enough risks in my working life. The fuel consumption gives me an ecological headache, but at least it runs on diesel. Are you getting cold?'

'A bit.'

'We'll go inside, get togged up, then go for a walk. There'll be more snow, but not yet awhile.'

As I got to my feet I felt the light touch of his hand on my elbow, guiding me discreetly between obstacles.

'Mmm … What's that wonderful smell? Wait, don't tell me – daphne?'

'Aye, it's growing against the wall just here. The scent's for me and the berries are for the birds.' I heard him inhale deeply. 'You could get drunk on it, couldn't you?'

'Keir, why *did* you bring me here?'

'Three reasons. I wanted to show you Skye.'

'But I can't *see*.'

'You can. You will. As much as anyone would. My hunch is you'll see more. And I wanted to show you my home and what I'm doing here.'

'Keeping the twenty-first century at bay.'

'It's a tough job, but someone's got to do it. A third of all plants and a quarter of all mammals face extinction in the century ahead.'

97

'Good God!'

'Well, no, not particularly. As deities go, rather a negligent God. Mind the step as you go indoors.' We stepped back into the fuggy warmth of the kitchen and he closed the door behind us.

'And the third reason?'

'Pure self-indulgence. You're a treat, Marianne. Like a box of chocolates.'

'Thank you. I *think*.'

'You're like a box of chocolates with the menu missing – the card that tells you what they are. I never know what I'm going to get with you: a soft, creamy centre, something chewy, or an explosion of alcohol.'

'I thought you didn't like living dangerously?'

'Unidentified chocolates I can handle.'

A few minutes later they are dressed for outdoor walking and standing in front of the house. As he shoulders a small rucksack Keir says, 'The terrain is uneven but we'll take it very slow. I'll make sure you don't fall.'

'Thanks. I'm used to falling. It's really not a big deal.'

'It is when you're as far from a hospital as we are. Have you ever used trekking poles?'

'No. I've rarely walked on anything other than pavements and footpaths.'

'Try one. Here – bend your arm ...' He slips the loop of one pole over her wrist and arranges her fingers round the handle. He notes the contrast between their hands: hers, small and slim; his own, twice the size, with thick, weathered fingers, nimble for their size, used to handling equipment in a North Sea gale or a desert sandstorm. When Marianne's fingers are finally arranged round the trekking pole, he envelopes her hand with his, briefly and superfluously.

'Now stand still while I adjust it for length. You have to have the handles quite high. You could use one pole and take my arm, or hand, or you could try going it alone using both poles. You won't be able to use them as you would your cane because snow will have covered a lot of obstacles. It's really a question of maintaining your stability. But even one pole will help with that. If you use two it will be impossible to fall over but you won't be attached to me in any way. It's up to you. The poles are telescopic and lightweight so we can collapse them and put them in the rucksack if you don't get on with them.'

'No, they feel really comfy. I think I might like them. If I walk along right behind you, it will be like following a path. I'll feel your footprints. Like King Wenceslas and the page. You'll have to remember to tell me if you stop or we'll collide.'

'OK, we'll give it a go. If it gets too much, just say and we'll have that snowball fight instead.'

'Where are you taking me?'

'We'll follow the burn, maybe as far as the waterfall, if the weather holds. We'll see how you get on with the poles. I hope we'll be able to move fast enough to keep you warm.'

'I'll be fine. Stop fretting.'

'You've got about fifty feet of clear terrain in the direction you're facing before we come to any trees. You can stride out for a while. There's a wee bit of gradient – going up – but the poles will compensate for that.'

They set off, slowly to begin with then, as Marianne gains confidence, they achieve a normal walking speed. This despite the fact that most of the time, unbeknown to Marianne, Keir is walking backwards to monitor her progress.

Marianne calls out. 'Does the waterfall ever freeze?'

'It has. But it won't be frozen today. It's not cold enough.'

'Ice is silent, isn't it?'

'You've lost me.'

'I was thinking of the burn and the waterfall, stopping in their tracks, transformed into ice. The water music would stop. When it does, the silence must be uncanny. Frozen music.' Marianne plods through the snow, seeking the indentations of Keir's footprints. He is complimenting her on the ease with which she walks, aided by the trekking pole, when he trips backwards over an unseen tree root. Snow falls around them in a sudden, slithering shower. Marianne turns her face upwards, laughing, and licks the snow that lands on her lips. Watching her, Keir steadies himself with a hand against a tree trunk.

'Are you walking backwards, Keir?

'No,' he replies, too promptly.

'Liar.'

'How did you know?'

'Your voice has been facing me. And then you tripped. Someone like you wouldn't trip. Not on home territory.'

'It's a fair cop, officer. I'll come quietly. Tell me more about this frozen music.'

'Face the way you're walking and I will.' As they set off again, Marianne resumes, 'It's how someone once described architecture to me. As frozen music. I found that quite helpful. Buildings are things I can never grasp, especially big ones. I can feel the texture of stone in a cathedral, but I can't get much of a sense of the building itself: light passing through stained glass windows, flying buttresses, the sheer scale of the thing. The *grandeur*.'

He doesn't reply for a moment, then stops walking and stands still. As she approaches he reaches for her arm. 'I've stopped.'

'Is something wrong? I don't need a rest yet.'

'OK, this is a long shot but d'you know Poulenc's organ concerto?'

'Yes, I do. Not very well. I find it an intimidating piece – a bit overwhelming, to be honest. Oh ...' Her voice fades. 'Is *that* –'

'Aye, it's pretty close, I reckon. It'll do for now anyway. I'll give it more thought. What's the matter?' She is standing with her head bowed, her body tense, as he remembers she stood once before in the Botanic Gardens before she told him about her dead husband. 'Marianne? Have I upset you?'

She turns up her eyes and he sees they are brimming with tears. 'No, I was just ... so *touched*. That you always try to translate things for me. And you do it so *well*. I'm really grateful, you know.'

'Aye, well ... As I said, when you get to my age, you dream of grateful women.'

Chapter Nine

'There's a couple of stepping-stones here, where the burn gets wider. We need to cross to the other side. Will I carry you over or d'you want to try and find them for yourself?'

Marianne pauses beside the stream. 'Are they flat stones?'

'Aye.'

'But wet, I suppose?'

'Possibly icy.'

'I'll let you carry me over. Piggyback?'

'Not worth it. Put both poles into your right hand and stand still. I'm going to put an arm behind your knees and another round your waist, then I'll lift you off the ground, OK?'

As Keir lifts her, Marianne hooks her free arm round his neck. She pats the rucksack. 'What have you got in here?'

'Waterproofs. Camera. Picnic.'

'A picnic in the snow?'

'At the tree-house. Setting you down now.' He straightens up and tugs gently at her arm. 'This way. Take it slowly. The tree cover is denser now. Keep a good grip on your poles. And you might want to shut your eyes to protect them.'

As they weave a path through the trees Marianne says, 'You said you wanted to show me what you were doing here. What exactly *are* you doing?'

'Planting trees, mainly. Looking after them. Trying to educate folk about trees. Trying to make them love trees, I suppose. *Know* them.'

Marianne plods on for a moment, then says, 'This is going to sound like a stupid question.'

'Try me.'

'Why?'

'Why trees, you mean?'

'Yes, why trees? Why not animals or birds?'

'It's a good question, not stupid at all. Trees encourage wildlife. They increase the space available for wildlife, like tower block flats for humans. Though personally, I'd rather live in a tree. Unlike tower blocks, trees increase the quality of that living space. Bark provides a habitat for insects, also for lichens and mosses and all the animals that live in and on those plants. A tree doesn't even have to be alive to enrich the environment. Dead or dying wood provides food and nesting sites for all sorts of insects, like bees and beetles ... and you've stopped listening, but you're far too polite to tell me I'm being boring.'

'No, carry on! I was the victim of an arts education, so science is a closed book to me. Go ahead and educate me.'

'I suspect you're merely humouring me, but I'll pretend I detect a note of genuine interest ... Deciduous trees provide shade and decaying plant material, which in turn provides homes for slugs, snails, earthworms, woodlice, spiders, millipedes, centipedes – och, how long have you got? And those invertebrates feed animals higher up the food chain, like birds, frogs and hedgehogs. It's an amazing symbiotic system. If you want to deal a body blow to local wildlife, just fell a tree.' Keir stops suddenly and says, 'We're here.' He removes the pole from Marianne's hand, and places her gloved fingers on a piece of hanging rope. 'This is the ladder. There are wooden rungs between two thick ropes. It's strong and it's safe, but you need to go up first because the ladder will swing unless I hold it steady at the bottom.'

'What will I find at the top?'

'A platform. There's a safety rail of sorts. Don't lean on it, just take it as a boundary. You'll be fine if you stand still.'

'How many steps are there on the ladder?'

There is a pause while Keir counts. 'Sixteen.'

'Goodness, it must be quite high up!'

'Aye. You wouldn't want to fall out.'

'Keir, I'm not sure I'm really up to this. Couldn't you haul me up in a basket or something? I'm sure that's what they did in *Swiss Family Robinson*.'

'There *is* a pulley system, but it's for goods traffic only.'

'Don't I qualify? As a box of chocolates?'

'Nice try. Just count the rungs as you go up. By the time you get to ten, your head should be about level with the platform. Climb on and wait for me.'

'And if I fall out of the tree?'

'I'll endeavour to catch you.'

'Thanks a *lot*.' As she grasps the rungs of the ladder, Marianne turns her head and says over her shoulder, 'There isn't much catching in shinty, is there?'

'Only of colds.'

Marianne

The wooden rungs were slimy with damp, and treacherous. My gloved hands slipped but my boots gripped. Even with Keir holding the ladder, it swayed and soon I was no longer climbing vertically but leaning backwards, pulling myself up, my wrists taking most of my weight. At first I was frightened, then I began to feel a creeping exhilaration. My head nudged a projecting branch and, seconds later, Keir cried out below.

I froze on the ladder. 'What's wrong?'

'Nothing. Just some snow down the back of my neck. You dislodged it when you hit the branch.'

'Sorry.'

'No bother. It was very refreshing. What are you grinning at?'

'I was just thinking about that snowball fight ... Oh, I've lost count now. Am I nearly there?'

'Your feet are on the tenth rung. It should get easier now. The ladder will feel more secure where it's attached to the platform.'

Reaching above me, my hand found wooden staging with a rough surface. It felt like chicken wire stretched over wood. I hesitated, wondering how I was going to haul myself onto this platform, when Keir called up, 'There's a handle to your right, on the platform itself. Have you found it? You can use that to pull yourself on.'

'I'm frightened I'll fall if I let go of the ladder.'

'You won't. Find that handle with your right hand. Now move your feet up a rung. And another. Keep going ... That's the last one. Now you can wait till I get up there, if you like, but the ladder will swing like hell as I come up. Or you can lift your left leg up and onto the platform. This is where those expensive sessions at the gym will really pay off.'

I clambered onto the platform trying not to think about how far it was to the ground and whether or not the snow would break my fall. Keir called out, 'That's right! You're on! You can stand up if you want – there's head-room.'

'No, thanks, I won't push my luck. I think I'll just sit quietly and wait for you to join me.'

'Coming up.'

The platform tilted slightly as he climbed and I clung to the handle for dear life. I heard him arrive, then he took my hands and helped me to my feet. Cowering, I said, 'Are we standing with our heads in the branches? I'm worried about my eyes. They may be useless but I'm still quite attached to them.'

'We're under a sort of wooden porch here. Part of the tree-house. There are no branches near your eyes. But if you come over here ...' He put an arm round my shoulders and propelled me forwards. 'You're out from under the porch. It's like being on a balcony. You're twenty feet up in the air.' He placed my hand on a branch the thickness of my arm. 'Up in the tree's canopy.'

I grasped the branch and bounced it up and down. There was a shuffling noise and a slap as snow fell from upper branches and landed on the platform.

'Did I get you that time?'

'No, you missed.'

'I always was a rotten shot. God, it's cold up here, isn't it? You can feel the wind.'

'Hot chocolate, madam? Brandy?'

'Is that what you've got in the rucksack?'

'Aye. Though it's the St Bernard that's so damn heavy.'

There was the sound of a latch being lifted, then an agonised creak as a door swung open on its hinges. I felt Keir's hand on my arm. 'Step this way, madam. Refreshments will be served shortly.'

'The space is probably small enough for you to navigate with your hands. But you've got plenty of head clearance.'

'Have you?'

'Enough. My grandfather was a big man. He built it for his children and grandchildren but he liked to spend time up here himself.'

Marianne removes her gloves and extends her hands, exploring. In the middle of the room she encounters a rough, curved surface. The sensation is familiar and she recognises it at once. She reels back, astonished, then extends her hands again, eagerly. 'This is the tree-trunk! The tree is growing *inside* the house!'

'Aye. There's a branch as well. It travels diagonally across the room.' Keir places Marianne's hand where trunk and branch fork. 'It forms a sort of room-divider. This side's the living room, the other's the sleeping quarters.'

'There's a *bed*?'

'Oh, aye. Grandfather didn't do anything by halves. There's two beds and hooks to sling hammocks. There's a collection of old blankets and eiderdowns in a wooden kist to the right of your feet. Mind you don't trip. I've brought your pole up so you can use it like your cane, if you want.' He hands her the pole and Marianne sweeps it in front of her, tapping the furniture.

'What else is there? Oh, this is *so* exciting!'

Keir turns his head, looks at her and grins. 'We've a small round table and some shelves with big lips on them to stop things falling off in a gale. Grandfather really wanted to set them on gimbals but I think the technology defeated him. The tree never moves that much anyway. The branches do, but not the trunk.'

'Have you been up here in a gale?'

'I've slept up here in a gale.'

Marianne exhales, her fingertips placed to her lips in a child-like gesture of wonder. Something catches at the back of Keir's throat and he swallows before continuing, 'There's plates, mugs, cutlery, plastic glasses – everything you might need for a picnic or a midnight feast. Are you ready for some hot chocolate?'

'You bet I am. Are there chairs?'

'Of sorts. Creepie stools. The crofter's equivalent of the occasional table. Stools you can sit on, eat off, rest your feet on – or a dram. Small, portable, one size fits all.'

He hands Marianne a sturdy, rectangular wooden stool and she sits. He places another in front of her, sets two enamel mugs on it and pours chocolate from a Thermos.

'That smells wonderful.'

'It's right in front of you. Are you hungry?'

'I can't be. I ate that huge bacon sandwich.'

'But somehow you *are*. I think it's this place. Tree-houses bring on severe attacks of the munchies.' He reaches down a tin from a shelf and rattles it.

'You keep food up here?'

'Bird food. And a little for humans. Tablet. It's not that old. I was up here two weeks ago, cleaning up. Hold out your hand.' Marianne obeys and he places a cube in her palm.

'You know, I wouldn't touch this stuff in Edinburgh. Instant tooth rot.' She pops the fudge-like sweet into her mouth. 'It's practically frozen! But it tastes really good.'

'Hunger is the best sauce,' Keir replies, his mouth full.

'Describe the tree-house to me. How on earth did your grandfather build it to accommodate live branches?'

'The house sits in the tree. It's perfectly safe but it's not attached. There has to be a certain amount of give to allow for gales and tree growth, so basically the house sits on a framework built around bits of the tree and there are sliding bolts that shift a few inches to accommodate movement.'

'But what about the girth of the trunk? That must have increased over the years. And the branch inside? I assume it passes out again through the roof or wall?'

'The holes he cut in the floor, roof and wall were all bigger than was necessary at the time. They're smaller now.'

'So are there gaps? I can't feel any draughts.'

'No, all the gaps are sealed with rope – anchor cable. It's

fixed to the house but not the tree. It's a kind of heavy-duty draught excluder. And quite decorative.'

'How clever! Will the tree outgrow the holes?'

'Not in my lifetime.'

'In your children's?'

'I don't have any.'

'I was speaking figuratively. Any nieces or nephews?'

'Not so far.'

'That's a shame.' Marianne sighs. 'A place as special as this should have children to love it.'

'I don't think I love it any less now than I did when I was a boy. And there was a time in my teens when I wouldn't go near it. Dismissed it as kids' stuff. I abandoned it to my wee sister and her dolls. She commandeered it as a sort of sanatorium for broken toys. Some of them are still lying around. The terminal cases. I should throw them out but I think they probably have as much right to be here as I do.'

'Describe them for me.'

'There's a wooden horse. The kind you pull along on wheels. Or you could if it still had any wheels. And there's the remains of a collection of wooden animals. The Lonely Hearts Club.'

'Why do you call them that?'

'They were pairs originally and they lived in an ark. Grandfather made them all himself and painted them. But over the years we lost some of them, so their partners ended up as singletons. Poor old Noah was accidentally used for kindling a campfire, so Mrs Noah became a harassed single parent and zoo-keeper.'

'A widow, in fact.'

He pauses then continues softly, 'Aye, I suppose so.'

Marianne sets down her cup of chocolate. 'I'm sorry. I've reminded you of Annie, haven't I?'

'And I reminded you of Harvey.'

After a moment she says brightly, 'Are there any wooden rabbits?'

'Aye, hundreds of the buggers.'

She laughs. 'Can I hold one of the Lonely Hearts Club members?'

Keir hands her an animal and says, 'Can you guess what it is?'

As Marianne runs her fingers over the wooden shape Keir studies her wide, expressionless eyes, a cloudy blue, like a sky threatening rain. Looking into them, unregarded, he feels like a voyeur until he remembers watching deer from the cover of trees, his gaze observant, but not invasive. He notes a flicker of an eyelid, a quiver at the corner of her mouth as she runs her fingers lightly over the wood, her head lifted, her throat exposed, like an animal scenting the air. She holds out her hand towards him, the toy cradled in her palm.

'Easy. A giraffe. I can feel the spots as well as the long neck.'

'Aye, it does have something of the look of a Dalmatian about it. Grandfather was good with his hands but not much of an artist. I think his style could best be described as *expressionistic*.'

As Keir reaches for the giraffe, his eye is caught by the branching veins at her wrist, blue against her pale, mottled skin. He lays his fingers on the veins, feels the surprised tendons flex, the chilly skin begin to warm under his hand.

'Are you taking my pulse?'

'No. But I can feel the blood in your veins. Just. Your wrist is so small, the bones so fine ... I wanted to touch. Sorry, I should have asked first.' He takes the wooden animal from her palm.

'*Should* I? I feel like I'm stalking an animal here. I'm always downwind of you and you never know what I'm going to do. It doesn't seem fair.'

'No, but that's how it always is for me. I'm used to men taking advantage of it.'

'I'm sorry.'

'Oh, I didn't mean *you*. I meant other men. Ages ago. Really, I can hardly remember ... I spend my life touching things, but very little touches *me* now. People, I mean.'

'Do you?'

'Do I what?'

'Do you mean people don't touch you?' He takes her hand and runs his thumb over her inner wrist again, smoothing the protruding veins. 'Or did you mean what you said? "Very little touches me now."'

Marianne stands quite still, her hand limp in his, her head bowed in thought. Eventually she says, 'There's music, I suppose. And my walks in the Botanics. There's your island. The *idea* of it, I mean. And ... there's you.'

He lets go of her wrist. After a moment he says, 'Do you want to touch me?'

He watches her lashes flicker with indecision, then the tip of her tongue as she moistens dry lips before replying. 'All the time. I can't work out whether it's just curiosity or something more. I want you to be more than just a *voice* to me ... Like my trees. I hear them. I know a lot about them from the noises they make – or don't make – but I want to know about their physical being. And the only way I can do that is by holding them. So I do. When I think no one's around, I lean against them. Sometimes I – I press my face to the bark and I ... breathe them in.'

His voice, barely a whisper, says, 'Show me. Show me what you do.'

They stand facing one another and she extends her palm in the direction of his voice, meeting the cold metal of a long zip, embedded in fleece. Pulling on the zip, she undoes his jacket and pushing it aside, lays both her palms on the ribbed woollen jersey beneath, placing them, with fingers spread, above his diaphragm. 'You're warm. And softer than the trees. I can feel the ribs of your jumper ... and they run in the opposite direction to *your* ribs ... There's a criss-cross pattern. And it's all moving, very slowly as you breathe ... in and out.'

She moves her hands under the fleece jacket, round to his back. Placing her palms on the projecting mounds of his shoulder blades, she turns her head to one side and lays her cheek against his chest. She inhales deeply but says nothing as her head rises and falls. After a few moments, she murmurs, 'I could drift off to sleep like this. Standing up. Like a horse.'

'Can I put my arms around you?'

'Yes.' He moves and she feels the contraction of muscle, the shifting of shoulder blades as he encloses her in fleece-clad arms. She's aware of a brief, gentle pressure on the crown of her head and guesses its significance. Curbing an impulse to lift her head and offer her mouth, she says, 'You prefer trees and animals to people, don't you?'

'I wouldn't put it like that. I feel more at home with trees. And I find animals easier to be with.'

'Why is that, do you think?'

'I had a dog who could read my mind and I could read his. That was a hard act to follow.'

'There's more to it than that, surely?'

He is still for a moment, then releases her. 'I'm just not good with folk. For a start I don't do a lot of eye contact – something you wouldn't be aware of. That's one of the reasons I find you easy to talk to. I don't have to look at you. Though I *do*, so I suppose I mean, I don't have to be looked *at*.'

'Why does it bother you? It's not as if you're ugly or disfigured. And I don't get the impression that you're shy. Reserved, perhaps, but not particularly so for a Highlander. In fact compared to some dour specimens I've met, you're the life and soul of the party.'

'Thank you.'

'So why don't you want to be looked at?'

'I suppose it's mostly the eye contact thing. Folk are unsettled by my eyes but they don't know why. And sometimes ... sometimes I see more than I want to.'

'What do you mean?'

Marianne hears him move away and the scrape of a stool on the wooden floor as he sits again. 'It's some sort of overdeveloped crap-detector. It must be the result of a lifetime spent watching animals and birds, registering tiny changes in behaviour, flight patterns, alarm calls ... I can stand very still for a long time – like a heron – and just ... take something in. When I look at folk they must feel as if they're being photographed. Hell, they probably feel they're being X-rayed.'

'I think I know what you're referring to. After she'd met you, Louisa said, "That man's eyes don't miss much."'

'Did she now? Well, I wouldn't mind betting Louisa doesn't miss much either.'

'You picked up on her sexual availability, didn't you? The

antennae waving. And you knew I'd lost someone close. You just stated it as a fact, as if you knew.'

'Seemed pretty obvious to me.'

'But most people can't read blind faces. We don't do expressions like sighted people. Especially not the congenitally blind. Our voices sound normal, but most people just see the dead eyes, feel very uncomfortable, then back off as fast as they can. The more socially skilled raise their voices and address us as if we're mentally defective.' She pauses, her head on one side. 'You've gone quiet. Am I ranting?'

'No, I'm just observing you. It's fast becoming one of my favourite occupations. Your expressiveness is concentrated around your mouth.'

'Is it?'

'Aye. Your mouth is fascinating. And very attractive. You touch it a lot. With your fingertips. And you touch it with your tongue. It's very alluring. You want to watch that when you're with those predatory types you mentioned. It maybe gives out a message you don't intend.'

Marianne's fingers fly to her lips. 'Oh dear. Do you think so?'

Keir laughs and lays his fingers gently on top of hers. 'See? You did it then. I think you react with your mouth the way other folk react with their eyes.' He removes his hand and watches the frown lines dance between her fair brows as she tries to assimilate new information.

'But this morning ... when you asked me if I wanted you to make love to me, you didn't know what I wanted?'

'Did *you*?' She is silent and after a moment he resumes, 'That was an emotional minefield and I was trying not to blow myself up. I thought I knew what you wanted but I wasn't sure if I'd been given permission. And I hadn't. That's what I mean about not being skilled with folk. I'm no good at playing games.'

'Apart from shinty.'

'Och, I'm not even that good at shinty! I'm certainly no good at the games you have to play with women. Men and animals are much more straightforward.'

'And blind women?'

'And blind women.'

'Except that you can't tell if they find you attractive.'

'No, but I'm a quick learner. For a man, that is.'

Marianne purses her lips and says firmly, 'Let's change the subject. I'm getting out of my depth.'

'Well, that was admirably straightforward.'

'Tell me more about your grandfather. And the toys.'

'Gladly. He loved to work with wood and made us wooden toys for our birthdays. The ark was mine. My sister asked for a wooden book when she was small, God knows why. He made her one with four painted plywood pages and canvas hinges.' Keir roots in a box, then says, 'I wonder, can you guess what this is?' He hands Marianne a flat piece of wood about the size of a small tea tray, irregularly shaped, but something like a starfish, or a bird with its wings spread. One side is smooth and featureless, the other is carved with wavy lines and indentations. In the middle, a series of raised lumps with serrated edges form a rough horseshoe shape.

'What on earth is it?'

'Something that's of more use to you than it ever was to me.'

'Is it some kind of sculpture?'

'In a way. It's a map. A wooden relief map of Skye. These winged pieces are the peninsulas: Trotternish, Waternish, Duirinish, Minginish and down here, this big piece, this is where we are, in Sleat.'

'And the bumps in the middle are the Cuillin?'

'Aye. They've lost some of their fine detail over the years. But then so have the Cuillin. Erosion takes its toll, of mountains as well as toys.'

'Is the map painted?'

'No, just carved and varnished. These long thin indentations ...' He takes her hand and guides her fingers over the wood. 'Can you feel those? They're rivers. And these depressions ...' He moves her fingers again. 'Those are lochs. The straighter lines are roads.'

'What a wonderful piece of work! But why? I mean, why a *wooden* map?'

112

'He'd seen one in Canada, made by the Inuit. They carried such things in their kayaks, maps of the coastline, carved from driftwood, so they could navigate by touch when they were at sea in the dark. The map was impervious to weather and floated if they dropped it overboard. A brilliant low-tech solution to a practical problem. That would have appealed to my grandfather. More chocolate?'

'Mmm, yes please.'

Keir refills her cup. After a pause in which they both drink in silence, he says, 'Marianne, if it's OK with you I'd like to go and ring Annie.'

'There's no reception here, surely?'

'No. None at the house either. I'll have to drive up to the main road. I could do with going into Broadford for supplies anyway. I didn't bring much. I prefer to shop locally. Would you like to come along for the very bumpy ride?'

'Well, I've had better offers. Will you be gone long?'

'A couple of hours. Maybe a bit longer. Depends how things are with Annie. And how many folk I meet in the Co.'

'The Co?'

'The Co-op. The social centre of the village. Shopping can take a while by the time you've caught up with all the news.'

'I think I'd rather stay at home. Sorry to be anti-social, but sitting and dozing by the fireside seems more appealing. I feel quite tired after all that trekking through the snow. And when everything is new to me I get worn out, trying to take it all in.'

'I can imagine. Well, I *can't*, but you know what I mean. Let's head back to the house, have some lunch, then you can put your feet up.'

Keir tucks the stools under the table and puts the empty mugs into a plastic bag inside the rucksack. He zips up his fleece, guides Marianne towards the door and opens it.

As the door complains again, she laughs. 'That creak is like something out of the Brothers Grimm.'

'Aye, I keep meaning to come up with an oil can to put it out of its misery.'

'Don't you dare. It's all part of the gothic charm. Does the tree-house have a name?'

'Of course. *Am Fasgadh*.'

'Which means?'

'*The Refuge.* Are you ready for the descent now?'

'As ready as I'll ever be. I've read enough about climbing to know that going down is just as dangerous as going up. That's when accidents happen.'

'Aye, so I'll go down first and hold the ladder steady for you. Once you're on, you'll be fine right enough, but take good care as you leave the platform.'

'Don't worry, I will.'

'Kneel down here and get your bearings.' She does so and he lifts her hand, placing it on the handle projecting from the platform. 'Remember to use this.'

'Can I put my hands on your shoulders as you move off the platform? It will help me orientate myself, then I can copy your sequence of movements.'

'Aye, hold on wherever you want. I'll move slowly so you get the idea.'

Marianne places her hands on Keir and feels his body twist as he lowers himself onto the ladder. As he moves out of reach she feels suddenly bereft and fearful. To maintain the contact she calls out, 'This has been such an adventure! Lou is never going to believe what I've been up to. She certainly wouldn't approve.'

Keir's voice travels up from below. 'Does that bother you?'

'Not in the slightest,' Marianne replies as, gripping the handle, she extends a foot into thin air in search of the doubtful security of a swaying ladder.

Chapter Ten

Louisa

Marianne would not approve.

That was my first thought when I woke up, the day after the mugging. Actually, my very first thought was, if my stomach was going to evacuate its contents before I managed to get to the bathroom, in which direction should I aim to minimise the damage?

As my eyes swivelled round the room in search of a suitable receptacle, I spied – with a shudder – a bottle of brandy and two empty glasses on the dressing-table. Then, as I completed a visual circuit of the bedroom, Garth came into view, horizontal, naked and fast asleep beside me.

That was when it occurred to me that Marianne would not approve. Not only would Marianne not approve, she wouldn't understand, since I don't even like brandy, but Garth had said brandy was what we needed after our ordeal, so I'd let him rattle around in the drinks cupboard being masterful, while I collapsed on the sofa and examined the damage to my poor feet and a new pair of Christian Dior tights, shredded as I'd run barefoot through the streets.

Garth had insisted I drink the large measure he'd poured and I did feel slightly better for it. At my request he checked the locks on all the windows, then checked the front door, putting the safety-chain across. He asked if I wanted to ring the police but we agreed that I'd done more damage to Magwitch than he'd done to us, so we decided not to bother. The thought of having to study a line-up of Magwitch clones in an identity parade made me start to shake again and I didn't protest when Garth refilled my glass.

I was halfway through the second brandy when, unaccountably, I started to cry. I just burst into hysterical tears and couldn't stop. Garth put his arm round me and said it was just shock, that I'd been 'a total star' and that he'd been very proud of me. He assured me I might well have saved both our lives.

I stopped crying then and started laughing, not at Garth's words, which were so sweet, but at the sight of his face, which looked truly awful. He looked like a panda, with eyeliner smudged round his eyes where we'd laughed till we cried after making our escape. His pale foundation was wearing off and beneath the make-up I could see what I thought at first was a virulent rash, then realised was a mass of freckles. His black, spiky hair, so carefully arranged for our evening out, had wilted and now hung low over his forehead. The damp night air had produced the suspicion of a curl. Looking at the wreckage of his face I wondered, possibly for the first time, what Garth really looked like and why he took such trouble to disguise his appearance.

He stared back at me. 'What you lookin' at then?'

'You. You look ghastly.'

'Well, you don't look a million dollars yourself, love.'

'I'm sure I don't! We need to clean ourselves up and get some beauty sleep.'

He gave me a sheepish look. 'D'you mind if I use your cleanser an' stuff?'

'Of course not. Help yourself to anything you need in the bathroom. My things are in the cupboard, Marianne's are on the shelf. Don't move anything of hers – it all has to be kept in the same position so she can find it.' I heaved myself off the sofa. 'I'll change the sheets on her bed. I'm sure she won't mind you sleeping in there.'

'Nah, don't bother,' Garth replied. 'The sofa'll do me. I'll wrap meself up in me coat. Russian army surplus, that is. Dead cosy.'

'I won't hear of it – not after what we've been through! You need a good night's sleep. We both do.'

116

But that wasn't, in the event what either of us got.

When Garth emerged from the bathroom with a naked face and wearing my red silk kimono, I didn't recognise him. His skin *au naturel* was as pale as ever, but creamy, not dead white, and he was covered in freckles. Completely covered, I assumed, as the casually belted kimono revealed constellations of them scattered across his narrow, almost hairless chest.

I know it wasn't the most tactful thing to say, but I'd had two large brandies and was completely shattered. I couldn't help myself, I was just so surprised.

'Garth, surely your hair must be red?'

He stood still and eyed me suspiciously. 'Yeah. It is. What of it?'

'You dye it?'

'Yeah.'

'Why?'

' 'Cos I 'ate it. 'Cos kids at school used to make fun of it – that an' me freckles. That's why I became a Goth. It meant I could dye me 'air and cover meself up with make-up.' He shrugged and helped himself to another brandy. 'It was that or be gay. An' I'm not, so becomin' a Goth was easier.'

I stared open-mouthed. 'What colour is your hair really? Carrotty?'

'Nah, sort of red setter colour. Carrot wouldn't be too bad, not up 'ere. Loads of Scots blokes 'ave 'air the colour of Irn Bru. But mine's pretty unusual. Me mum said the colour's called titian. Like that helped,' he added, staring morosely into his glass. 'An' it's curly an' all. If I'm not careful, I look like a bleedin' King Charles spaniel.' He tugged self-consciously at long black locks that were beginning to coil like springs. 'I've been mistaken for a woman from behind 'cos I'm not that tall. 'Ad me arse pinched by drunks needin' glasses. Pretty embarrassin'. So I straightened it an' dyed it black. But that looked ridiculous with all me freckles. Weird, like I'd got some sort of plague or somethin'. But I 'ad this girlfriend, see, an' she was a Goth. She did me face one day, just for a laugh, like. An' I loved it! So I stuck with it.' He grinned. 'Aven't 'ad me arse pinched since.'

117

As I struggled to assimilate a new Garth, I noticed his lovely even teeth and large green eyes. (I could have sworn they were hazel.) His appearance was really quite arresting. Not what you'd call handsome, not by a long chalk, but in an odd way, attractive.

'Garth, I'm seeing you in a whole new light! I realise I've never really looked at you before. I just saw the daunting Goth exterior, not the man beneath. You know, you have beautiful green eyes and I've never even noticed!'

'Yeah, people don't really see you, they just see the gear. Suits me. I got stared at enough as a kid to last me a lifetime.'

I stood up and set off uncertainly towards the bathroom, then, as the room did a pirouette, thought better of it. I steadied myself with a hand on the back of the armchair and peered at Garth. 'I wish I could see your hair in its natural state. I'm trying to imagine it ... It sounds gorgeous!'

He snorted and took another mouthful of brandy. 'Me aunties used to ruffle me 'air an' say, "Wasted on a boy." Charming, eh? At least I could punch the morons at school.'

'Oh, I could murder the brats who teased you! Why do children have to be so cruel?'

'You know what kids are like – if it wasn't me 'air, it would've been somethin' else, I expect.' Garth took a step towards me, his head bent. 'You can see the real colour at the roots. It needs doin' but I 'aven't 'ad time lately.'

He stood in front of me and raised his arms, parting his thick black hair. As he did so, the kimono belt slipped undone and the scarlet silk gaped open. Garth looked down. So did I.

'Ah – there you go!' he said and pointed. 'It's that colour!'

After a simple lunch of cheese and oatcakes, Keir makes a shopping list, tends the stove, and brews a pot of coffee for Marianne.

'I'm away to Broadford now.' He lays a hand on her shoulder, registering with an odd pleasure how the curved bone fits neatly into his palm. 'The stove won't need any attention for a few hours. You'll take care now?'

'I'll be fine. I'm safer here than on the streets of Edinburgh.'

'What will you do?'

'Vegetate. Fall asleep in a chair beside the stove, probably. Or if I'm feeling energetic, I might sit outside and listen to the sounds of Mother Nature at work. What's the weather doing now?'

'The sun's shining but there could be more snow on the way. The weather changes fast on Skye ... You'll find a dish by the back door with bacon scraps. On the windowsill on the right. If you throw those down round your feet, you'll not be short of company. The robin feeds from my hand but I doubt he'll do you the same honour. You might get the weasels though.'

'*Weasels*?'

'Aye. There's a nosey pair that come to the back door. You know how folk use "face like a weasel" as a derogatory term? Well, let me tell you, it's a calumny. They have bonny wee faces with big, soulful eyes. So listen out for anything that doesn't sound like a bird. It'll be a weasel ... Right, I'm away. I'll be back as soon as I can.'

'Stop fretting! I'm not going to get mugged by a pair of weasels, am I?'

'Not if you feed them.'

Marianne

I took a mug of coffee and the dish of bacon rinds out into the garden. Sitting on the bench, I tossed the scraps down and waited for visitors. The sun was weak but welcome and I turned my face upwards, shutting my eyes. Without the distractions of Keir's voice and physical presence, I was at liberty to absorb the sounds and smells around me, foremost among which was the daphne, under-scored by a strong scent of vanilla that I couldn't place. Another shrub in flower, perhaps, or was it just the effect of sun on the snow? I thought of a time when I was small and tried to make ice-cream with a mixture of snow and strawberry jam, a culinary experiment I remember whenever I eat sorbet, which I think of as fruit snow.

Basking in the sun, surprised I felt no need for coat or hat, I considered the information Keir had given me over lunch. The house had been built in a clearing among the remnants of old, decaying woodland. Keir's grandfather had chosen the spot because it was sheltered but still had a view of the sea and, in good weather, of the Cuillin mountain range beyond. (I asked Keir if he could suggest a musical equivalent for the Cuillin, mountains being even more beyond my grasp than cathedrals. He was silent for some time, then said, 'The third movement of the *Hammerklavier*.' To my astonishment, he'd named the longest and most beautiful *adagio* Beethoven ever wrote for the piano. I hoped I wasn't falling in love with this man. I was resigned, however, to falling for his mind.)

Keir said water was supplied to the house from a tank filled by a spring which never dried up. Dead and dying trees provided a constant supply of fuel, as did the sea, turning up all manner of combustible material and even some of the furniture. He was now regenerating the woodland, systematically planting trees – fast-growing birch alongside slow-growing oak. His planting had now reached the stage where thinning was required and the trees planted as shelter for slower-growing specimens now had to be felled to provide more light and space for larger, longer-lived varieties. I knew Keir wouldn't live to see many of his trees reach maturity, so I'd asked him about his motives.

'I want to put something back.'

'Back?'

'Give back to the Earth. In recompense for what I've taken out.'

'Your "carbon footprint", you mean?'

'Partly. But I work in the oil industry. I've spent my whole working life screwing the planet for resources so that oil-greedy Westerners can live in mindless comfort. It's ecological rape and pillage. And I'm not, as you may have gathered, one of life's Vikings. By the time I woke up to the mess we were making of the world, I could see the oil industry itself was an endangered species and there weren't going to be too many job options for me. It's not a career path young folk pursue any more. When I went into it, the money was good and there was the lure of travel. There's no security, but you don't think about that when you're young. It seemed like a good idea at the time for a geologist who didn't know what the hell he wanted to do with his life. But there's no future in oil. It's dead. It's an industry full of guys in their forties, like me.'

'If there's no future in oil, what will you do?'

'Good question. There's still work in my field – oil and gas exploration. The oil is almost gone and there's now an undignified scramble to find and grab what little is left. And one of the effects of global warming is that hazard prediction has become something of a growth area. That's my field too. That could be the way I go, but it would mean spending even more time abroad.'

'And you don't want to?'

'Och no, I've had enough! I get homesick on the other side of the Skye Bridge. If I had my way I'd live here year-round, but I don't know what I'd do to pay the bills. There's very little work on Skye apart from the tourist industry, and that's not year-round anyway. A lot of folk who live here are retired incomers or elderly natives. The young move away to the mainland for work. They have to. I had to.'

'What about ecological tourism? Teaching people about wildlife, woodland management, living a greener life? That's a growth area too, isn't it? There must be lots of townies who'd like to create the sort of idyll you have here. Couldn't you exploit that?'

'Aye, I've thought about that ... It's tempting. But this place would be no good as a base. It's inaccessible and it's not big enough. I'd need to provide some sort of residential facility and it would need to be on a good road. It's something I think about. But I can't see it happening.'

'Wouldn't it be marvellous if children could come here – school parties, I mean – and stay for a week and learn about wildlife. And the stars ... And wouldn't they just *adore* the tree-house!'

'Aye, I've had similar thoughts myself. This place would be an excellent teaching resource because of the variety of habitats.'

'And you wouldn't mind sharing it? Having noisy teenagers tramping through your personal Garden of Eden?'

'I was a noisy teenager once. Kids wouldn't be noisy if they had a reason to be quiet. Silence, watchfulness is a natural response to wildlife. It's man's hunting instinct. It's a survival instinct too. You can run, or you can be still and silent. If city kids could see the stars here on a clear winter's night, they'd be struck dumb. *Anybody* would. Stars forbid you to speak ... Och, I have my dreams, but not the resources or the will to live them. But I've made a start.'

'Regenerating the woodland, you mean?'

'No, bringing you here. It's enabled me to see what I could do. What I probably *should* do ...'

Marianne

A fluttering at my feet told me some birds had braved my unfamiliar presence. I sat completely still, my hands cradling the warm coffee mug. Behind me I could hear a constant drip from the gutter as the sun melted the snow on the roof. With a noisy flapping of wings, the birds suddenly took flight, even though I hadn't moved a muscle and there had been no sound to disturb them. Had a weasel appeared? I felt nervous and wanted to withdraw my feet, place them under the bench, out of the way of small mammals, but I sat still and tried to imagine – as best I could – their 'bonny wee faces'. But it was Keir's face with its angular, slab-like planes that came to mind; his face I remembered in the tips of my fingers.

There was a change in the quality of the silence. Without knowing why, I reached for my cane, then remembered I'd left it indoors because my hands were full and I wouldn't need it – I was only going to sit on the bench.

I'll never know if I actually heard something before the grating noise above my head or whether I just sensed movement. Was there a creak? Did the dripping accelerate? I don't know, but when I heard the strange grinding noise above and behind me, I was already anxious. It's not often I hear a noise I can't identify and I stood up, ready to go back indoors. As I turned towards the back door there was an almighty *rushing* sound and I sensed a current of cold air on my face and pressure moving towards me. Terrified, I turned and ran, my arms extended in front of me.

I hadn't moved far when the noise resolved itself into a long hiss, a thump and a wet splashing sound. Snow from the roof.

There had been an avalanche of snow falling from the roof above the bench where I'd been sitting. The bench was probably covered in snow now. I laughed at myself a little nervously and walked back the way I'd run.

Except that I didn't. I can't have, for my hands met a tree I hadn't encountered when I'd fled from the bench. I stood still and took stock for a moment, cursing myself for not bringing my cane out. I must have lost my sense of direction after running. I'd panicked and stupidly lost my bearings. Now I didn't know if I was facing the house, so I would just have to find my footprints in the snow and trace them back to the bench.

I bent and felt the ground with my bare hands, tracing the depressions. I followed these carefully but, after a minute or two, it dawned on me that these weren't my footprints. They were too large, too deep and too widely spaced. These were Keir's. I'd been following Keir's footprints, not mine, and I had no idea where they'd led me. Feeling in the snow, I could detect only one set of footprints. An outward journey, no return. So these would probably lead to the steps down which Keir had carried me when we arrived, or they might lead to the winding path that he'd said led down to the house. Either way, this set of footprints was not going to take me back the way I'd come.

The sun went in and I felt the temperature drop several degrees. I was beginning to feel a little concerned, but not frightened. How could I lose a *house*? It couldn't be far. I turned round and re-traced my steps to the tree. My extended hands found it and I told myself I couldn't be far from the house and my bench, I just didn't know in what direction they lay.

I bent down and felt in the snow for something to throw. My fingers were practically numb now with exploring the snow and my legs were damp where I'd kneeled to read the footprints. I tried to ignore the uncomfortable fact that I was very cold and getting colder. My frozen fingers found a stone. I clasped it and stood up, trying to work out in which direction I thought the house lay. I hesitated before throwing, wondering if I might smash a window. Aiming low, I hurled the stone, hoping that the sound of it hitting something would tell me if it was a wall, a door or just a tree.

Nothing. I heard the stone land with a distant sigh in the snow. It must have missed the house altogether. I found another stone and threw that in a different direction. There was a dull thud. Not the crack of the stone hitting a wall. Perhaps the bench? Or maybe just another tree? I set off in the direction of the sound, striding purposefully in an attempt to get my circulation moving again. My foot slipped on something smooth. Arms flailing, I skidded and lost my balance. There was a hideous crack as the ground gave way beneath me, plunging me to my knees into icy water.

I'd walked into a frozen pond. The cold was so intense, I screamed. I stepped back out of the pond and stood still, shivering convulsively, furious with myself, but now frightened as well. My feet and legs were soaked up to my knees. My hands were numb. I had no hat, no coat. I was wearing a woollen jumper, not even a sensible, wind-proof fleece. And I was lost. I might be a matter of metres from the house and a wood-burning stove but, to all intents and purposes, I was lost. Keir had said there were no boundary hedges or fences here. The garden blended into its woodland surroundings, so I had nothing at all to navigate by, nothing to contain me.

I'd no idea how long Keir had been gone, nor when he would be back. But he *would* be back. Eventually. I was in for an uncomfortable couple of hours – no more than that, probably – but as long as the weather held, I told myself I couldn't come to much harm. I turned my face upwards, hoping to feel once again the blessing of the weak February sun.

Instead I felt flakes of snow as they drifted down and settled on my cheeks, like a chilly caress.

I knew about hypothermia. Harvey, a Skye man, had been a keen hill-walker and climber and he'd accompanied me to the top of Ben Nevis on a sponsored walk to raise money for charity. This was not a particularly spectacular achievement, even for someone who was blind. Children and people with all manner of physical disabilities make the ascent every year, following a well-trodden path. But every year there are cases of hypothermia, walkers dressed inadequately for the altitude, tourists who get wet, cold and hungry and who, by doing so, put their lives in danger. Hypothermia is a killer and it can kill quite quickly.

Without a hat I was losing one fifth of my precious body heat via my head. I could hardly feel my feet or hands. I was shivering uncontrollably but I knew that was a good sign. The body shivers to generate heat. If I stopped shivering, then I would really start to worry. To conserve energy the body stops shivering and goes into survival mode, then shutdown. I also knew that as I got colder, I would become confused, even more disorientated than I was now. I needed to find the house or, failing that, some shelter. And in a hurry.

I stood still and listened, all my senses straining, but all I could hear was the convulsive chattering of my teeth. I thought longingly of the stove and wondered if I could smell the wood smoke and trace it back to the house? Then I recalled the sweetly perfumed daphne by the back door, but I imagined the sun's warmth was no longer drawing scent from the shrub. I could smell nothing but the mud and stagnant pond-water that had drenched my clothes.

I needed to move to keep warm but I was frightened to move until I knew I was going in the right direction, so I stood, stamping my feet, trying to think, becoming colder by the minute as I stood out in the open while it snowed. It was then that I conceded a kind of defeat and stopped trying to be brave. Something snapped and I yelled at the top of my voice, 'Keir!' It was a futile and quite hopeless gesture but it was easier to call out Keir's name than the words I shouted next: 'Help me! Somebody – please help me!'

There was a flapping sound as a couple of birds took off above me. I knew I must be standing among trees. If I was among trees I probably wasn't very near the house, so I decided to walk, to set off in a random direction. I told myself walking would not only keep me warm, it would help me think.

I walked with my arms extended, my hands freezing in the cold air. I stumbled as my numb, wet feet failed to register variations in the terrain. As I made my slow progress, I listened out for the sound of the Land Rover but I knew Keir probably hadn't even got as far as Broadford yet. Perhaps if I kept going I would hit the road and come across another vehicle? As I listened out for distant sounds of a car, I caught instead a cheerful, gurgling sound – literally music to my ears. The burn. At last something to navigate by, something that would give me a sense of direction! The burn flowed downhill, towards the sea, Keir had said. It also flowed around the house. Surely with all this information I could find my way back?

The snow was heavier now. Large flakes had settled on my head and shoulders, wetting my hair, seeping into my clothes. I brushed it off, alarmed to feel how much there was. As I did so, I walked smack into a tree. Stunned, I sank down at the base of the tree, forgetting as I did so that this would soak one of the few parts of my body that was still dry, but I was tired and just wanted to curl up in a ball. Harvey had said something about that ... Conserving core body heat ... You should hug your knees, curl up in a foetal position and wait for rescue. Wandering around only wastes energy. That's what he'd said ... I hugged my wet knees and waited. I listened to the burn singing its aimless, endless song and waited for Harvey to come and find me.

Not Harvey. *Keir*. Harvey was dead, long dead ...

The burn was singing to me now, constantly repeating a refrain: 'Follow me down, see where I go ... Follow me down, see where I go ...' In the end, the sound got on my nerves and I yelled, 'For God's sake, shut up!' The burn took no notice but carried on burbling. I pressed my back against the tree trunk, trying to derive some comfort from its solidity. I thought of Keir again, the warmth of his big body, the strength. How he'd lifted me – as if I weighed no more than a heavy rucksack – and carried me across icy stepping-stones to the other side of the burn, on the way to the tree-house.

The tree-house ...

Shelter. Blankets, Keir had said. And tablet in the tin. My mouth filled with saliva at the thought of the sugary fudge dissolving on my tongue. I struggled to my feet. If I could find the burn ... If I could find the stepping-stones ... It wasn't far from the stones to the tree-house. We'd walked for only a minute or two and I remembered the route as a straight line. Keir had set me down on the other side of the burn, saying, 'It's straight ahead,' and we were there in no time at all, standing at the foot of the ladder.

But even if I could locate it, how could I follow the burn without falling into it? Supposing there was more than one set of stepping-stones? What had Keir said about them? ... They were flat. He'd said I could attempt them, so they couldn't be that widely spaced. How many were there? Could I remember how many steps he'd taken? More than two ... I remembered lurching through the air, clinging on round his neck. But not many more than two. He'd taken maybe three or four steps, but the last one would have been on to the opposite bank. So I was trying to find three flat stepping-stones. *Maybe.*

But how do you find stepping-stones in the middle of a burn when you're blind? I started to laugh at my own idiocy, lost my balance and reeled into a low-hanging branch. It scratched my face and I seized hold of it angrily, yanking it down. To my surprise it came away from the trunk easily. I staggered back, almost falling, but regained my balance at the last moment, using the branch like a walking-stick.

Now I had a cane.

I could trail my branch through the burn without getting myself wet and it would tell me when it encountered obstacles. Like large, flat stones. Stepping-stones. Stones which would take me across the burn to the tree-house where I could lie down and rest, where I could curl up in an old eiderdown, with all the wooden animals, with the spotty giraffe and Mrs Noah. Poor, lonely Mrs Noah, waiting patiently for a husband who isn't ever coming home because he burned in the fire ...

My face felt hot suddenly and I touched it with my fingertips. Warm water was running down my cheeks, cheeks that felt as cold and dead as stone. I rubbed my useless eyes with my sleeve and set off. Trailing my branch through the snow I walked towards the sound of the burn. I found it – as I'd feared – by walking into it. I heard a loud splashing noise but my feet felt nothing, nothing at all. I stood dripping on the bank, struggling to order my thoughts. The tree-house was on the other side. But *where* on the other side? Should I walk up- or downstream? I didn't know. Keir knew, but he wasn't here ...

Sod it.

Sod it, sod it, *sod* it!

My shivering seemed to have got much worse. I wrapped my arms around my shaking body and realised I was crying, my body racked with sobs. I heard it then: a shriek, a terrible animal cry. A name. Harvey? Keir? I don't know. It didn't matter, not any more. I lifted my branch and plunged it into the burn. Dragging it along beside me, I trudged upstream.

After some time, I don't know how long – it took all my concentration just to put one foot in front of the other and keep hold of a branch I could neither see nor feel – there was a jarring sensation in my arms and I knew the branch had struck an obstacle. My co-ordination was poor now. I bent over, then, stumbling, fell to my knees. Stretching my hands out over the water, I tried to find the obstruction. One flattish stone. Were there more? I poked with the branch. It felt as if there was another, but without my cane I could get no precise feedback.

I stepped cautiously on to the first stone and used the branch to find the next. Stepping carefully again, my spirits lifted a little. Maybe this *was* where Keir and I had crossed? There was a third flat stone and that was the last. I could feel the expanse of ground on the other side of the burn. As I swept it with the branch it struck me that I was removing any trace of the footprints that would tell me if this was where we'd crossed. When I reached the other side, I dropped the branch, got down on my hands and knees and felt for depressions in the fresh snow. Perhaps they would have been filled in by now anyway? But surely not Keir's? His would have been deep, especially while he was still carrying me.

I found a hollow, then another, then lots of them, some large and deep, some smaller and shallow. These must be our footprints. I turned back to retrieve my branch, ripped off a long slender piece of wood to use as a more sensitive cane and swept it in front of me, bending over so the wood reached the ground. The line of footprints was straight and easy to follow. I paused as one of my feet fell into Keir's footprint, like a foot sliding into a large Wellington boot. I stood, swaying, wondering how I was

128

ever going to find the strength to lift my foot, let alone climb a rope ladder, then with a lurch, I fell forwards and was moving again.

The footprints stopped. The snow was churned up and there was no longer any trail. Was this where we'd stopped, where Keir had explained how I was to climb? I extended my makeshift cane, sweeping the air in front of me. It hit something. Not something solid, something that yielded. Oh dear God, *please* ...

I walked forwards, a hand stretched out in front of me. It collided with a piece of slimy wood at chest height. Smooth, worn wood. With ropes passing through it at both ends. The rope ladder.

I clung to the ladder as if I'd found a friend, hugged it to me, weeping with relief and pride that I'd found it using nothing more than common sense and some twigs. I grasped the rungs, remembering Keir had said the ladder would swing unless he held it steady. It did. It swung wildly, but I climbed slowly, counting the rungs out loud to stop myself thinking about the drop.

Hauling myself onto the platform was easier than I remembered and, crawling around, I soon located the door. But I found I couldn't get to my feet. My legs had given out completely with the effort of climbing the ladder. I reached up with my hand, searching for the door handle, turned it and, as the door opened with its familiar groan, I fell into the room.

My nose was assailed by a delicious smell. Chocolate. The chocolate we'd drunk here this morning. (This morning? Was it really only a few hours ago?) I pushed the door shut behind me and leaned against it, trying to remember where Keir had said the bedding was kept ... *'There's a collection of old blankets and eiderdowns in a wooden kist.'* I crawled across the floor in search of something that felt like a wooden box. I found one and lifted the lid. I plunged my hand in but instead of the warmth and softness of textiles, I met hard edges, corners, a jumble of wood and metal. The toys. *The Lonely Hearts Club.* I grasped one of the wooden figures, clutched it, as if it were some sort of talisman. I sat back on my haunches, no longer cold, no longer feeling any sense of urgency. A vague calm had settled on me. All that seemed to matter was whether my frozen fingers could identify the wooden figure in my palm. It had curves. An elephant? A hippopotamus? No, a small head. And a face. A human face. It was Mrs Noah. Mrs Noah, waiting for her husband.

Still clutching the figure, I found another box. Lifting the lid I smelled a mixture of camphor, lavender and old sweat. I knew what the box contained even before I put my hand inside. I dragged the blankets and quilts out on to the floor and lay down. With the last of my strength, I rolled myself up in them and curled into a ball. I could feel the figure of Mrs Noah under my chin, her head digging in to my jawbone. It hurt, but I couldn't find the strength to move. I told myself it was a good sign, that I could still feel something, feel pain. It meant I was alive.

So we lay together, Mrs Noah and I. Waiting.

Waiting for our men-folk to come.

Chapter Eleven

When Keir arrives in Broadford, he pulls into the car park, performs a neat, fast three-point turn, pulls out again and sets off, back the way he has come. Murdo MacDonald, walking slowly on the arm of his wife Katie, stops to raise a frail hand in salute as the Land Rover speeds past. Unusually, Keir fails to acknowledge.

Murdo turns and follows the speeding car with his eyes, then resumes his gentle pace. 'That was Keir Harvey. Back home again.'

'Oh, aye? He was in a mighty hurry.'

'Aye, he was. Looked as if he'd seen a ghost.'

'Och well,' says Katie placidly. 'If it was Keir Kenneth Harvey, maybe he *had*.'

The Land Rover slews to a halt and Keir jumps out, landing softly in several inches of snow. He pulls on a hat and heads for the steps leading down to the house. They are still visible but now snow-covered. He scrambles down, using his hands for extra speed. Arriving at the bottom of the steep slope he jogs towards the house, then stops suddenly. He looks round, peering through the trees and calls, 'Marianne?'

There is no sound, not even wind. He runs to the house, opens the door, leans in and calls again. Barely waiting for an answer, he slams the door and runs round to the other side of the house. Despite the fresh fall, he can see the old snow has been churned up and a great pile has slid from the roof, narrowly missing the bench. Footprints travel back and forth, criss-crossing the garden. One line of prints leads to a black hole in the ground. Seeing it, Keir swears and calls Marianne's name again, louder this time.

He scans the garden looking for a trail of prints leading out into the woods. As he does so, he tries to estimate how old the prints are, how long Marianne has been lost in the snow. He follows a track away from the house, one that leads straight into a tree. At its base the snow is alternately churned and compressed where Marianne has reeled backwards, fallen and tried get her bearings again. Reading the eloquent pattern in the snow, something tightens in Keir's stomach and he smashes a gloved fist against the trunk of the offending tree. Oblivious, he is showered with snow.

He picks up a trail leading in another direction. Alongside this set of footprints is another track, of something being dragged. Keir looks back at the tree and notes the jagged edge of a broken branch. He murmurs, 'That's my girl ... ' under his breath and runs through the trees, following the broad sweep of the branch through virgin snow.

Keir follows the trail but he already knows where Marianne was trying to go. Did she get there? He stops for a moment and lifts his head, as if he's surveying the woodland, searching, but his eyes are closed. He breathes, 'Hang on, Marianne ... ' and runs upstream, following the course of the burn.

When he enters the tree-house, all Keir can see at first is a pile of blankets heaped on the floor. As his eyes adjust to the low level of light he sees a projecting foot and registers a pool of muddy water that has leaked out of Marianne's shoe on to the wooden floor. He kneels and tries to locate her head without removing the covering of blankets. Spotting a long coil of wet hair, he removes his fleece hat, uncovers Marianne's head and puts the hat on her, pulling it down over her ears. She stirs. Keir removes his gloves and reaches into a pocket. Flipping open the blade of a Swiss army knife, he slices through the sodden laces of her shoes, pulls them off, then peels off her wet socks. He pushes each of her icy feet into one of his gloves and then

132

covers them again. Feeling under the blankets for her torso, his hands meet cold wet wool. Alarm catches his breath as he realises she isn't wearing a coat.

He tries to rouse her. 'Marianne, wake up. Can you hear me? It's Keir.'

She groans. 'Go away ... I need to sleep.'

'Marianne, I need to find out how cold you are. I'm going to put my hand under your jumper and feel your tummy, OK?'

As he delves under the blankets she wriggles away from his exploring hands. 'Stop that! What are you doing?' A wooden figure falls from her hand and rolls across the floor.

'I'm sorry, but I need to know your body temperature. Listen, Marianne – I'm going to ask you a question. It'll sound pretty stupid but can you answer anyway? Who's the Prime Minister?'

'Get your hands *off* me, Keir!'

'The name of the Prime Minister, Marianne. Tell me. Please.'

'Tony bloody Blair! Now will you just bugger off and let me sleep?' She shrugs her way under the blankets again.

'Marianne, you're suffering from hypothermia and we have to get you back to the house and get you warm. You got lost in the snow, you fell in the pond and you're very, very cold. So listen to me – Marianne? Are you listening?' He shakes her gently. 'I'm going to lower you down. There's a pulley system. I won't be able to carry you down the rope ladder – especially if you're not going to co-operate,' he adds under his breath. 'So I'm going to put you into a kind of sling. It's a tarpaulin on a rope. You can sit in it and I'll lower you down to the ground. You'll be quite safe. Then I'll climb down the ladder and carry you back to the house.'

'But I'm *tired*, Keir. I just want to sleep.'

'When we get back to the house you can sleep, I promise. Now I'm going to pick you up. Try not to move, I want you to stay wrapped in the blankets. We need to conserve what body heat you have left. I'm going to take you outside and then you'll feel me putting you down on a piece of canvas. It'll close up around you when I pull the rope and you'll feel as if you're in a kind of bag. It won't be for long. I'm going to hoist you off the platform and then swing you round, out into the air. But you'll be on a rope and I'll be at the other end of it, so you'll be quite safe. Then you'll feel me lower you to the ground. When you get there, just sit still and wait for me. D'you understand? That's important. Just sit still. You've no shoes on, so don't try to walk away.'

'Where *are* my shoes?'

'Never mind. We'll get them later. Can you count backwards from one hundred?'

'Of course I can. What a stupid question!'

'Do it.'

'Why should I?'

'Because if you can, it's a good sign. So show me you can do it, then I'll stop worrying. Backwards from one hundred. Ninety-nine ... Go on.' Keir opens the door, turns back and lifts Marianne, swathed in blankets.

'This is ridiculous, Keir!'

'Just do it. Ninety-eight ... *Please*, Marianne.'

She feels a wave of cold air on her face, the touch of snowflakes on her cheek. 'Oh, for goodness' sake ... Ninety-seven ... ninety-six ... ninety-five ... '

'Keep going.'

'Ninety-four ... ninety-three ... '

Keir sets her down on a bench beside a hanging tarpaulin. He lowers it onto the platform and pulls the rope till the tarpaulin gathers. He lifts Marianne again and sets her down inside the canvas bag. 'I'm going to hoist you up, then swing you out. Don't be frightened – you're perfectly safe.' He pulls on the rope and grunts, 'Keep counting.'

Marianne's voice is muffled. 'I've lost count.'

'Ninety-four.' Keir swings the load round so Marianne dangles in the air.

'Ninety-five ... ninety-six ... '

'No. Backwards. Ninety-three ... '

'Ninety-two ... ninety-one ... ninety ... '

Her voice fades as Keir passes the rope slowly through his hands. He feels her touch the ground, lets go of the rope and scrambles on to the ladder, descending quickly, jumping the last few feet. Disentangling Marianne from the tarpaulin, he pulls her hat down firmly again and wraps her tightly in the blankets, ignoring her protests.

'I'm quite capable of walking!'

'Not without shoes. Anyway, this'll be quicker. We'd be quicker still if you'd stop wriggling. What happened to the counting? Come on, eighty-nine ... '

'I passed that ages ago. On the way down. I'm into the seventies.'

'Good. Carry on.'

'*Why?*'

'Because it will make me very happy. Seventy-nine ... '

'Seventy-eight ... Seventy-seven ... It's still snowing, isn't it?'

'Aye. But we'll soon have you tucked up in bed. Seventy-six.'

'Seventy-five ... seventy-four ... ' Her head flops suddenly onto his shoulder. 'I'm so *tired*, Keir.'

'Aye, I know. You've had a hell of a time and I was a stupid bastard to leave you behind. But you're going to be OK. Seventy-three.'

'Seventy-two ... I wasn't scared. Not very. I knew you'd come. I knew you'd find me somehow. How did you know where I was?'

'It's a long story. I'll tell you later. Seventy-one ... '

The stove is still alight and the house feels warm as Keir carries Marianne up to the bedroom. Sweating with the exertion, he sets her down on the bed, still swaddled in blankets. He kneels in front of her and takes her by the shoulders, raising his voice to be heard over the chattering of her teeth.

'Listen to me, Marianne. We have to get you warm, and quickly. I want you to take off your wet things – your jeans and jumper. I'm not going to look at you, I promise.' She sheds the blankets and fumbles with the zip of her jeans. Keir turns away and unzips his jacket. 'I'm taking off my fleece and jumper now and I want you to put them on because they're warm and dry. Or ... if you'll let me, there's a better way.'

'What?'

'I can warm you up much quicker with my skin.'

'I don't understand. What do you mean?'

'I mean, I can get into bed with you and get you warm. I'm the warmest thing we've got. And after carrying you, I'm very warm. And,' he adds, 'there's a lot of me.'

She frowns, then her face crumples. 'Keir, what's happening? I don't remember where I am!'

'Don't cry! You're going to be OK, I promise. Just take off your wet clothes now and get into bed.'

As she peels off her jeans, a sob turns to a snort. 'I've got gloves on my *feet*.'

'Aye, I had to improvise.'

She struggles with her jumper for a moment, then gives up and whimpers, 'My head's stuck. My hands are *useless*!'

'Here, let me.' He helps her out of the wet wool, retrieves the hat and replaces it on her head.

'*Now* what are you doing?'

'Putting your hat back on. To keep your head warm. Under the duvet with you now.'

She sniffs. 'I must look a complete idiot.'

'Wouldn't know, I'm not looking.'

Marianne climbs under the duvet and lies on her back, shivering violently. 'What are you doing now?'

'Taking off my jumper. But not my jeans. Now don't be frightened – this isn't what it looks like. Ach, sorry! You know what I mean. I'm going to get under the duvet with you and use my skin to warm you. Believe me, it's the quickest way. Standard procedure, in fact.' He lifts the duvet and she feels the mattress subside as he gets into bed beside her. 'Lie on your side, facing me. I'm going to put one arm round your waist and put my hand in the small of your back. Like that ... And this one – lift your head now – I'm going to put round your neck and shoulders. Now ... I want you to press yourself up against me.' Marianne hesitates, then edges across the mattress. She feels him flinch. 'Christ Almighty, you're cold! Try and get as much of your skin in contact with mine as you can ... That's right, that's good! We'll have you warmed up in no time. Then I'll

136

make you a hot drink and get you some food. Are you comfortable?'

'The hair on your chest is tickling my nose.'

'You can feel your nose? Och, that's a good sign. Turn your face to one side. Lay your cheek against my chest. Better?'

'Mmm ... Shouldn't I be moving about though?' she asks drowsily. 'To get the circulation going?'

'No, it's not safe to do that. The warm-up has to be gentle. You're very, very cold. Your body is struggling to keep your core warm. We mustn't take blood away from your organs.'

'How do you *know* all this?'

'I've friends in the Mountain Rescue team. And I've heard tales of folk being treated for hypothermia.' He moves his hand gently over her chilled flesh. 'Your back's still really cold. Turn over, we'll try a different position.'

She turns away from him and says with a weary sigh, 'This is like the *Kama Sutra*.'

'Now *that* would get your circulation going. Draw up your knees.' He curves his body round hers, enfolding her with his arms. 'I'm going to put a hand here, on your midriff and I'm going to leave it there. Press your back up against me. Aye, like that!'

They lie still, breathing in unison, until Marianne says, 'I walked into the pond. Fell straight through the ice.'

'I know, I saw. You must have given the frogs a hell of a fright. But the pond's not close to the house. Why did you move so far away?'

'I was frightened. Snow fell off the roof. It was like an avalanche. I just heard a strange noise ... and I ran. Ran away from the house. Then I couldn't find it again.'

'But you managed to find the tree-house.'

'Eventually. I followed the burn. And I managed to find the stepping-stones. It was just luck.'

'Don't you believe it! That was excellent navigation and hill-craft. You're a wonder, Marianne.' He squeezes her gently. 'A bloody wonder.'

'Thank you.' He feels her body relax against him and wonders if she's falling asleep when she announces, 'I'm *starving*. I hope you bought us something nice for supper.'

He hesitates before saying, 'I didn't do any shopping. I got to Broadford, then turned round and came back. I'm afraid it'll be baked beans on toast. Unless you're any good with loaves and fishes.'

'You caught some *fish*?'

'I was thinking more tinned sardines.'

'Sardines on toast is one of my favourites. But Louisa can't stand the smell,' she says absently. 'Keir, I don't understand. Why did you come back early?' She is aware of his chest rising and falling behind her, feels the pressure of warm air on the back of her neck, as if he has let out a great sigh, but he doesn't reply. 'I suppose you heard me ... Calling out.'

'Aye. In a manner of speaking.'

After a moment, she turns her head and says over her shoulder, 'You can't have! Where from? You heard me shout from *inside* the Land Rover? Up on the *road*? But you must have been miles away by then.'

'Lie still now ... It's hard to explain. And I don't think you're going to understand anyway. I picked up a kind of ... distress signal. I thought you might be in trouble. So I turned back.'

Marianne struggles to grasp the meaning of his words. 'Are you saying you can read *minds*?'

'No. It's not like that, I just ... pick things up. Hear things other folk don't hear. It's like when you get a hunch about something. I get hunches. Lots of them. Really strong ones. And they're always right.'

'*Always*?'

'Aye.'

'So you didn't actually hear me?'

'No. It's a kind of ... radar, I suppose.'

'Does it only work with people you know?'

'No. I knew you were in trouble when we first met. *Before* we met, in fact. That's why I stopped. I sensed it walking along the street. Some folk give off really clear signals. You're one of them. I suspect it's something to do with being blind. You transmit as well as receive. Like bats.'

'But you can't actually read my thoughts, can you?' she asks anxiously.

138

She feels his chest move again and senses silent laughter. 'No, it's not that specific. It's more ... moods. Emotions. Like music. It's like picking up music on long wave radio. Faint. Crackly. Then it comes over loud and clear for a wee while.'

Marianne is silent for a moment, then says solemnly, 'That must be terrible. I can't imagine feeling that ... vulnerable.'

Keir struggles with a mixture of emotions: relief and something he can't quite place, which he thinks might be gratitude. 'Och, I think *you* probably can.'

'Do you pick up big things? Earthquakes? Tsunamis?'

'I do in my job. I look and listen for geological hazards. And I predict when and where they might happen.'

'But you do that using state-of-the-art equipment, don't you?'

'Aye. And by following some very unscientific hunches. So yes, I do sometimes pick up big things.' She is silent again and he feels the question form as her body tenses. 'Aye ... I saw Piper coming.'

Marianne says nothing, then turning in his arms, exclaims, 'But if you *saw* –'

'If I saw it coming, why didn't I say something? *Do* something? I've lived with that question for eighteen years now and I haven't come up with a satisfactory answer. I saw it coming, but I'd no idea what it was! So what could I do?'

'I don't understand!'

'No, neither do I. Look, this is all going to sound crazy, but you're alive because of it. I don't talk about it, except sometimes to local folk who ... *accept* it. If you came from these parts, you'd know what I'm talking about.'

She clutches at his broad hand spread on her tummy. 'You have *second sight*?'

'Aye.'

'Oh my God ... How *awful*.'

'Well, I'm glad I don't have to explain that part! As you seem to realise, the sight's not a gift, it's a burden. You know something's going to happen and you know who it's going to affect, but you don't know when and you don't know exactly how. And you see it, you *receive* it until ... until it's over.'

139

He is aware of Marianne's fingers moving gently on the back of his hand, as if reading the complex data of skin, tendon and bone. The sensation soothes him and he's overwhelmed with a desire to sleep.

'Keir, did you know about Mac? Before it happened.'

'Aye ... You remember when we met at the opera? We were talking. And I disappeared.'

'You told me you'd seen someone you knew. I remember now, you said something rather odd. You said you'd seen someone ... who shouldn't have been there. Oh, God –'

'I saw Mac. Standing in the middle of the bar in his working gear, with his helmet smashed in and his face covered in blood. So I went to make a call. In a hurry. I phoned Annie. Mac wasn't even offshore. So I knew it wasn't something that had happened, but something that was *going* to happen. But I didn't know when.' She lifts his hand and, in a gesture that almost unmans him, lays the palm against her mouth. He feels her lips move, then she replaces his hand on her waist. Swallowing, he continues softly, 'I always pray I'm going to be wrong. I used to hope I was just ... *mad*. Hearing voices, seeing things. But I knew. It's not uncommon in the islands. My grandfather had the sight too. My family just accepted it, but didn't talk about it. You don't. What is there to say? What's for you, will not go by you.'

'Did Mac know you'd seen –'

'Och no, I never *tell* folk! Nobody knows about it except my family and a few folk on Skye. I told a woman once ... Someone I felt a lot for. I thought we'd maybe marry, so I decided I'd better tell her about ... my wee problem. She was completely spooked. We lived together for a while but it didn't work out. She couldn't handle it. Said I was a living *memento mori*. It was like living with an undertaker, she said, only worse. At least an undertaker would know when the funeral was and who was to be buried. I could see her point. You'd be for ever asking yourself, "What has he seen? Who's next?" Och, it's no way to live! So I never talk about it. And I don't get involved with women, except on a pretty casual basis.'

The room is dark now. Being careful not to lift the duvet off

140

Marianne, Keir sits up in bed. The stove needs attention but he's loth to move. He feels the flutter of Marianne's fingers on his naked back, reaching for him – a touch that, for the first time that afternoon, travels straight to his groin. He turns away from her and swings his legs out of bed. 'I'll make us a hot drink and see to the stove.'

'Keir, you said you saw Piper Alpha ... before it happened.'

He sits hunched on the edge of the bed. 'Aye. But I didn't know that's what it was. I'd seen it for years. I'd grown up with it. My parents told me it was a recurring dream, a nightmare, but I knew it wasn't. I only ever saw it when I was awake.'

'How old were you?'

'When I first saw it? About eight or nine, I suppose. It didn't make any sense to me. The picture I saw. It was just ... an impression. I never knew what it meant, just that it was bad. Very bad. By the time I was in my late teens, I sensed it was something that would happen, but I didn't know what, or where, or when.'

'What did you see?'

He doesn't answer. She lays her palm on his back and, after a moment, she feels the hard ridge of bone retreat as his spine straightens.

'I saw the sea ... and it was on fire.'

Marianne sits up, searches with her hands for his face, for his eyes, finds the eyelids tight shut, the lashes wet. She takes him in her arms and he lies down beside her, not moving, not speaking, for in the end there is no need for words.

Spring 2007

Chapter Twelve

Louisa

Keir delivered Marianne to the door late at night. She looked even paler than usual, apart from a bruise on her forehead where I suppose she must have collided with something. Keir looked hollow-eyed with tiredness. Remembering with a flush my recent wakeful night and the cause of it, I wondered if his exhaustion was a positive sign, but his face looked drawn, the lines much deeper than I remembered. His smile was warm enough, but it didn't reach those strange, inscrutable eyes, which barely met mine. He wouldn't come into the flat, claiming his boots were too muddy, that he was jiggered and needed his bed.

Marianne didn't kiss him goodbye and Keir didn't kiss her, but I noticed her hand reach for his arm and rest there a moment as they said their brief farewells. After I'd shut the door, Marianne announced that she needed a long hot bath and then sleep. Clearly, girly chats over a nightcap were not on the agenda.

To be honest, there's not a lot to be gained from asking Marianne about things she's done or places she's been. She can really only tell you what she's experienced, which is fascinating, of course, but the traffic is one-way. You can't really compare notes. We went to Venice last year and when we got back Garth asked us for our impressions. I trotted out all the usual Canaletto clichés (well, what is there left to say about Venice?) but Marianne said nothing. Garth turned to her and said, 'Did you do St Mark's, then? The Piazza? What was that like?' Marianne thought for a moment, then said, 'The sound of pigeons' wings beating incessantly ... Like a heavenly host. The air was never still. And there was a pervasive scent ... of the sea ... and sweat ... and limoncello.' Silence descended after that. (Marianne often has that effect on people.) Eventually she took pity on us and changed the subject.

It's not that Marianne can't enter into our world. Far from it. It's that we can't enter into hers. I wondered if Keir had made any headway.

Marianne seemed very odd once she was home. Quiet or, rather, preoccupied. She also seemed more bad-tempered than usual, but perhaps I was being more irritating than usual. I too was preoccupied with a man and hadn't yet found either the opportunity or the courage to tell Marianne what had happened with Garth. I hadn't yet found an opportunity to discuss it with Garth. I was waiting, in time-honoured fashion, for him to ring me, but since I was also his employer, I knew he might have been waiting for me to make the first move.

I hadn't a clue about the sexual mores of twenty-five year olds. Perhaps he would pretend nothing had happened? For all I knew, he made a habit of sleeping with lonely middle-aged women, though to judge from his diffident bedside manner, I thought not. In the heat of the moment he'd been enthusiastic and affectionate, but the morning after, he'd seemed subdued. (Thankfully, not embarrassed.) A hangover, plus having to face the world minus his war paint could have accounted for low spirits. (Male Goths don't seem to travel with their make-up kit. Lack of handbag, I suppose.)

Marianne simply wouldn't be drawn on the subject of Keir. She told me about his home, the tree-house, the clever ways he found to share his world with her, and she told me about his family (although I gathered she hadn't actually met any of them). I asked her about the bruise on her forehead. Her face clouded over and she said she'd been for a walk in the garden on her own and bumped into a tree. Well, you didn't need to be Hercule Poirot to see that she wasn't telling the whole story. As to her relationship with Keir, whether it was on a new and better footing, *or whether everything had gone pear-shaped, I didn't know. Nor, it would seem, did Marianne want me to know.*

When I helped her unpack I found a pair of muddy shoes in a polythene bag. They were sturdy lace-ups, minus their laces. I said, 'What happened to your shoes?' She replied, 'They got very wet.' Since I was holding them this was hardly news to me, but I said nothing more. Then I came across a woollen scarf I didn't recognise – bottle green, a colour Marianne never wears. It was cashmere and I presumed it must have been a gift from Keir, but I thought it best not to enquire. I was beginning to realise that the topic of Keir was off-limits as far as my sister was concerned.

I left her putting things away and went to make some tea. When I passed her open bedroom door a few minutes later I happened to glance in and saw Marianne reflected in the wardrobe mirror. (She wouldn't have known I could see her. Not surprisingly, Marianne has never really grasped the concept of mirrors and reflections.) She was sitting on the bed with her face buried in the scarf. I thought for a moment she must be crying and was about to go in when she raised her head. I saw that she was, in fact, quite composed. She stroked her cheek with the scarf, then buried her face in it once again, inhaling audibly.

Then it dawned on me. The scarf wasn't a gift. It was Keir's.

Marianne had never been the weepy type. She'd been an adventurous, resilient child, always falling over and righting herself cheerfully. Nor had she ever been prone to self-pity, not even when she lost her husband and baby in quick succession. She said she cried herself out for ever with the miscarriage. (I never asked if some of those tears were relief mixed with grief, but I had my suspicions.) So I was surprised to find her so unsettled after she came back from Skye. The slightest thing seemed to upset her and she was easily moved to tears. I braced myself for what looked like the onset of an early menopause and resolved to broach the subject of HRT the next time she dissolved.

I didn't have to wait long.

Keir was back in Norway, inside the Arctic Circle. This much information Marianne had volunteered. She received no phone calls from him (or none that I knew about), but when she'd been back in Edinburgh a couple of weeks she received another of his audio-postcards. I confirmed for her that it was a cassette from Keir and she retreated into her bedroom to listen to it. She was gone a long time and, although I'd heard Keir's voice at the beginning of the tape, it had soon fallen silent. I wondered if she was having trouble with her ancient cassette player, which was on its last legs.

I knocked on her door and received an indistinct reply. I went in and found her sitting on the bed beside the machine, clutching a handful of tissues, tears running down her face. The tape was still playing but it just sounded like radio interference. I could hear no words, only whistling sounds and a hissing noise that sounded like rain falling in a forest. There was the odd weird hoot and a sinister whooshing noise that for some reason made me think of a fire-breathing dragon. This racket went on for another minute or so, then Marianne pressed the Stop button and wiped her eyes.

I sat down and put my arm around her. 'Is the tape faulty? Oh, darling, how disappointing! Why on earth didn't he check before sending it?' Marianne still didn't speak but felt for the cassette player and pressed Rewind, then when the tape stopped she pressed Play. After a few seconds we heard Keir's voice.

'Hi, Marianne. This is a postcard of the Northern Lights which I've been watching for the last couple of nights and I'm telling you, it's a grand sight. Did you know some folk say they can hear the lights? Technically, this is impossible because where they're coming from – about a hundred kilometres above the Earth – it's almost a vacuum, so sound can't travel. Nevertheless some folk claim to have heard sounds while observing the lights and the Saami word for them apparently refers to "audible light". It's possible, I suppose, though I can't quite get my head round the physics of it.

'I haven't been able to record an Aurora Borealis Symphony for you, but what I can offer is a recording made by a magnetometer hooked up to an audio recorder. Try to contain your excitement now, while I explain ... A magnetometer measures variations in the strength and direction of the geomagnetic field – variations due to electric currents in the upper atmosphere. The electrons and ions that produce the Aurora also cause these *currents, so a magnetometer measures a quantity that is directly related to the Northern Lights. The variation in sound you're about to hear is the variation in the magnetic field caused by incoming solar particles. The stronger the magnetic variations, the greater the auroral activity ...*

'Och well, that's the best I can do for now. Give it a whirl. After a few plays you might find it grows on you. Like Pink Floyd. Personally, I like that "screaming swifts" effect. If you can, listen on headphones and you might get a wee feel of the night sky full of random coloured lights. Like a cosmic firework display ...'

Keir's voice changed then, as if he was about to say something more personal. Marianne's hand shot out and pressed the Stop button. I sat not knowing what to say. I hadn't understood much of what I'd heard and I still had no idea why she was so upset. She blew her nose, sighed, then said, 'I'm sorry, but I just can't cope with the kindness of the bloody man. Nor,' she added faintly, 'the onslaught of his imagination.'

Still at a loss for something to say, I decided to tell her about Garth. I thought it might provide us with a little light relief. In a way, it did. Marianne laughed until she cried.

Marianne deposits a mug of coffee on the table where Garth is working, then takes her own to the sofa. 'Louisa tells me you've given up the Goth glad rags.'

He slits open an envelope, scans a letter and places it on top of a pile of correspondence. 'Yeah. You wouldn't recognise me now. Well, *you* would, 'cos me voice is still the same. She didn't, though.'

'Really? She didn't tell me *that*.'

'I turned up on 'er doorstep with some flowers an' she thought I was a delivery man. You should've seen 'er face! Oh – sorry, Marianne. I wasn't thinkin'.'

'Don't be silly – I'm not that sensitive. You must look quite different then.'

Garth opens another envelope, then drops the contents into a waste paper bin. 'I do. Me own mother wouldn't know me. I got me 'air cut, really short, so what's left is me natural colour. Seemed easier than dyein' it all. An' I leave me face natural now. 'Aven't stopped any clocks with it so far ... An' I did what I've been meanin' to do for ages. Bought meself a suit.'

'Good gracious! What made you do that?'

'Well, Lou's been sayin' she wants me to go to business meetin's. 'Er agent's been talkin' about film deals, merchandisin' an' stuff, an' Lou says she'd feel 'appier if I was there, for moral support, though as it 'appens, I do know a bit about the film biz. Me brother's a cameraman. But I knew she wouldn't want me there lookin' like somethin' out of one of 'er books, minus the muscles. So I decided, what with one thing an' another, it was time I cleaned up me act. Acted me age, not me shoe size.'

'Well, good for you! How marvellous, to just re-invent yourself like that. Does Lou approve of the new you?'

'Seems to.' A faint flush tinges Garth's pale cheeks and, forgetting his embarrassment is unobserved, he bows his head over the pile of mail. 'She says I look a lot older now. Which is probably a good thing ... under the circumstances. She won't get quite so much stick. About me, I mean.'

'Oh, you don't need to worry about that. Lou wouldn't care. She's very thick-skinned. Has to be, to cope with the scathing reviews she gets. She doesn't give a damn what people think, never has. But I'm sure from a career point of view – *yours*, I mean – the transformation will prove to be a good move. People do seem to jump to conclusions about appearances. Sighted people, anyway. But I have to say, I miss the jingling.'

'What? Me chains?'

'Yes.'

'Yeah, so do I! I thought I'd miss all me black gear an' the convenience of not 'avin' to decide what to wear in the mornin'. Or me make-up. I thought that'd be 'ard, facin' the world without all me slap on. But in fact I got over all that in a week. But I still miss the sound of me chains rattlin'. Some'ow they used to keep me company.'

'Yes, it was a cheerful sort of noise. Friendly.'

'Yeah, it was! An' it followed me around. Like a dog. To tell you the truth, it's a bit quiet without it, but I can't say as I really registered the sound before it wasn't there.'

'It was *you*, that sound. I'd know you were in the room even before you spoke. I'd hear the little jingle.'

'Yeah.' Garth shuffles a pile of letters and tidies them into a folder. 'You know, when me dad died a couple of years ago I thought I'd miss 'is laugh or 'im grumblin' at me to cut me 'air, but what I miss, what's missin' when I go and see me mum, is Dad's *wheeze*. 'E was asthmatic, you see, all 'is life, and it was pretty bad for the last few years. Even when 'e didn't say much – an' 'e was never much of a one for chit-chat, me dad – you were always aware of 'im breathin', strugglin' for air. We were all so used to it, we never noticed. I didn't really register it till 'e wasn't there any more ... Bet if I was to 'ear someone wheezin' now, it'd crack me right up. Memories of poor ol' Dad would come floodin' back ... Funny thing, memory, innit?'

'Yes,' Marianne replies, sipping her coffee thoughtfully. 'Very funny.'

Marianne

I don't know why I didn't confide in Louisa about Keir. After she'd told me about Garth it would have been the obvious thing to do, but I couldn't. I didn't want to explain about getting lost in the snow. There seemed no point in worrying her and I still felt a complete idiot about having let it happen. I suppose, if I'm honest, the experience was too terrifying for me to want to relive it. Being lost and then found was an event now shut away in the vaults of my memory, along with other horrors; something that happened, then was over. Finished. I was in a different place now, geographically and figuratively.

And so was Keir.

Some memories of my time on Skye were vague, elusive; others so vivid they seemed almost tangible. I could still sense their reverberations in my body. The scent of daphne on the cold, damp air; the sharp, oily taste of the sardines I wolfed down at breakfast, ravenous after my ordeal; Keir's body lying beside me, massive, inert, like a felled tree. These details I could remember, but what had actually *happened* between Keir and me, why, or what any of it meant, I didn't know.

Perhaps I didn't want to know. It was bad enough knowing that

151

on the last day, when I'd come across his scarf hanging on the back door, I'd taken it without asking and stashed it in my suitcase. When I got home, I'd hidden it in my bedside drawer.

I tried not to take it out more than once a day. Mostly I failed.

I received another packet a few days later, which made me wonder if Keir was seriously under-employed in the Arctic. It was a CD this time and Louisa said it was labelled 'Rautavaara's *Cantus Arcticus*'. She read me the short note from Keir, which said, 'You'll either love this or think it a musical abomination. I'm hoping that blindness will incline you towards the former, a position I occupy. Beware – listening to it is strangely addictive.'

The piece was unknown to me so while I ate my breakfast Garth kindly read the descriptive notes Keir had written for me. *Cantus Arcticus* is a concerto 'for Birds and Orchestra'. Rautavaara is Finnish and the bird sounds were apparently taped in the Arctic Circle. The first movement is called *The Marsh* and represents bog birds in spring. The second movement is called *Melancholy* and the featured bird is the shore lark. The third movement is called *Swans Migrating*.

Those are the facts. I barely know how to describe the music or its effect on me. It was – as far as I could tell – like *being* there. I have no sense of distance or colour, little sense of height, depth or even shape when it comes to anything bigger than I can hold, but to listen to this music in the warm sitting room of our Edinburgh flat was to be surrounded by wheeling flocks of birds. It was as if I'd been transported to a cold, northern wasteland. I felt a sense of vastness, I had an inkling of what people mean when they talk about sky. The bleak beauty of it all was inexplicably moving.

I've never held a live bird. I've never seen one fly and have no concept of the movement of birds in the sky, either individually or as a flock. (My mother told me birds flew in the sky the way fish swam in the sea; that a shoal of fish was something like a flock of birds. I was none the wiser. I put my hands into our aquarium to see if I could feel the fish swimming, but all I felt was the occasional slimy touch of something slithering through my fingers, like seaweed.) I know some people are moved by the sight of a skein of migrating geese and I've listened to a mathematical computer buff talk about modelling the flight patterns of roosting starlings, but until I heard this music, it was all just so many words to me. I had no sense of birds in their context.

Cantus Arcticus revealed to me not the form of a bird – its feathers, its wingspan, the way it moves – but the movement of the flock, the emptiness of their natural habitat, its scale. Birdsong alone could not have done this for me. Nor could music. I'm familiar with pieces such as *The Firebird* and *The Carnival of the Animals* and never much cared for them, even as a child. A musical friend said you needed to know what birds and animals look like and how they move to appreciate how clever Stravinsky and Saint-Saëns were. Their music assumes prior knowledge. These composers aren't trying to depict animals for someone who has never seen them. Nor, I am sure, was Rautavaara, but that is what he managed to do for me.

I've stood beneath cascades of flapping pigeons in Venice and Trafalgar Square; I've lingered in Edinburgh squares at dusk to listen to the gossipy chatter of roosting starlings. I heard them move, but never saw. I never saw patterns, formations of birds moving against the sky.

The first time I listened to the concerto I was stunned, barely able to respond. The second time, I was fighting back tears and I didn't know why. I thought it must be something to do with Keir. The third time, I allowed myself to weep because I knew I was crying tears of joy. And gratitude.

Chapter Thirteen

Louisa

Marianne seemed a little more settled after receiving her two parcels but she still looked peaky. She didn't seem to know when Keir was due back and tried to make light of the matter, but she didn't fool me for one moment. She played that maddening bird CD non-stop until I thought I was living in an aviary. I took to wearing headphones when working, so Garth had to semaphore when he wanted my attention. He pointed out that it was Marianne who should be wearing the headphones, but I explained that she depended too much on her ears for 'seeing' ever to exclude ambient sound. I didn't really begrudge her the strange music as, oddly enough, it did seem to lift her mood.

Choosing my moment carefully, I suggested she go and talk to Dr Greig, our female GP, about coping with the onset of the menopause. I expected resistance but, to my surprise, met none. Marianne said she'd been wondering whether that was what was wrong with her, especially as her periods seemed to have become erratic. I said that was a sure sign and it was obviously time to start thinking about HRT. It was ridiculous to have to put up with all the ghastly and humiliating symptoms of the menopause as young as forty-five!

Before she could change her mind about going, I rang the surgery and made an appointment for her the next day. We strolled round to the surgery together and I sat in the waiting room, happily leafing through back-numbers of OK! and Hello!, wondering how she was getting on.

*

Marianne thinks she must have misheard. More and more, she seemed to be succumbing to what Louisa referred to as 'senior moments'.

'I'm sorry, could you repeat that? I didn't quite catch ...'

Dr Greig looks over the top of her spectacles at her blind patient and enunciates clearly, but not unkindly, 'I said, the commonest cause for the cessation of periods in a woman your age, in good health, and in the absence of other symptoms, is pregnancy. It would also account for the mood swings, feeling faint and so on. Is it possible, Mrs Fraser, that you could be pregnant?'

Marianne blinks several times before answering. 'Yes ... Yes, it's possible.'

'Then I suggest a pregnancy test. If the result is negative we'll think again, but I think you'll probably find you get a positive.' Dr Greig notes with some concern her patient's pallor. 'I take it this would come as something of a shock to you and your husband?'

'It comes as a shock to me. My husband will no doubt take it in his stride.'

'Well, that's good to hear.'

'He's dead. He died eighteen years ago.'

Dr Greig removes her spectacles and searches Marianne's impassive face. 'I see ... And the baby's father?'

'He's somewhere in the Arctic Circle. But it might as well be the Seventh Circle of Hell. It doesn't really matter where he is, he's just the biological father.'

'This would be ... a *casual* relationship then, I take it?' Dr Greig says carefully.

'Yes, it is. I mean, it was.'

So ... you've no partner currently?'

'No. I live with my sister.'

Dr Greig glances at Marianne's notes. 'And you're ... let me see now – forty-five?'

'Yes.'

'Do you have any children?'

'No.'

'Does your sister?'

'No. Not unless you count her lover. He's not long reached years of majority.'

'I *see*,' says Dr Greig, only just managing to keep the surprise out of her voice. She replaces her glasses and resumes her professional manner. 'Well, Mrs Fraser, assuming you *are* pregnant, you have various options. You'll no doubt want to give them some thought. Single parenthood is a challenge at any age, but given your added *difficulties* ... As I expect you're aware –' Dr Greig lowers her voice tactfully, '– at your age, there is a greater risk of miscarriage.'

'Yes. That's what happened last time.'

'So you've been pregnant before?'

'Oh yes. Many years ago. But I miscarried. They said it was probably the shock of my husband's death. That caused the miscarriage, I mean. But perhaps I would have miscarried anyway. I was told it's a very common occurrence. One in five pregnancies, I gather. Nature is very wasteful, isn't it?' Marianne hears herself chattering away like a demented type-writer and wonders if this signals the onset of hysteria, even mental breakdown. Realising Dr Greig is speaking again, she makes an effort to assimilate the information.

'Miscarriage is indeed very common, much more so than people realise. There's also, as you'll no doubt be aware, a higher risk of abnormality at your age. But we're jumping the gun. Let's do a pregnancy test, then we'll take it from there. We can do one now if you could provide us with a urine sample?'

'Thank you.' Marianne stands and gathers her handbag and cane. 'I can probably manage that if you'd care to direct me towards the loo.'

'No bother at all.' Dr Greig rifles in a drawer, then places a plastic container in Marianne's hand. Taking her arm, she walks her to the door. 'You have someone waiting for you, I take it?'

'Yes. My sister. Oh, but please don't mention this to her. I'd rather she didn't know. For now. She'll only make a fuss.'

'Mrs Fraser, do you not think confiding in your sister might be a good idea?'

'No, I don't. Believe me, telling Louisa would only compli-cate matters.'

'And there's no chance that the baby's father–?'

'No,' Marianne says firmly. 'No chance at all. Really, I'd rather deal with things in my own way, if you don't mind.'

'Of course. That's your prerogative.' Spotting a nurse, Dr Greig calls out, 'Peggy, could I have a wee word? I'd like you to assist Mrs Fraser here.' Turning back to Marianne, she says, 'I'm handing you over to Nurse Peggy now. She'll do the necessary. Now come back and see me if there's anything you'd like to discuss. *Anything* at all,' Dr Greig says with a meaningful but wasted look. Thrown by the vacancy of Marianne's expression, she pats her arm and says, 'Good luck, Mrs Fraser.'

'Thank you. It seems I might be needing it.'

Marianne

At some level I suppose I must have known. Known it was a possibility. But if I'd admitted pregnancy was a possibility, I would have had to admit how little I actually remembered about the encounter that had led to my interesting condition.

I remembered waking up and finding, when I moved, that Keir was lying beside me, audibly asleep. I could remember taking him in my arms the night before, but not what had made me do it. I thought I remembered tears. But were they mine or his? As I moved slightly in bed, I became aware of my own tender flesh and a moistness that left me in no doubt as to what had happened, but I had no memory of anything said, least of all any discussion about a condom. If you'd asked me, if Keir had asked me – and perhaps he *did* – I'd have said that, at nearly forty-six, my chances of conceiving were so remote as to be not worth considering.

Life always has the last laugh, doesn't it?

The harder I tried to remember what had happened, the less I could recall. I couldn't remember anything in detail but a conviction was forming in my mind that I could have died and that Keir had probably saved my life. But I knew gratitude wasn't the reason I'd taken him into my arms, into my body. I *did* remember – with some embarrassment – just how much I'd wanted him, how suddenly, how fiercely.

I'd woken early the following morning, but instead of turning to Keir, waking him, making love again, consciously, I'd got out of bed without disturbing him and gone downstairs to shower. By the time he woke, I was dressed and drinking coffee. I heard him walk slowly downstairs and into the kitchen. It must have been dark still. I heard him fumbling with matches and then the scrape of an oil lamp's glass chimney. He must have stood still for several moments, trying, I suppose, to gauge how things were between us. My nerve broke and I said, 'It's not fair. If you don't speak or move, there's nothing for me to *read*.'

Eventually he said softly, tentatively, 'Marianne ... I have to go back to Norway. Next week.'

'For long?'

'A couple of months.'

'Oh ... I hope you'll send me one of your postcards. I do so enjoy them.'

After another long silence he said, 'Yesterday ... Was – was it not what you wanted?'

'Yes, it was. It was what I wanted. *Then*. I thought I'd nearly died. It was what I wanted.'

'But now?'

'You mean, what do I want if I'm not going to die? I don't know. I remember so little about what happened, I think it probably best to act as if it *didn't*. For now.'

He was silent again, then I heard a great intake of breath and he spoke in a rush. 'If I misread the signs, I'm very sorry. I thought – I mean, you made it pretty clear – '

'Yes, I'm sure I did. Please don't feel badly, Keir. I don't remember the details but I do remember how much I wanted you. I'm not saying it shouldn't have happened, all I'm saying is, now that it has, I haven't the slightest idea where it leaves us. Especially if you're off to Norway. I think I've done my fair share of waiting for men to come home to me. Or *not* come home to me.' He didn't reply. I could hear that he hadn't moved. I knew he must be staring at me, uncomprehending. Sensing the intensity of his gaze, I felt more naked than when we'd been lying in bed together. Relenting, I said, 'Keir, I wonder if you'll understand if I say my body got way ahead of my mind?'

159

'Oh, aye. Men live like that all the time.'

'My mind needs time to ... catch up. Assimilate.'

'Aye ... I'd a notion that bed was where we were headed, it was just a question of ... timing. Looks like we blew it. I'm sorry if I rushed things. I should have – '

'Would you mind if we didn't discuss it any more? For now? I don't know if it's delayed shock or exhaustion or what, but I feel rather wobbly. I think I'd just like to sit quietly by the stove for a while.'

'Surely. I'll see to the fire. Then can I get you some break-fast?'

'Yes, that would be nice. Would you mind?'

'There's no bacon left. You'll remember I didn't get as far as the Co-op. Beans on toast? Or those sardines I promised?'

'How did you know I liked sardines?'

'You told me. Yesterday.'

A memory stirred. 'Did I?'

'Aye. You said Louisa hated the smell.'

'I must have been rambling.'

'Aye. Hypothermia takes you like that.'

Another memory tugged at my brain and I shivered, but not with cold. 'Keir, I didn't dream it, did I?'

'Making love?'

'No. What you said about ... the things you see.'

I heard him exhale, then the sound of his bare feet shuffling on the floor. When he finally answered, he sounded tired. 'No ... You didn't dream it.'

'You knew somehow that I was in danger?'

'Aye, I did.'

'You know, I think I really *do* need to sit down ...'

There was, of course, no question of my keeping the baby, even if I did manage to carry it to term, so I didn't even ask myself if I wanted it. There was no point. My age, my blindness and my circumstances were such that I couldn't entertain the idea for a moment, and so I didn't. My dilemma wasn't so much what to do, but how best to do what undoubtedly had to be done. I didn't see myself coping with an abortion and its physical and emotional

160

aftermath unaided. In the absence of a partner or close girlfriend, the obvious course of action was to confide in Louisa (who was in fact my closest friend), but this I was reluctant to do and I wasn't sure why.

I thought she probably had a shrewd idea of the nature of my entanglement with Keir. Apart from the fact that she seemed well aware of his attractions, it was what she would have wished for me, and Lou was ever the optimist. So my present difficulties wouldn't come as a complete shock to her, nor did I fear her censure. Louisa is and always has been tolerant by nature. She has needed to be since I can't have been the easiest of flat-mates, nor was I the most affectionate of sisters.

Even if Louisa *had* had the slightest inclination to disapprove of my carelessness, she scarcely had a leg to stand on since she herself was engaged in an unaccountable relationship with a man half her age. That she'd always been fond of Garth, that she regarded him as a good friend, was not news to me. I knew they enjoyed each other's company, that they shared a sense of humour, but I had no idea how they'd moved from camp matey-ness to being lovers. Or, rather, I understood how it could have happened *once* (I knew from recent experience how extreme circumstances can produce uncharacteristic behaviour), but I couldn't really grasp how and why the relationship was ongoing. What I would have dismissed as a drunken fling – and Louisa had had a few of those in her time – now appeared to be something more serious, not least because Garth appeared to be making her seriously happy. I think that was why I couldn't talk to Louisa about an abortion. I didn't want to spoil things by burdening her with my problems.

On the other hand, it's possible I couldn't face confiding in Lou simply because she seemed so very happy and I was so very, very miserable.

Garth lies on his back in bed, his shorn head pillowed on thin, white arms, his freckled brow furrowed with concern. 'She's cryin' again.'

Louisa stirs, groans and opens her eyes. Grey light at the window tells her it's very early or another dreich Edinburgh

161

day. Perhaps both. 'Oh, God ... It *must* be her hormones. Either that or she's fallen in love with that wretched man.'

'I thought you liked 'im? What's 'e done?'

'*Nothing*. That's the point. He doesn't ring, he doesn't write, he's stuck out in Norway somewhere and she's here – pining.'

Garth replies in a high-pitched, nasal voice, 'Pinin' for the fjords?'

'Oh, shut up. You weren't even born when that sketch was written.'

'Well, look at it from 'is point of view: not much point writin' to Marianne, is there? Not unless 'e's got a Braille typewriter 'andy.'

'He could ring her!'

'P'raps she told 'im not to.'

'Why would she do that?'

'Dunno. 'Cos she doesn't want to be over'eard by us? She's a very private person, is our Marianne.' Garth sits up in bed. 'Can you 'ear what I 'ear?'

'What?'

'Listen ... There! Did you 'ear that?'

'*What*? Garth, don't be infuriating. You know my hearing isn't as sharp as yours.'

'*That*! It's Marianne. In the bathroom. She's throwin' up.'

'Oh, poor thing! She really is under the weather these days. It's just one thing after another! I'd better go and see if she's all right. Put the kettle on, would you? Be a love and make us some tea.'

As Louisa gets out of bed, Garth places a restraining hand on her plump arm. 'Lou, 'ang on a minute.'

'What is it now? Hurry up, Marianne might need me. She's obviously ill.'

'Nah, I don't think so ... I suspect everythin' is in full workin' order.'

Louisa rolls her eyes heavenwards. 'I don't care what you say, I *must* be getting old. Sometimes I haven't a clue what you're on about! Look, I'm going to see how she is. Get that kettle on, please. And I'm requesting that as your *employer,* not your besotted paramour.'

Garth raises a hand to his forehead in derisory salute. 'Yes, ma'am.' As Louisa hurries out of the room fastening her dressing gown, he throws back the duvet and mutters, 'But I think you might be needin' somethin' stronger than tea, ladies ...'

Chapter Fourteen

Louisa

Marianne was pregnant. My little sister was pregnant.

Was I shocked? 'Does the Pope have a balcony?' as Garth would say. 'Pole-axed' doesn't begin to describe my consternation. Marianne emerged from the bathroom, white-faced and haggard, her nightdress splashed with vomit. The sight would have made a stone weep. I said, 'Marianne, is there something you aren't telling me?' She didn't bother to deny her condition, excuse it or prevaricate, she just burst into tears and wailed, 'Oh, Lou – I'm so sorry!' I threw my arms around her and we stood in the hallway – Marianne crying her eyes out – until Garth appeared at my shoulder and said, with ineffable tact, 'Tea's up, girls.'

I don't know when I last saw her so unhappy. Certainly not since she lost Harvey's baby. Her misery made a delicate situation more difficult to handle than it might otherwise have been. Although I wanted to sympathise with my poor sister's plight, see things from her point of view and offer much needed support, try as I might, I couldn't disguise the fact that my feelings about this pregnancy were quite unequivocal.

I was completely and utterly thrilled.

The breakfast table is a curious but comforting sight. Garth has laid a clean linen tablecloth and placed on it a large pot of tea, two bowls of porridge and a bottle of brandy. He kisses Louisa on the cheek, then disappears to the kitchen to wash up. Louisa pours them both a brandy and insists her sister drink it. To her

165

surprise, Marianne finds the brandy settles her rebellious stomach.

Louisa sits and contemplates her congealing porridge. 'We really ought to make an effort, you know. As Garth has gone to all this trouble.' She spoons some into her mouth. 'How many weeks are you?'

'Six. No – nearly seven now. Time flies when you're having fun.'

'And there's no doubt? You've done a test?'

'Two. At the surgery. Dr Greig was very helpful. She's given me all the information I need about a termination. Now I just need to stop crying – and vomiting – long enough to get it done. You don't need to worry, Lou, everything's in hand. I had hoped you'd never know.'

'Well, I'm very glad I found out! I *hate* to think of you going through all this on your own.' Louisa looks at her sister for a long moment, then says, 'You have to tell him, Marianne.'

'No, I do not. What would be the point?'

'It's Keir's responsibility as much as yours.'

'No, it isn't. It's my body that's been hi-jacked, not his.'

'All the more reason why he should share the responsibility.'

'For what? Getting rid of it? Do you seriously think he's going to fly back from the Arctic to hold my hand? For heaven's sake, Lou, be realistic. He's a man! He's an *oil* man.' Marianne reaches for her brandy and takes another sip. 'And he's a bloody Highlander. They don't do feelings.'

'But Keir isn't like that!'

'How would *you* know? You've only met him twice.'

'If he were as you describe, he wouldn't have sent you a CD of Arctic birdsong or a tape explaining the Northern Lights. I mean, he took a *blind* woman *sight-seeing*! You can make a case for Keir being eccentric, even insane, but not insensitive. If he were the clod you make out, you surely wouldn't have slept with him!' Marianne is silent. Louisa pours her a cup of tea and places it by her right hand. 'Drink some tea. You'll be dehydrated with all that vomiting.'

'*Please*! Don't even mention the word or I'll start again.' Marianne feels for her cup and lifts it carefully to her mouth

166

with both hands, warming chilly fingers on the bone china. 'Keir doesn't need to know I'm pregnant and there's absolutely nothing to be gained from telling him. I certainly don't need his support to go through a termination.'

'I realise that, darling, I just thought that if you saw him again – oh, God, I'm sorry – I mean if you *met* with him again and explained ...' Louisa's voice tails off. Tight-lipped now, she begins to trace with a finger the pattern of embroidery on the tablecloth.

'What, Lou?'

Louisa registers the warning note in her sister's voice but decides to ignore it. 'I thought perhaps you might change your mind. That *Keir* might change your mind.'

'What do you mean?'

'I thought if you had his support ... you might not *want* a termination.'

Marianne sits quite still and says nothing. Louisa remembers a time when, as a girl, she'd hidden under the dining table to avoid her little sister's wrath and randomly flung missiles. She is considering this option again when Marianne speaks, her tone and bearing imperious.

'Do I understand you correctly? Are you suggesting there is the faintest possibility that I could *keep* this baby?'

Louisa resumes her close inspection of the tablecloth and says in a small voice, 'Yes, I am.'

'You must be out of your mind.'

'Well, perhaps I am. I'm sure some people think so. I write books about vampires and sleep with a man half my age who until recently *looked* like a vampire.' Louisa reaches for the teapot and refills her cup, splashing tea into the saucer. 'Wanting to become an aunt, or a sort of surrogate mother at fifty-one is no doubt further proof that I'm losing my marbles. But that doesn't necessarily mean I'd be an unfit mother. Does it?' she adds doubtfully, stirring her tea.

'Let me get this straight – you're saying you want me to have this baby so *you* can raise it?'

'No, I want *you* to raise it! But if you don't want to, or feel that you can't, then I'm saying *I* would raise it. With your help,'

167

she adds. 'Let's face it, darling – it's the Last Chance Saloon for both of us. But we could do this! Do it together! They say children don't need two parents, just consistency of care, a loving family background. Between us we can provide that!'

'Lou, we are both middle-aged women. And one of us is blind!'

'So what? Some women my age are still giving birth.'

'Not naturally. Their reproductive lives have been extended with IVF and hormones. They're biological freaks.'

'No, they aren't, they're just desperate women.'

'And is that what you are? Desperate?'

'No, not at all! I have a fulfilling career, pots of money, a man I'm very fond of and all the sex I can use, thank you very much. But I would *love* an addition to our family. I would love you to have a child! To make up for the one you lost and the husband who was taken from you. I would love a baby for me, but mostly I want it for *you.*'

'No baby could possibly make up for losing Harvey.'

'No, of course not, I realise that. I'm sorry, I didn't choose my words very well. But I think you know what I meant. *The Lord giveth and the Lord taketh away.* He's taken away rather a lot from you, Marianne. I think it's payback time.' Marianne doesn't reply and Louisa sighs. 'Won't you try some of this porridge? It's still hot. Sugar's to your left.'

Marianne doesn't move. 'It would be totally insane. And I would be the world's worst mother.'

'Oh, very probably.'

'And blind.'

'It wouldn't be easy, I do admit. But you'd have me. And maybe Garth if he sticks around. He knows an awful lot about babies and children. He's the eldest of six, did you know? Between us we would manage somehow, I'm sure.'

'What about when you're away? How would I manage then?'

'We'd employ a nanny.'

'There's no room for a nanny!'

'There's no room for a *baby*! We'd have to move. The child would need a garden to play in ... fresh air ... trees to climb.'

'Stop it! Stop this *fantasy*! For God's sake, Lou, stop scheming! This isn't the plot of one of your books. We aren't fictional characters deserving a happy ending. This is real life! *Mine*!'

'Yes. It's also the baby's.'

'That's emotional blackmail.'

'I know. But it's also true.'

'I refuse to be manipulated. I do not feel guilty about being pregnant, nor do I feel guilty about getting rid of it.' Marianne swallows some more tea. 'I'll probably miscarry anyway.'

'Ah!'

'What do you mean, "Ah!"?'

'I mean, ah, I see why you're so dead-set on getting rid of it. You think you'll lose it anyway. So you're getting your retaliation in first.'

'Well, I probably *will* lose it. I'm forty-five!'

'But you're fit. You have the body of a much younger woman. Our mother was forty when she gave birth to you. And what about Cherie Blair?'

'Dr Grieg said the chances are high that the baby would suffer from some abnormality.'

'Well, she has a duty to warn you, I suppose, but the chances of the baby being normal are much higher. And there are all sorts of tests they can do these days.'

'They can't detect everything.'

'No, I know, but if there's something badly wrong you probably *will* miscarry. Anyway, who are we to play God and decide who's fit to be born? You were born "handicapped", as they used to say in the bad old days. Has anyone ever loved you the less for it, or wished your life away?'

'If Keir happens to be a carrier for my condition, this baby could be born blind. There's no pre-natal screening for LCA.'

'You know perfectly well that it's a one in two hundred chance of that happening. You're more likely to be knocked down by a car on the way to the antenatal clinic. Tell me,' says Louisa, scraping the last of the porridge from her bowl, 'Did you go through all this soul-searching when you found you were expecting Harvey's baby?'

169

'That was different. I was married to Harvey. There were two of us. We were in it together.'

'There are two of *us*! If you gave Keir a chance, perhaps there would be three.'

'No!'

'What have you got against this baby?'

'*I don't want it!*'

'I don't believe you, Marianne. I don't believe you've even asked yourself if you want it. Or, for that matter, if you want Keir.' Louisa pushes her bowl aside and leans across the table. 'Do you know, I've always thought you were the bravest person I've ever known. And *that's* what's knocked me for six. Not the fact that you're pregnant, the fact that you're scared to look into your heart and ask what you actually want from life. God knows, you might not get what you want – which of us does? – but *please* don't be afraid to want more than you have! I know some cynics think the secret of a happy life is low expectations, but I refuse to subscribe to that. It's mean and small-minded. I wouldn't raise a child to believe that. Would you?'

'No.'

'Nor, I suspect, would Keir. Tell him, Marianne. Give him a chance. *Please*.'

'No, Lou. And that's final.'

Marianne

I had several reasons for not wanting to tell Keir I was pregnant. Louisa knew some of them but not all.

The very last conversation I had with my late husband was a row. A terrible row. A row so bad, we hadn't even telephoned each other to kiss and make up before he died in the Piper Alpha conflagration. I still remember the last words he ever spoke to me, although I've spent eighteen years trying to forget them.

I'd told Harvey I was pregnant.

When my period was a week late I'd gone to the chemist and bought a pregnancy test. Harvey was away so I'd asked a friend, Yvonne, another oil wife, to come round and read the test result for me. We sat together in nervous silence waiting for the result to

170

show. Eventually Yvonne said it was a positive but that you could get a false positive, so I should leave it a few days before doing another test. They came in packs of two so I put the other test away in the bathroom cabinet to do when Harvey came home. I wanted him to be the first to know, know for certain, and I wanted him to be the one to tell me.

We'd never discussed having a family except in vague terms. Harvey had asked if any children I had would be blind. I said they wouldn't, not unless I'd had the misfortune to fall in love with an unwitting carrier of Leber's Congenital Amaurosis and the chances of that were about one in two hundred. Any child of mine would be a carrier of LCA but not necessarily blind.

At the time of his death, Harvey was thirty-three and I was twenty-seven. Decisions about parenthood hadn't seemed particularly urgent. His job in the oil industry was well paid but insecure. He was often away. I doubt he ever thought fatherhood was a real option for him. I was blind; my parents were dead; his widowed mother had gone back to live in Canada; my sister lived more than a hundred miles away in Edinburgh. I didn't make friends easily and had no support network, just the casual and often temporary friendships offered by oil wives like Yvonne, women who were passing through, who preferred the company of women like themselves, women who could see.

Harvey never asked if I wanted children and I never said that I did. I didn't think I *did*, but I realised afterwards that wasn't true. I just hadn't asked myself the question. Harvey – so I discovered – didn't think we could afford a child. He had a point. He liked the good life: holidays abroad, a smart car, meals in restaurants, decent clothes. We had a comfortable flat in Aberdeen and the mortgage repayments were punitively high. Harvey earned a lot of money but we spent a lot of money. He was right. We couldn't afford a child, not without making big changes to our lifestyle. All this I knew before Harvey said it, but I hoped he would say something different. I hoped he would *feel* differently, as I had done once fate had taken a hand.

I was on the pill and took it conscientiously. There was no element of deceit, something Harvey accused me of in the heat of the moment. I'd had a gastric bug and spent a day vomiting. I would have brought up one pill and was late taking the next. My routine was thrown by illness and since I never *saw* my packet of pills, I was dependent on my memory. Missing two pills must have been enough. I found myself unintentionally pregnant, simultaneously thrilled and appalled.

Harvey was just appalled. To begin with he wasn't angry. He spoke about it calmly, as if it was an unfortunate accident, a problem that had to be dealt with, like the car breaking down. He didn't realise at first – because of the impassivity of my face, I suppose – that I was pleased, that I actually wanted the baby.

That was when he got angry, although I think actually what happened was, he panicked. The pregnancy was unplanned, so Harvey didn't feel he was in control of the situation. He wasn't used to his blind, nominally helpless wife surprising him, let alone standing up to him, wanting something different from what he wanted, so he did what men do. He blustered. He dug in his heels, took up a position and wouldn't budge. He wouldn't even listen. My feelings weren't taken into consideration. They were subsidiary to the two irrefutable arguments against having a baby: we couldn't afford one and Harvey hadn't been consulted. (He talked about my pregnancy as if it were some kind of immaculate conception, as if he hadn't been around at the time.)

I got very upset and then I got angry. Harvey hadn't often seen me angry because I didn't get angry, and never with him. I don't remember exactly what was said but I do remember his last words, the last words he ever spoke to me before he slammed the front door, late for his helicopter flight – his last one – out to Piper Alpha. He said, 'I'm sorry, Marianne. You're going to have to get rid of it. And that's final.'

And it was.

After breakfast Louisa insists that Marianne go back to bed and rest. Marianne offers no resistance. Beyond her bedroom door she can hear Garth and Louisa talking in hushed tones, moving quietly around the flat as if there's an invalid in the house. Unable to discern words, Marianne can nevertheless detect the tenor of the conversation as her sister's high-pitched, anxious chatter is undercut by Garth's phlegmatic, sometimes forceful responses. Louisa calms down. There is a long silence followed by a girlish giggle, a sound unfamiliar to Marianne. As she drifts off to sleep she wonders, with a little envy, what kind of intimate moment has passed between her sister and her unlikely lover.

Garth stands at Marianne's bedside holding a tray of coffee, with a newspaper tucked under his arm. As she stirs he registers the plainness of her room, the interior of which he has rarely seen. Marianne sleeps under an antique whole-cloth quilt, faded to an anaemic shade that might once have been pale blue. Thousands of tiny stitches form a ghostly design of swirls and knots, creating a complex pattern of light and shadow that Marianne can never see but is able to feel. There are no table lamps, no pictures on the walls, no family photographs. There is no dressing table, just a desk with toiletries arrayed in regimental order, like a shop window display. On either side of the double bed are small chests of drawers cluttered with CDs and tapes, labelled in Braille. Built-in shelves house books, more CDs and tapes and various objects chosen for shape and texture: shells, stones, driftwood, glass ornaments, small sculptures. The room is tidy, the floor carpeted but clear even of rugs. Furniture and possessions have been placed at the perimeter. Emanating from a vase on the windowsill, the heady scent of narcissi permeates the spartan room.

Surfacing, Marianne props herself up on an elbow. 'Lou?'

'Nah, it's me. I did knock but you were out for the count. 'Ow you doin'? I've brought you a nice cup of coffee and some biccies. Lou says they're your favourite – gingernuts. Me mum says, eat little an' often. That's the way to keep the nausea at bay – an' believe me, she should know.'

Marianne hears pillows being plumped and rearranged behind her. 'I had no idea you came from a large family. Lou tells me you have a lot of siblings.'

'Five at the last count. An' I sincerely 'ope that's the lot, 'cos birthdays an' Christmas are gettin' to be a major expense.' Garth pours two cups of coffee and puts one in Marianne's hand. 'Biscuit's on the saucer.'

'Thank you. What are they all called?'

Garth pulls up a chair and sits beside the bed. 'After me there's Rhodri, Hywell and Aled and the little ones are Rhiannon and Angharad. They're twins. Me mum said she was gonna keep goin' till she got a girl, then she 'it the jackpot an' got two.'

'All those names are Welsh, aren't they?'

'Blimey, Marianne, you don't miss a thing.'

'That's enough of your cheek. You're not to take advantage of my debilitated state. Garth sounds Scandinavian to me. Old Norse, or something. Why have all your brothers and sisters got Welsh names and you haven't?'

'Ah well, that's me dark secret.'

'What is?'

'Me name. Mum 'ad me christened – wait for it – *Geraint*. Well, no way was I goin' to step outside Wales with a name like that, so when I was packed off to school – posh English boardin' school it was – I lost me accent an' changed me name to Garth. I thought that was dead cool. Garth Vaughan. Thought a six-stone weaklin' needed a big butch name. I mean, would you mess with a guy called Garth Vaughan?'

'No, you have a point, I don't think I would.'

'Unfortunately the name didn't totally offset me carroty 'air and freckles, so I still got it in the neck, but at least they never knew me name was Geraint.' Garth shakes his shorn auburn head. 'Jeez, I'd've been dead meat.'

'Oh dear, it sounds really grim. Poor you.'

'Nah, it made me the mature, well-adjusted individual I am now. Ready for a refill?'

'Mmm, yes, please. You know you really are a tonic, Garth. You're such a positive person to have around.'

'Thank you. That's what 'er ladyship says an' all. I do me best. Now, 'ow's about I read to you from the paper? That'll take your mind off things. Or would you like some of your music on?'

'Read me the paper, if you wouldn't mind. That would be a treat. Not depressing news, though. I don't think I'm quite up to

174

that at the moment. The music reviews, perhaps. Or the popular science bit. I really ought to educate myself a bit more.'

Garth reads aloud a scathing review of an opera production and then offers to read an article claiming the greatest threat to the ozone layer is flatulence in cows.

Marianne chokes on her gingernut. 'Oh, now you're pulling my leg!'

'Nah, it's true! Listen ...

'Bovine flatulence is responsible for a quarter of the UK's methane emissions. In Scotland, where there is a greater concentration of agriculture, sheep and cows produce 46% of all emissions. A single dairy cow produces about 400 litres of methane each day.

'Stone the crows ... I dunno why you're laughin', Marianne,' Garth says sternly, trying to suppress a grin. 'This is dead serious. The *Guardian* reportin', no less. The 'eadline says "Farting Furore" in great big letters.'

'It doesn't!'

'You're right, it doesn't. My mistake.'

Helpless with laughter, Marianne pleads, 'Oh, move on to something else, before I wet the bed.'

'Right ... 'Ow about this, then?

'The discovery of a parrot with unparalleled powers to communicate with humans – both verbally and telepathically – has brought scientists up short. The bird, a captive African grey called N'kisi, has a vocabulary of 950 words and, like a human child, he invents his own words and phrases when confronted with new ideas for which his existing repertoire has no word. N'kisi also appears to be able to read his owner's mind. In an experiment, the parrot and his owner, Aimée Morgana, were put in separate rooms and filmed as she opened random envelopes containing picture cards. When Aimée opened a picture of a man with a telephone and looked at it, N'kisi called out, 'What ya doing on the phone?' When Aimée looked at a picture of a couple embracing, the

*parrot said, 'Can I give you a hug?' Analysis showed that
N'kisi had used appropriate keywords three times more often
than would be likely by chance.'*

Garth lays the newspaper aside. 'Amazin'! Mind-readin'
parrots! It's straight out of *Doctor Dolittle*. Mind you, I dunno
why I'm so surprised – I used to 'ave a dog that knew when I
was comin' 'ome. Whatever time it was, me mum would always
know I was on me way 'cos Spike would go an' sit on the
doormat an' stare at the front door.'

'Keir had a dog he thought could read his mind. He was called
Star. But he also had another name, a secret name. Sirius ... Keir
told me about the stars, you know. When I was on Skye. He
described Orion the hunter and his dog, Sirius. I was so moved.'
Marianne's voice is unsteady and Garth watches her anxiously. 'I
can't really explain why. He went to so much trouble for me.'

'I'd like to meet this Keir. From what you an' Lou say, 'e
sounds quite a geezer.'

'I don't know if you will get to meet him now. Things have
got rather ... complicated. But I would have liked you two to
meet. I think you'd get on well.'

'What's 'e like, then?' Marianne is considering how to
change the subject when, without waiting for an answer, Garth
says, 'I mean, what kind of bloke listens to a bird concerto? A
bird-lover or a music-lover?'

'Keir's both. He's a polymath. A geologist who's interested
in zoology, astronomy and music. He'd never admit it, but he's
also something of a poet, I think. He's a gentle giant. And
lonely, I suspect. He sees himself as something of a misfit. He's
an acutely sensitive man working in a world populated by
stoical tough guys. I think there are two Keirs and he keeps
them carefully compartmentalised.'

'Sounds tricky.'

'Yes, I think it probably is. He views the world holistically,
as an entity. He doesn't really make divisions. That's why he
can describe colour in terms of smell; why he sees landscape in
terms of music. But he splits himself into his component parts
and lives divided.'

'Why?'

'A survival mechanism, I suppose. Self-protection. Well, you'd know all about that. He never exposes all of himself, just the bits he's prepared to show you. He offered someone the whole show once and she didn't want to know. I suspect he clammed up after that. I think most of Keir's feelings are shut away in a metaphorical toy-box. They're things he's done with, they belong to his past. He occasionally takes them out to handle, for old times' sake, then they go back into the box.'

''E sounds fascinatin'. Complex. For a *bloke*, I mean.'

'He's not like anyone else I've ever known. When I first met him I actually thought he was a figment of my imagination. He didn't seem real somehow, he was so strange. Then, as I got to know him, I couldn't understand what he would see in someone like me.'

'Well, there you go. "As a man is, so he sees." That's William Blake, another visionary. This Keir sounds like a bright guy to me. 'E obviously sees beyond the surface of things.'

'Oh yes, he does. Way, *way* beyond the surface ...'

Chapter Fifteen

Marianne

Louisa bought me a homeopathic remedy for morning sickness, which helped a little, and Garth's mother suggested starting the day with camomile tea and a Digestive biscuit. It was apparently important to consume these before getting up, so Louisa – and sometimes Garth – took to waiting on me first thing in the morning. I was very touched and grateful for their support. As the sickness abated, I felt I was coping better with my predicament.

Although I sounded as if my mind was made up, my feelings about the termination were mixed, largely because I seemed unable to separate my feelings about the pregnancy from my feelings for Keir. At times I was certain I wanted the man, but not the baby; at others I was convinced I didn't want the man, but possibly wanted the baby. Under the circumstances, a clean slate seemed to be the only sensible plan. As I'd so far failed to miscarry, it looked as if I was going to have to make a decision and take belated responsibility for my rash actions.

Louisa had insisted on booking me into a private clinic. We both thought privacy and comfort would be desirable, not least because of my blindness, and I was to stay in for two nights. I packed my case, leaving the CD of *Cantus Arcticus* on the bed. I was trying not to pack it – a symbolic act of severance. I put it in, then hurriedly took it out again, rearranging a packet of sturdy sanitary towels which Louisa had tactfully pointed out I would need. I hadn't worn such things since I was at school and my heart sank at the thought of them, then tears came to my eyes as I thought about why I was going to need them, what I was about to do.

Overwhelmed with grief and shame, I sank down onto the bed, on top of *Cantus Arcticus*, cracking the CD case. I swore aloud, glad of a reason to be furious with myself, to chastise myself for stupidity, sentimentality and all-round incompetence. As I worked myself up into a lather of self-loathing, the phone rang.

And I knew it would be him.

'Marianne?'

'Oh ...'

'It's Keir.'

'Yes. I recognised your voice. Where are you?'

'Oslo. The airport. I'm on my way home. Well, back to Edinburgh. How are you?'

'I'm ... I'm very well, thanks. Thank you for the parcels. I did enjoy them. It was kind of you to think of me.'

'No bother. Thinking of you is one of my preferred recreational activities – there's no hangover ... You're sure you're OK?'

'Yes. Why do you ask?'

'Och, no reason. You sound a wee bit fragile, is all. Are *you* hung over?'

'No, I was just surprised. Hearing your voice after so many weeks.'

'We agreed we wouldn't ring. That was what you wanted.'

'Yes, I know, I didn't mean it as a criticism. Why are you ringing now?'

'I just wanted to know if you were OK. You *are* OK?'

'Yes, I'm *fine*! A bit low in spirits, perhaps.' When he doesn't respond, Marianne wonders if they've been cut off. 'Keir? Are you still there?' Her stomach lurches in the second's silence before he replies.

'Aye, I'm here.'

'Oh. Good. I've been wanting to ask you ... Why *do* you take so much trouble?'

'The parcels, you mean? It's no trouble.'

'No, I mean, why do you take the trouble to share so many things with me? What's in it for you?'

When Keir answers, Marianne hears a different note in his voice: something raw and unprepared. 'There's no one else I can share these things with.' She hears an intake of breath, then his voice, louder now, energised, resumes its customary bantering tone. 'You're a captive audience and I exploit you mercilessly. Who else wants to know about Rautavaara's *Cantus Arcticus* – apart from Mrs Rautavaara, all the wee Rautavaaras and Pilkku the dog?'

'*Pilkku*?'

'It's Finnish for Spot.'

'You're pulling my leg.'

'Honest to God, *Pilkku* is Finnish for Spot. I've been working with a Finn and he told me that was his dog's name and translated it – aye, and showed me photos too. It was a Dalmatian. A fine specimen.' Keir sighs, then says, 'Och, I know, I really should get out more. But it *was* the Arctic.'

'I have to say, Louisa was unimpressed with the bird concerto, but Garth and I are completely hooked. I play it almost every day.'

'Aye, it gets you that way. I did warn you.'

'I love what he does with the brass in the final section. It's so unexpected.'

'Aye, that's genius!'

'You were right about Garth and Louisa, by the way.'

'You're kidding me.'

'No. Love's young dream. I was sceptical to begin with, but actually they're very sweet together. Garth is an exceptional young man, I think.'

'I'd like to meet this guy.'

'He's not a Goth any more, I'm afraid. He's gone straight. He tells me he looks quite ordinary now.'

'Presumably Louisa doesn't think so.'

'No, I suppose not. But then love is blind.'

'Is it love, d'you think? Already?'

'Far too early to say. But they seem to be having fun in the meantime.'

181

'Good for them. Though that must leave you feeling like a spare part.' She doesn't answer and, after a moment, he says, 'I'm flying back to Edinburgh this afternoon. I won't be there for long, I'm on my way to Skye. I was ringing to say ... you're very welcome to come with me. To Skye. No strings. And no snow either. It will all be gone now, except on the Cuillin. That sometimes hangs around until May.' She says nothing and he continues, 'No pressure, I just thought ... Och, hell – how d'you say to a blind person, "Do you want to see me again?" when see doesn't mean *see*, but "resume our tentative and decidedly weird relationship"?'

'I think you say, "Do you want to see me again?" and hope the blind person can read minds.'

'Do you?'

'Not as well as you.'

'I meant, do you want to resume where we left off?'

'Not *exactly* where we left off, Keir.'

'No, no strings ... Just lunch, as they say.'

'Sardines?'

He laughs. 'Whatever floats your boat.'

The thought of sardines provokes a sudden wave of nausea. Marianne breathes deeply and says, 'Keir, can I think about it? I'm not sure ... I've been a little unwell lately.'

'I'm sorry to hear that. When I asked earlier, you said you were fine.'

'Yes, I know. I think I was a bit flustered. Hearing your voice ... and I was in the middle of something.'

'Aye, well, I won't keep you from it. But something's wrong, isn't it? Your illness – it's nothing serious?'

'Oh no, I'm not *ill*, exactly. Just ... a little run down, that's all. I'm not sure if I'm up to the rigours of Skye. Can I let you know? When are you setting off?'

'Soon. Day after tomorrow, probably. I was going to spend a day catching up with sleep. And my family.'

'You have family in Edinburgh?'

'Aye, I've a wee sister. She keeps a spare room for me to crash in. I leave all my work gear there. I'm taking her and my brother-in-law out to dinner tomorrow night. We're celebrating.'

'What's the occasion?'

'She's pregnant. I'm going to become an uncle.'

'Oh ... Congratulations. Are you pleased?'

'Aye, I'm fair bursting with excitement! I've opened an account with Toys "R" Us and I fully expect to become one of their best customers.'

Marianne fights down another wave of nausea. 'Keir, I'm sorry, I have to go. The doorbell just rang and I'm the only one in. It's probably Garth, forgotten his key. I'll ring you tomorrow. Bye.'

Marianne puts the phone down, feels for an armchair and sinks into it. She leans forward and covers her face with her hands. Eventually she raises her head and says softly, but with feeling, 'That bloody man ... That bloody, *bloody* man.'

Marianne

My case was already packed. It seemed easier to go to Skye with Keir than check in to a clinic and abort his baby. *Much* easier. I was aware of a drastic element of procrastination but knew if I turned him down, Keir probably wouldn't invite me again. At some point he would give up on me and I didn't want him to do that. (I may not have known what I wanted, but I knew I didn't want *that*.)

I extracted my cotton nightdress and replaced it with cosy fleece pyjamas, added a pair of jeans, a couple of jumpers, some thick socks and gloves. I also packed Keir's scarf in the hope that I'd be able to return it without his noticing or, depending on how things went, tell him why I'd taken it.

My hand fell once again on the plastic packaging of the sanitary towels. I'd heard that lovemaking could cause a miscarriage or start labour if you were due. Was sex likely to be an option? The decision would probably be mine. Would Keir notice I was pregnant? What was there to notice? I was only nine weeks gone and there was surely nothing to see. My inability to face breakfast meant I was thinner now than when we'd made love. My breasts felt fuller, but I knew my waist hadn't thickened yet because I could still do up my jeans. Observant though he was, I thought it unlikely Keir would notice any change in me. In any case, the problem was easily avoided. I simply had to refrain from going to bed with the man.

Which was possibly easier said than done.

Keir arrived to collect me and, since Garth was in the flat, introductions had to be made. Keir didn't kiss me in greeting but I felt his rough, warm fingers enclose both my hands for a moment. He fell oddly silent but the room was still full of him: his hawthorn scent; the movement of air displaced as his large body moved around the flat, greeting Louisa, reaching past me to shake Garth's hand. As they shook hands I raised mine to tidy some loose hair behind my ear, a gesture I'm wont to make when nervous. As I lifted my hand the backs of my fingers brushed Keir's arm. It was only a glancing touch but my skin remembered the jumper from the tree-house. At least, I thought it was the same one. Soft, ribbed and warm to the touch (but that was no doubt Keir's body permeating the wool). I remembered holding him in the tree-house – it seemed such a long time ago now – and I felt an impulse to lay my head down again on his chest, let go of all my anxiety and just listen to him breathe.

Louisa, in stridently cheerful hostess-mode, was offering us coffee. She must have been nervous too. Her behaviour towards me seemed over-solicitous and I suspected this might be her way of alerting Keir to my condition. I seethed inwardly until I remembered she'd fussed around me (and Keir) in exactly the same way the last time he was in the flat. It was just her way of expressing affection. I might be the one who was pregnant, but it was Louisa displaying maternal tendencies.

She went off to clatter about in the kitchen and I said, in the direction of Keir who I thought was still standing beside me, 'Is the sofa empty?'

'Aye. Garth's gone to help Louisa in the kitchen.'

'How very tactful. We get to have a *tête à tête*.' I sat down on the sofa and Keir seated himself beside me. 'How was your sister? Well, I hope?'

'Aye, she looked bonny! It was grand to see her looking so healthy and happy. They've been trying for a while and she's miscarried twice. Time was running out for them.'

'How old is she?'

'Thirty-seven.'

I fought an urge to burst out laughing, then said, 'Oh, that's no age at all. Not these days. When is she due?'

'September.'

'Will you be around then?'

'I don't know. I never really know. I take the work when and where I can get it.'

There was a lull in the conversation during which I could hear Louisa humming. Lou never hums. As coffee was still not forthcoming, I said, 'Are you wearing your brown jumper?' I felt Keir turn suddenly to face me.

'How the hell did you know that?'

'I recognised the feel of it. You wore it that day in the tree-house. And I held you. Don't you remember?'

'I remember you holding me. I don't remember what I was wearing.'

'You told me it was a brown jumper. I think it was this one.'

'But ... you haven't touched me since I arrived.' Was that a note of reproach in his voice? Or just disappointment? 'My clothes, I mean. I held your hand earlier.'

'My fingers brushed your arm. Or it might have been your shoulder. When you shook Garth's hand.'

'And that was *enough*?'

'Yes. That was enough.'

'Blimey, 'e's a big feller.'

'Sshh, he'll hear you!'

'Nah, 'e's only got eyes 'n' ears for Marianne. I don't think we even register on 'is radar.'

'Well, that's not my impression,' Louisa hisses, rattling saucers. 'So I'll thank you to keep your voice down.'

'Sorry!' Garth replies in a stage whisper, then shakes the biscuit barrel. 'You're low on biscuits. Marianne must be gettin' through 'em.'

'No, that's me, I'm afraid. I eat two for every one she manages to get down. I think it must be anxiety. It brings on severe attacks of the munchies.'

'That's your story.'

'And I'm sticking to it.' She looks at her watch. 'How long do you think we can string this out for? I want to give them time to chat. You know, I'm really worried she's going to change her mind.'

'About the abortion?'

'Sshh! No, about going to Skye.'

'Well, unless you want them to be 'ere all day, it might be a good idea to switch the kettle on.'

'Oh, God, yes.' Louisa flicks a switch. 'Thank you. I don't know what's got in to me today.' She grabs a cloth and, humming, begins to wipe down an already clean worktop. With Zen-like calm and precision, Garth arranges biscuits on a plate.

Marianne

Coffee finally appeared and the conversation became general again. I sat back on the sofa, content to listen while I debated yet again the wisdom of another trip to Skye. It seemed Garth knew Skye from childhood holidays and he and Keir struck up a conversation about the advent of wind farms and their impact on bird life. Despite the subject being close to his heart, Keir sounded ill at ease and I remembered what he'd said about not feeling comfortable with people. But then the circumstances *were* rather strange. Keir and I were seated side by side on the sofa, lovers who had barely touched after nine weeks apart. I couldn't see him and I imagined he wasn't looking at me. He wasn't even talking to me, but answering questions about sea eagles from a surprisingly well-informed Garth.

Finding myself tongue-tied by the awkwardness of my situation, overwhelmed by a lassitude that I assumed was hormonal, I was happy to leave social niceties to Garth and Louisa. My befuddled brain was busy coping with the fact that I was pregnant with Keir's child and he was the only person in the room who didn't know.

They say their goodbyes and Keir carries Marianne's case downstairs to the echoing hallway. As they reach the massive

186

front door, he puts the case down, turns to Marianne and says, 'You're sure now? You do want to come?'

'Of course! Why do you ask?'

He shrugs. 'The Ice Maiden performance, I suppose.'

'*Ice Maiden*? What do you mean?'

'Your behaviour. And you're dressed head to foot in white. '

'*Am* I? Damn! It was meant to be black. I don't know *what's* happening to my memory these days.'

'You look untouchable. It's very alluring, but hardly encouraging. And it's not just your clothes. You seem ... unreachable somehow.'

'*You're* the one who's unreachable.' Marianne raises her hand in the direction of his voice and finds his face. Her fingers falter for a second when she encounters stubble. Standing on tiptoe, she cranes to press her lips against his rough cheek, then, navigating her way across his face with her fingertips, she kisses his mouth and notes a film of sweat on his upper lip.

When he speaks she can hear his smile. 'If I'd thought you'd do that, I'd have shaved. Your double messages are coming over loud and clear, Marianne.'

'I'm sorry. I am pretty confused.'

'*You're* confused? Here, let me clarify.' He lays his hands on her shoulders and pulls her towards him. She lifts her head and her mouth is grazed by his, not unpleasantly. He releases her and they stand facing one another, not speaking, not touching. Eventually he murmurs, 'You've no need to come. I'll still want to see you. It's not a test. Some kind of Outward Bound bonding exercise.'

'I think we already did that. In the snow.' He laughs and she raises her hands, spreads the palms on his chest, as if steadying herself. 'Can we just take it one step at a time, Keir? Make no assumptions. But be honest with each other?'

'Oh, aye. I'm not thinking about the future. I try not to. You know why.'

'Let's go to Skye and – and see what happens. Can we just ... play it by ear?'

'Aye, that's fine with me.' He cradles her face with his hand. 'You hum it, Marianne, and I'll play it.'

Chapter Sixteen

Marianne

I was a fool. A complete fool. A fool to go back to Skye, a fool to think I could control the situation, control my body, keep that man out of my bed. Did I think I'd be able to hide my feelings? From *Keir* of all people?

I was a fool to think I would be able to resist the island: the scent of daffodils, gorse and primroses; the pitiful bleating of day-old lambs; the symphonic dawn chorus; the knowledge that, a few metres from my muddy, booted feet, grazing in the evening sun (could I actually hear them munching?), were a pair of hares. When they moved away, Keir drew my hand down quickly to the flattened grass where they'd sat, 'looking like tea-cosies', and it was warm to the touch.

Everywhere we walked, everywhere we sat, there was teeming life, scents and sounds to make one swoon. We walked in wind, rain and surprisingly strong sun, till my muscles screamed for mercy. But the only mercy Keir showed was to carry me, laughing, up the stairs to bed.

'This *is* what you want?'

'Oh, yes. You can have it in writing, if you like. Give me a pin and I'll punch it out in Braille.'

'That won't be necessary.'

She hears sounds of clothing being removed, falling to the floor. A zip. The scrape of his watch as he slides it across the bedside table. Unbuttoning her shirt with clumsy fingers, she

189

asks, 'Is it still light? I feel a bit nervous ... about you looking at me. I'd rather you didn't light the lamp.'

'I wasn't going to. It's dusk. But I can see you. Just. You look beautiful.' The mattress sinks as he sits beside her.

'Well, it's all relative, I suppose. The last time you made love to me I was wearing a woolly hat and had gloves on my feet.'

'Och, I knew I was missing *something*.'

She reaches a hand out towards his voice and meets his naked chest. She lets her fingers trail down through curling, springy hairs, over his chest, his belly and into his lap. 'That reminds me,' she says thoughtfully. 'You never showed me the drumstick primulas. In the woods. I wanted to feel them.'

Keir's mouth is close to hers. 'You were flagging. I took pity on you and brought you home. You'll have another botany lesson tomorrow.'

She lifts a hand in search of his face and lays it on his cheek, fingering the ridge of bone. 'So what's this, then? Sex education?' She feels the muscles of his face contract into a smile.

'Play-time.' He leans forward and kisses her. 'So ... I have your permission to do this?'

'Yes.'

'And, presumably, this?'

'Yes ...'

'And ... *this*?'

Marianne's reply is indistinct. Keir assumes something in the affirmative. His lovemaking is gentle at first, considered, as if compensating for the excess of exhausted, despairing passion that fuelled their previous encounter. He is surprised, then excited by the eagerness of her responses, flattered by her hunger for him. He feels every part of his body touched by her seeing hands; feels her mind reaching out towards his, but he senses something, somebody between them, some barrier.

Used to seeing death in the midst of life, Keir assumes it must be Harvey.

Marianne lies in the crook of Keir's arm, her head pillowed on his shoulder. She has spread her fingers so they lie in the shallow grooves between his ribs, rising and falling gently.

190

Feeling the tug of sleep, she stirs, reluctant to waste a moment in unconsciousness. She turns her head, kisses his chest, then murmurs, 'Where exactly do you see your visions? Are they inside your head? Like memories? Or are they outside, in front of you, "before your very eyes"? It's hard for me to imagine how sight works. Let alone *yours*.'

He doesn't reply at once. She feels his lungs inflate and then, with a jerk of his diaphragm, he speaks abruptly, his voice too loud for the intimacy of the bed. 'What I see seems real enough. I mean, it appears the same as reality. Mac appeared to be in the theatre bar. He didn't look like a ghost. Not that I know what ghosts look like. But my visions are ... *layered*. As if one kind of reality is being superimposed on another.'

'That's a bit hard for me to understand.'

His arm tightens around her and his voice softens. 'It's hard for *anyone* to understand and that includes me. Think of an orchestra playing. When a new musical theme is introduced, the sound becomes layered. The instruments blend, but they also have their own music which exists independently. Given a good acoustic, you hear them both separately and together. How I see is something like that. I can try to concentrate on the tune – the violins and violas – but I can't shut out the cellos and double basses underscoring. They affect how I hear the other strings. The vision is both inside my head and outside it. Like the music. It surrounds me. I can *see* it being played and it's taking place *inside* my head. It's being played on the tiny bones of my ear, sending impulses to my brain, to the centre of my being.' He sighs. 'Did that make any sense at all?'

'Yes, it did. I think I'm beginning to get an idea ... But are you all right talking about it?'

'Aye, I suppose so. To be honest, I preferred our previous activity.'

She checks his roving hand and says, 'I've exercised my muscles – and yours. Now I'm trying to exercise my brain cells. Believe six impossible things before breakfast. How long did you know about Mac? Before it happened, I mean.'

'I saw him when I was talking to you at the opera. That was

the beginning of January. The accident happened on the third of February.'

'So you had about a month of knowing.'

'*Thinking*. I never *know*.' He removes his arm from behind her head and sits up in bed. Drawing up his knees, he hooks his arms over them and stares into the darkness. 'I always hope I'm going to be wrong.'

'Have you ever been wrong?'

His laugh is short and humourless. 'How can I be? If they're still alive, they just haven't died yet. I'm not given a timetable.' Keir lifts his head and gazes out through the window at the night sky where his eye is caught immediately by Arcturus. Noting its position, he computes automatically and registers the late hour. They must have slept for some time.

Behind him Marianne stirs and says, 'So ... you had about a month of treating Mac – how? Differently?'

'Aye, I suppose so.'

'What was different?'

'I laughed at his jokes. Mac tells – *told* – jokes. Badly. But in that last month, I laughed.'

She says tentatively, 'You know, it *is* a kind of gift. A gift of time. Time to make a difference. Time to put things right if need be.'

'It's a gift I don't want.'

'But that doesn't seem to be an option, does it? And if that's the case, don't you just have to accept it?'

'That's what I've been trying to do for more than thirty years,' he replies wearily. 'I've not made much headway.'

Marianne sits up and slips her arms round his waist, resting her cheek against the curve of his back. She listens to him breathing for a moment, then asks, 'Have you ever foreseen the death of a family member?'

'No.' The sound is low, a growl from deep inside his body.

'Not even distant family?'

'No.'

'Do you know of anyone who's foreseen the death of a family member?'

'No.'

192

'That's interesting. Maybe something blocks it.'

'Such as?'

'Love?'

'Why would love block the visions?'

'I don't know. Because love is blind?'

'Coming from you, that's very funny.'

'So you've never foreseen the death of anyone you loved?'

'No.'

'But that's your greatest fear, I would imagine?'

After a pause he says, 'Aye.'

'You're a scientist, Keir. Look at the evidence! Or rather lack of it.'

'Aye, I know! I'm paralysed by a bloody hypothesis.'

She releases him and lies back on the pillows. 'Your hypothesis is that it's possible you'll foresee the death of a loved one and feel utterly helpless. My hypothesis is that such visions are blocked by feelings of love. Or fear. The brain will not admit something so appalling. It won't allow the eye to see it. My evidence for this? You've never foreseen the death of a loved one and you don't know of anyone who has. What's the evidence for *your* hypothesis?'

'I don't have any.'

'It's just a fear that it could happen?'

'I suppose so.'

'So you're prepared to allow primitive superstition to outweigh a complete absence of verifiable evidence. Call yourself a scientist?'

He turns and lies down again beside her, propping himself up on an elbow. 'I'm also a visionary. A seer. Science tells me what I am doesn't exist. *Can't* exist. When I told my parents what I saw, they said I was imagining things. I wanted to believe them and I tried but ... I knew what it was. So did they. Eventually we just stopped talking about it.'

'But just because we fear something – fear it *terribly* – doesn't mean it's likely to happen! People regularly gather in their hundreds on hilltops to await Armageddon, but the world still turns. There's no correlation between fear and likelihood. It just feels as if there should be.'

193

'Marianne Fraser, you're a woman of profound good sense.'

'There you go again, making me sound like something out of Jane Austen.'

'I don't think Austen heroines do what *you* were doing twenty minutes ago.'

'Oh, I don't know. I think all that bluestocking propriety was just longing to be corrupted by something broad-shouldered in a pair of well-fitting breeches. Look at Lydia Bennet and Wickham. Once she was off the leash it must have been a sexual marathon.'

'Speaking of which ...'

'Yes?'

'If you're not completely debilitated by the day's strenuous activities –'

'Not *completely*.'

'I was wanting to ask you ...'

'Yes?'

'What d'you do for an encore?'

Marianne

I was a fool. A fool to indulge, however briefly, in the fantasy of Happy Families; to think my future held more possibilities than I had imagined. Then, when the fantasy came crashing down around my ears, I didn't even handle it with a good grace.

I was a complete, bloody fool. A pregnant bloody fool, brain addled by hormones, sex and what even a blind man could see was love.

After breakfast Keir looks out the kitchen window and announces that the rain has stopped. They don boots and fleeces.

'Where to today?'

'The beach, I think. It's not too wild now.' He takes her hand and as they let themselves out the door, the wind chime bids its cheerful farewell, a sound Marianne never tires of hearing.

Keir leads her through the garden, over springy rough grass pierced by the leaf-blades of flag iris, down to the seashore. He offers to carry her over the large boulders above the tide-line, but Marianne enjoys clambering over the rocks on all fours, removing her gloves so she can feel the rough textures of the different rocks. Keir eyes her anxiously, ready to spring towards her if she falls. Pausing for a moment, Marianne lifts her head.

'What's that bird called? The piping sound, a bit like a piccolo.'

He doesn't need to look. Still watching Marianne, he says, 'An oystercatcher. Down by the shoreline.'

Marianne turns her face up to face the emerging sun. 'Shall we just sit for a bit? I'd like to listen to the sea. This feels like a nice flat rock. Come and describe the view for me.'

He sits down on her windward side to provide some shelter. 'We're at the top of the beach, which becomes pebbles, then eventually sand. The tide's going out. We're looking northwest, facing a stupendous view of the Cuillin. There's a wide stretch of sea – pretty choppy today – and beyond that there's the mountains, their peaks covered in snow. The ridge looks serrated, something like holly leaves. Have you ever felt those?'

'Oh yes. At Christmas.'

'Aye, well, the Cuillin ridge is doubly serrated in that the "holly leaves" themselves are serrated. Erosion has given the ridge sharp teeth.'

'Can you translate the view for me?'

'Into music?'

'Anything. Well, anything I can relate to.'

Keir is silent for a moment, then says, 'I think you've finally stumped me. It's just too big for any music I know. Too deep. Possibly too beautiful.'

'So is there nothing? Nothing like it in the world of sound?'

'I don't think so.'

'You once said the Cuillin were like the *Hammerklavier*.'

'Aye, I did. But the Cuillin covered in snow, viewed across the sea, from a viewpoint at the bottom of my own garden, on an April day in bright sunshine ... Ach, it moves me so deeply, makes me feel so proud. Yet at the same time so ... *insignificant*. I'm sorry to disappoint you, but I don't know how to translate it. Into music. Into anything.'

'Thanks for trying. I know I ask a lot.' She reaches out and meeting his thigh, runs her hand absently over the long expanse of muscle. Registering the hard warmth, she places her other hand flat on the cold rock beside her. Marianne fancies she can feel the blood pulsing through Keir's arteries, that she can feel life with one set of fingertips, deadness with the other. The contrast excites her and she leans over to kiss him, aiming where she hopes his mouth will be.

He puts an arm around her and pulls her towards him. 'Hell, I *do* know what it's like.'

'What? Your wonderful view?'

'Aye. It's like making love. Don't laugh, I'm serious! I don't know what sex is like for anyone but me. But how this view makes me feel, it's ... like orgasm. Well, mine, anyway. You feel the biggest and strongest you've ever felt. *And* the smallest and weakest. Vulnerable. And full of wonder.'

'Is sex always like that for you?'

'No. Not always.'

'Was it like that for you with me?' she asks shyly. 'And I'll know if you're lying.'

'Aye, it was. That's what made me think of it ... You OK? You've gone very quiet.'

'Struck dumb by the view.' She gets to her feet unsteadily and says, 'Come on. Let's walk.'

Keir takes her hand. 'If we go closer to the water's edge we can walk on wet sand, which will be easier for you, but it's more exposed.'

'Will it be very windy?'

'Aye. It'll blow away a few cobwebs.'

'Let's walk down by the sea then. Until we get too cold. '

He leads her out of the shelter of the bay, down towards the sea. Marianne feels the ground level out, the pebbles become smaller, until with a sense of relief she feels firm, wet sand beneath her feet and walking becomes easy. 'Oh, yes, this is much better!'

'I'll let you set the pace. Do you want the wind in your face or at your back?'

'In my face. I like to feel the wind.'

Keir turns and repositions himself on Marianne's other side. 'I'll walk by the sea so if a rogue wave comes in, I'll see it coming. It's not yet the weather for paddling.'

'Thank you.'

'No bother.' He turns and studies her profile as the wind whips her hair back from her pale, exhilarated face. He notes the rosy tip of her nose and how the cold has turned her ears a glowing pink. He feels a tenderness mixed with an urge to protect, emotions he rarely feels for people, only birds and animals, sometimes trees. As a strong gust of wind buffets them, she lifts up her head and laughs. He laughs too, without knowing why. 'Cobwebs gone?'

'I'll say! You know, I've touched cobwebs. Hateful things, all stretchy and sticky. And to think of all those paralysed insect bodies caught in the web – *horrible*! Yet people say spiders' webs are beautiful.'

'So they are.'

'You can't touch them without destroying them, can you? Like bubbles. Something else I can't imagine. A hollow sphere, made of water? Impossible!'

'Cobwebs *are* very beautiful, especially if you're of a mathematical turn of mind. Fiendishly delicate. Or perhaps I mean delicately fiendish. Think *The Well-Tempered Clavier.* On a harpsichord.'

'Oh, what Lou calls knitting-needle music. She knits Fair Isle sweaters, you know. If you stand still long enough she'll measure you up for one. She'd love to get a tape-measure round *your* chest.'

He stops walking and tugs at her hand, drawing her into his arms. She buries her face in his fleece, inhales the warmth of him and strains to hear his heart beating. They sway slightly in the wind and, with a sudden sinking of spirits, Marianne remembers what stands between them – literally now. She's about to say the speech she has prepared when Keir, his voice a low murmur in his chest, says, 'Marianne, there's something I want to say. Something we need to discuss.'

'Oh? Well, as it happens, there's something I want to tell you too.'

197

'What?'

'No, you go first.'

'I'm going away again. To Kazakhstan.'

'*Kazakhstan*?' She lifts her head from his chest, her body stiffening. 'That's a very long way, isn't it?'

'Aye. Central Asia. If I went much further I'd be on my way back. It's one of the few places left with any significant deposits of oil. I'm going to be looking for them.'

She wriggles out of his arms and turns her face into the wind. 'Are you going for good?'

'Och, no! Three months.'

'And you won't be coming back in that time, I should imagine?'

'No.'

Fighting a sudden wave of nausea, she swallows a mouthful of acrid saliva. 'Don't you think you might have mentioned this earlier? Perhaps before I came back to Skye?'

'Aye, maybe I should.'

'Why didn't you?'

'Because if I had, you'd have had to deal with what you felt about me. And then you wouldn't have come.'

'Dead right, I wouldn't.' She shivers and folds her arms across her chest.

'I didn't pressure you to come, Marianne. And I didn't have to drag you into bed either. The terms were yours. You asked if we could play it by ear. That's what we've done. I think that's how we should continue. Och, I don't see what else we can do! I have to earn a living. But I'll want to see you when I get back. I'll want to send you tapes while I'm away. I hope you'll let me ring you. But other than that ... you're free. No strings. I hope when I get back we can pick up where we left off. If that's what you want,' he adds.

'Let me get this straight – are you asking for my permission to sleep around?'

'No. I'm giving *you* permission to sleep around.'

'Oh, thanks. I'm glad you brought that up. I was wondering how I'd cope. I'm so in demand, you know. The phone never stops ringing.'

198

'Marianne, I don't think I've handled this very well.'

'No, I don't think you have. But if you'd told me all this earlier it would just have sounded like a sex-with-no-strings speech. Which is what it sounds like now, so there was really nothing to be gained by being frank. And this way we probably enjoyed the sex more. It certainly sounds as if *you* did.'

In the long silence that follows Marianne realises that she too isn't handling the situation well and considers apologising or, alternatively, bursting into tears. Instead she stands silently, her body tense, and awaits Keir's indignation which doesn't come. Eventually she says, 'Oh, for God's sake, Keir, *say* something! You can't make a worse mess of things than I just did.'

When he finally speaks his voice is even, the words measured, but Marianne hears the effort neutrality costs him. 'I haven't been dishonest. You knew about my work. About my lifestyle. I'll be gone three months. We've just spent two months apart, but we were able to pick up where we left off.'

'You think so?'

'Don't you?' She doesn't answer and he continues, 'In any case, I think this is my last trip.'

'Why do you say that?'

'I've had enough. I want out.'

'Not because of me?'

'No. I've wanted out for a while. A long while. You knew that.'

'What will you do?'

'I don't know. But I thought three months in Kazakhstan might focus my mind.'

'So you expect me to wait for you.'

His composure breaks then. 'No, I *don't*! That's why I said the no-strings stuff! You're *free*.'

'And so are you.'

'Yes, I'm free too.' Keir looks out to sea, narrows his eyes and watches as a gannet folds its wings into an arrow formation and drops vertically, like a stone, plummeting head first into the sea. He waits for it to surface, then says, 'I don't do the future, Marianne. You know why.'

'And I don't do the past. I had hoped we might be able to

come to some arrangement about the present. But with a conti-
nent or two between us, I think that would be a tall order.'

'Are you not up for a challenge, then?'

'Oh yes! Never let it be said that plucky little Marianne lacks
courage! But I think I have enough on my plate at the moment.
Coping with my condition.'

'Your condition?'

She hesitates for a moment, contemplates her future once
again and comes to a final decision. 'Leber's Congenital
Amaurosis. My blindness.'

'I see.'

'And I *don't*. Can we go back to the house, please? I'm
getting cold.'

'Aye. Sorry, we should have kept moving. Will you take my
arm?'

They turn their backs to the wind and set off along the beach.
After a few moments Keir asks, 'What was it you wanted to tell
me?'

'Oh, it doesn't matter now,' she replies, her voice leaden.
'The moment has passed.'

Chapter Seventeen

Louisa

I think Garth spoke for us all, summing up our feelings of utter dismay when he exclaimed, 'Where the 'ell is Kazakh-bleedin'-stan?' To make matters worse, I had the temerity to ask Marianne if she'd actually told Keir about the baby. My sister is incapable of a withering look but she more than compensated with the scourge of her tongue.

It seemed she regarded her relationship with Keir as over and said this made everything easier. I didn't really understand, but assumed she meant having the abortion. I assured her that, more than ever now, Garth and I would do what we could to support her and I offered to make another appointment at the clinic. She prevaricated, said she was too exhausted to think and retired to her room, from which she barely emerged for three whole days.

You can usually judge Marianne's state of mind by the music she plays. Over the years I've learned to interpret her mood through her choice of music, much as you might read someone's facial expression. (Not an option with Marianne.) She'd been through a Puccini phase recently, which I'd quite enjoyed, then she'd played Beethoven's Hammerklavier *piano sonata, the one that sounds like a sort of pianistic shopping list – a snatch of all the sonatas Beethoven might have written had he not decided to ditch the piano in favour of string quartets. Not exactly easy listening. Then she became obsessed with the Finnish bird concerto. There was always music of some kind in the background and I suspected that, lately, it had all been connected with Keir. The worrying thing was, after she got back from Skye the second time, she didn't play anything, not even her birds.*

The only time I could remember Marianne entering a seriously silent period like this was after Harvey died. I couldn't believe that breaking up with Keir had been an event of that magnitude, but my sister was always hard to fathom, and not just because of her blindness. As the days went by and still no clinic appointment was made, I began to wonder whether what she was processing (rehearsing in a way) was death and grief: the death of her husband, the death of two babies and the loss (which was after all a kind of death) of a man she'd realised, somewhat belatedly, she loved.

Marianne lay on the bed in her room, in silence, eating and drinking little and saying less. Garth did his cheerful best with her but in the end she sent him away. Then one morning, about a week after she got back from Skye, she emerged from her room, showered and dressed, and started moving purposefully around the flat. She made a pot of tea and as she poured herself a cup she announced, 'I've come to a decision.'

I braced myself, but tried to sound casual. 'Oh? And what is that?'

'Don't get your hopes up, Lou. In a way I think what I've decided makes things harder for you. Probably for me too. But it feels like the right thing to do. And in a way the easiest. Certainly the most humane.'

'Darling, you know you can count on me. Whatever. Garth too. He thinks the world of you, you know.'

'Yes, I do know. I can't think what I've done to deserve such loyal support. I think it says rather more about your generosity than my deserts. But God knows, I think I am going to need you.' She took a deep breath and said, the words tumbling over one another quickly, 'I've decided to go through with the pregnancy and put the baby up for adoption. Don't go hoping I'll change my mind when it's born – I have no attachment whatsoever to this child, only to its father. And though I know what I should do is get rid of it, make a fresh start, I just cannot bring myself to abort that man's baby. It would be like killing him. A part of him. And I can't

do it. I've had too much to do with death. And so has Keir,' she added softly. 'So I'm going to let Nature take its course. If the baby lives, it will bring happiness to another couple. That seems to me to make some sense of the appalling mess that currently constitutes my life. But if I'm to see it through, I'm going to need your support. And I know that's asking a lot.'

'Well, I'd be lying if I said I don't hope you'll change your mind about adoption, but I can promise you faithfully I'll never mention it, never put any pressure on you. But I think you know that would be my dearest wish.'

'Yes, I know. Which is why I think all this might be harder for you than for me.'

'Oh, that doesn't matter! Whatever you decide to do, it's you who have to live with the consequences for the rest of your life. I did think Keir had a right to know, but if he's going off to Kazakhstan ... and God knows where next ... Well, it's nobody's business but yours now.'

'Thank you.' Marianne shook some muesli into a bowl and started to peel a banana. Assuming the subject was closed, I turned away and was about to leave the kitchen when she said abruptly, with a strange little catch in her voice, 'I do love you, you know. I'm such rubbish at telling people how much I care for them. But that doesn't mean I don't feel it.'

'Darling, I know! Honestly, I do understand. In any case,' I said briskly, 'your bark has always been a lot worse than your bite.' I saw her lip tremble and threw my arms round her – as much as anything to give her an excuse to cry, poor thing. We stood in the kitchen, hugging each other, weeping and wailing for I don't know how long. When Garth let himself in, he stopped in his tracks, took one look at us and said, 'All right, then – 'oo's died?'

Marianne

Keir and I didn't discuss what we felt for each other. It was a tacit agreement. Perhaps we *couldn't* have discussed it. I doubt we would have known how to describe what we felt, what to make of the mixture of intensity and reserve, a sense that we hardly knew each other at all, and had always known each other.

Oh, we talked. Talked and talked, but not about *us*. Not until that last walk on the beach when I learned the geographical whereabouts of Kazakhstan. Instead we made love. And that was overwhelming. Or rather, we were overwhelmed by our need for each other, the sense of urgency, our inexplicable but visceral connection that seemed to lead naturally and often to making love. And in some unlikely places.

We sheltered in the tree-house on the way back from a woodland walk. Rain was turning to sleet and Keir pulled at my hand and led me to the foot of the rope ladder. I hesitated as the memories flooded back but his voice was at my ear, reassuring. 'It'll be OK.' I climbed up, like an old hand, while he held the ladder.

Inside the tree-house we stood in silence, listening to a sudden fusillade of hailstones on the wooden roof. Keir laughed, I've no idea why. He didn't laugh very often but when he did, it was somehow infectious. I laughed too, then he kissed me, without any serious intent, I thought. But then he bent his head again and took my face in both his hands and kissed me in a way that was unfamiliar, so raw and needy, I felt shocked. But shock didn't prevent me from responding. His hands pushed their way inside my fleece, up under my jumper and T-shirt, and tugged at the zip of my jeans.

We didn't even undress. I heard him drag something soft out of a box and throw it onto one of the makeshift beds where it settled with a sigh. Then he pushed me down, supporting me in the crook of his arm while his other hand must have been busy with his clothes. As he lowered me on to the makeshift bed, cradled like a baby on his arm, I felt both completely secure and as if annihilation might be imminent. My hands touched an old quilt, soft and damp beneath me. I felt the weight and pressure of Keir above, then the breath was knocked out of me – not just by the violence with which he made love to me, but by the strength of my feeling for him and my absolute need for his body. I was aware of a random, ghoulish wish that this man might procure the abortion of his own baby and with that thought I clung to him, my arms round his neck, my fingers clutching the bones of his skull. I cried out something, I don't know what.

It was over in minutes. Afterwards Keir apologised for behaving 'like a bloody adolescent'. I said there was no need for apology. I'd never felt so desired or desirable in my entire life which, I added, wasn't bad going for a woman of forty-five, but he apologised again and seemed bothered by what had happened. After a long silence he said, 'I wish I knew what you wanted, Marianne. What you need. You must tell me. I want things to be good for you.'

'That *was* good for me. Short and very sweet.'

I heard him laugh softly. 'Aye, but did the earth move?'

'No ... The tree did.'

Louisa

Marianne kept herself busy. I thought she was engaging in some sort of fitness regime to keep her weight down and build up physical stamina for the later stages of pregnancy and the birth, but when I mentioned this to her she said her long walks, the swimming and the sessions at the gym were intended to give the baby every opportunity to miscarry. As she passed the thirteen week stage at the beginning of May she announced that, 'It looked as if the little bugger showed every sign of being as strong and healthy as its father.'

So we went back to see Dr Greig, to talk about adoption and preliminary wheels were set in motion. Marianne asked me to go with her – she had become quite clingy since she'd returned from Skye – and I also attended antenatal appointments with her and sat in on the midwife's visits. I was down on the forms as Marianne's official birth partner but I was spared antenatal classes. Marianne said she wasn't prepared to mix with happy couples half her age, although Dr Greig assured us it was unlikely Marianne would be either the only elderly mother or the only single one. 'But,' Marianne replied, with some asperity, 'I will be the only mother intending to dump her baby the minute it's born.'

Garth or I would sometimes accompany Marianne on her walks in the Botanics. I don't think she relished our company particularly. I suspect she just wanted to avoid being prey to her own thoughts, which must have been pretty gloomy. Dr Greig had explained that mothers sometimes changed their mind about adoption, before and often after the baby was born, so Marianne should perhaps regard her arrangements as provisional. Dr Greig also warned of the possibility of depression. She said pregnancy was something of an endurance test, an ordeal made bearable

205

by the thought of a healthy baby at the end of it. Marianne received all this in silence, her face expressionless as usual, and it was left to me to thank Dr Greig for her concern.

Well, I don't know about Marianne feeling depressed, but I could have howled. We walked home arm in arm, saying very little. I suspect she must have sensed my abject mood. When we arrived home it was only 4.30 but she headed straight for the drinks cabinet and declared, 'Sod the baby – I'm going to have a gin and tonic. Will you join me?'

I fetched some ice, Marianne poured monster gins, we kicked off our shoes and collapsed into armchairs. I knew things must be bad when she took the unprecedented step of enquiring about the progress of my latest book. I waffled vaguely and Marianne soon lost interest. I didn't have the heart to tell her I hadn't lifted finger to keyboard in weeks. I just sat staring at the screen, my mind elsewhere.

Kazakhstan mostly.

We'd discussed the scan. We both knew that when the baby was scanned, the radiologist might be able to determine the baby's gender and offer to tell us. Marianne had told me she didn't want to know, there was absolutely no point in her knowing, and that it would only make life harder for me because the baby would seem more like a person. (As far as I was concerned it already was. On some days I envisaged a little boy; on others, a little girl. I'm ashamed to admit I'd even given them names, but perhaps as a writer I can be forgiven this lamentable self-indulgence.)

We had to go to the hospital for a scan when Marianne was fifteen weeks. It was mid-May and Edinburgh was sunny and fragrant with blossom. As we walked through the hospital grounds she stopped suddenly. I thought perhaps she was bottling out, but she said she just wanted to smell the hawthorn blossom. I looked up at the foam of creamy flowers on a May tree and felt pleased she was still able to take pleasure in simple things. My spirits lifted a little but sank again as soon as I saw all the high-tech equipment.

I tried not to look at the screen. (Marianne, of course, couldn't.)

It must have been written into her notes about adoption because the radiologist didn't try to describe anything to her or offer to turn up the volume on the heartbeat, she just informed us that everything appeared to be normal. And then came the moment I'd been dreading. The girl said, 'Would you like to know the baby's gender?' I braced myself and when Marianne didn't answer I averted my eyes from the screen and launched into an explanation, but Marianne cut me off.

'It's all right, Lou. There's no need.' The radiologist looked at Marianne expectantly and so did I. 'Yes,' she said. 'I would like to know.'

'It's a boy. And it looks like he's going to be a big one.'

'Ah,' said Marianne. 'That doesn't surprise me. Thank you.'

Stunned, I waited while Marianne got dressed. When she emerged from her cubicle she took my arm, but before we set off she said, 'I'm sorry, Lou. I suddenly wanted to know. I've felt all along that it was a boy and I just wanted to know if I was right. Silly really.' I wasn't able to reply. She squeezed my arm and continued, 'It's all for the best, you know. Just imagine a boy being brought up by a couple of old spinsters. It wouldn't be right, would it?'

'No ... I suppose not.'

For what must have been the first time in my life, I thanked God Marianne was blind and couldn't see my face.

Marianne

Hawthorn blossom. His smell. Life has a way of waiting till you're down, then giving you a good kicking.

I've always been a martyr to my sense of smell. When I finally agreed to let Louisa help me clear out Harvey's wardrobe, I insisted on being present. Don't ask me why. When you've had no body to bury, you invent a variety of rituals, partly to show respect for the dead, but mostly in an attempt to achieve some sort of closure. I agreed with Lou there was no point in my actually handling Harvey's clothes, but I wanted to be present while she sorted, to tell her where I wanted stuff to go. (Some things we gave to the night shelter in Aberdeen, the better quality stuff went to charity shops.)

I suppose I must have been stupid with grief not to have realised that Louisa handling Harvey's clothes would bring him back, would bring him into the bedroom, in as vivid a way as if he'd been resurrected from the dead. I stood it for as long as I could. (Another ritual. If I bore the pain, it would begin to cancel out the pain Harvey must have suffered when he died.) Eventually I ran out of the room, overcome.

That May morning in the hospital grounds, the scent of hawthorn blossom stopped me dead. Keir was beside me. *Inside* me.

I didn't faint, but it was a close call.

Louisa

By the end of May I'd more or less come to terms with the results of the ultrasound scan. I'd abandoned my pretty-in-pink fantasies and was doing my best to quell the blue version. Marianne didn't relent, she didn't waver for a moment. She still referred to the baby – when she had to – as 'it', which for some reason I found distressing. I suppose it was necessary.

Although I agreed that raising a son between us would have been even more of challenge than raising a daughter, I couldn't help wondering if the baby's gender had actually made life harder for Marianne; if the baby seemed even more a piece of Keir now. She never mentioned it, of course. The baby was discussed only in terms of its health, when she got the results of tests. Occasionally she would mention something to do with the adoption procedure. You would have had no idea we were discussing a person. But I suppose, to Marianne it – I mean, he – wasn't a person. She couldn't allow him to be.

One day I'd hit the gin long before the sun was over the yardarm (well, if you waited for the sun in Edinburgh you'd die of thirst) and I was sitting with my feet up, thumbing mindlessly through a fashion magazine, when Garth put his head round the sitting room door and said in a whisper, 'Is Marianne in?'

'No. She's gone for a walk. She should be back soon. Why do you ask?'

He crooked his finger and beckoned. 'Come an' take a look at this.'

I followed him into the study where he stood beside the PC and indicated the chair. 'Sit down. It's probably nothin' but I thought I'd better show you, just in case Marianne gets wind of it.'

There were lots of windows open on the screen and Garth leaned over, clicked the mouse and maximised one. It was a news website. I peered at the text. The item was headed BRITISH OIL WORKERS KIDNAPPED IN KAZAKHSTAN.

'Oh, my God! It's not Keir, is it?'

'Dunno. There's no way of tellin'. So far it's just breakin' news. As they 'aven't released any names I suppose the families don't know yet. Do we know 'oo Keir works for?'

'Well, I don't. I dare say Marianne does, but we can hardly ask her, can we?' I looked back at the screen and skimmed through the article. 'It probably isn't him ... I mean, there must be hundreds of British oil workers in Kazakhstan – mustn't there?'

'Possibly. An' I suppose a lot of 'em would be Scots.'

My stomach turned over. 'Why do you say that?'

Garth leaned across and maximised another window. 'Because this blogger mentions the kidnap an' 'e describes the oil workers as an American an' two Scots.'

'Oh, no! Is this a reliable source of information?'

'Couldn't tell you. It appears to be a blog written by a scientist. A Kazakh livin' in Aberdeen. This guy thinks the oil workers 'ave been kidnapped by a group of Kazakh conservationists.'

'Conservationists?'

'Yeah. Militants. You know, like Greenpeace. He thinks they'll be 'oldin' the guys to ransom.'

'For money?'

'Doubt it. Political leverage, more like. This blogger says a lot of Kazakhs aren't very 'appy about what's goin' on in their country.' Garth clicked on another window. 'The scramble for oil an' gas is causin' a lot of damage to the environment, apparently. Particularly the Caspian Sea. It's become a chemical dustbin.'

I stared blankly at the screen. 'How can we find out if one of these Scots is Keir?'

'I don't think we can without their names bein' released or askin' Marianne. Does she know any of 'is family?'

'No, I don't think so. She said he'd talked about them, but

she's never mentioned meeting any of them ... Oh, she said he has a sister who lives in Edinburgh!'

'Do you know 'er name?'

'No. She was married anyway, so she probably wouldn't even be called Harvey.'

'If we knew 'oo Keir worked for we could try an' contact them without Marianne knowin'.' Garth shrugged and plunged his hands into his pockets. 'Maybe we should just tell 'er. Ask if she's got any contact details for Keir.'

'No, we can't tell her! There's no sense in worrying her unnecessarily. I mean, it probably isn't even him!'

'Nah, probably not. But I thought I'd better show you. It'll turn up on the radio soon. TV an' all. She could get to 'ear about it.'

'Well, we'll just have to cross that bridge when we come to it.' I stood up wearily and kissed Garth on the cheek. 'Thanks for researching all this. You are an absolute angel. At least we're prepared now. But it probably isn't Keir ... And if it is, they wouldn't harm him, would they?'

'Can't see why they should. This'll be a political gesture. They'll want publicity for their cause. Concessions from the oil companies. Compensation. Representation in the decision-makin' process, that sort of thing. Anyway ...' He smiled at me briefly then, reaching for the mouse, turned back to look at the screen, his pale brow contracted into a frown. 'It probably isn't Keir ... '

Chapter Eighteen

Louisa

But it was. It was Keir. They released the names the following day. Garth found them by Googling Keir's name and 'Kazakhstan'. In desperation I said, 'Perhaps there are two Keir Harveys?' Garth swung round on his chair and looked up at me, his green eyes sad and patient. 'Both workin' in oil? In Kazakhstan? Both Scots? Suppose it's possible, but personally, I wouldn't put money on it.' He folded his arms and looked back at the screen. 'So ... do we tell 'er?'

I sank into an armchair beside my desk, closed my eyes and tried to think. 'Is it on British news websites yet?'

'Not yet. I've set up a Google Alert for 'is name, plus "kidnap" an' "Kazakhstan", so that should bring any news straight into your inbox.'

'Do we know why he's been kidnapped?'

'It's like I said, they're militant Greens. They want the oil companies to clean up their act. And the Caspian Sea while they're about it.'

'So it really isn't likely they'll harm him, is it? I mean, people who care about pollution aren't violent, are they?'

'Depends if they're fanatics. Animal activists can be a bit dodgy. But this crowd,' he said, tapping the screen, 'they sound like environmentalists. Probably young too – they're thinkin' about the future. If they speak any English – an' they probably do – they'll talk to Keir an' find out 'e's a diamond geezer. On the same wavelength.'

'So should we tell Marianne?'

Garth turned to face me. 'It's over between them, right?'

'Well, that's what she says, but I don't believe a word of it.'

'The only way she'll find out is on the radio or TV.' He picked up a pen and started to tap the desk with it, his eyes fixed on some imaginary point in the distance. 'We could say one of them wasn't workin', but not both. She'd never swallow that.'

'We rarely have the TV news on. She prefers the radio.'

Garth raised his pen. 'What if I remove a fuse from the radio plug? Then it'd be dead when she switched it on.'

'She'd just think the fuse had gone and ask me to change it.'

'Yeah, I know. Then you fiddle about with it – or I will if I'm 'ere, that'd be better. She trusts me to be technologically minded. I'll say I've mended the fuse but the thing still isn't workin'. Then I'll take it away to get it fixed. An' that could take a couple of days.'

I was feeling slightly encouraged by Garth's plan and, as ever, grateful for his calm competence, when I remembered something. 'No, that won't work. She's got a little portable radio in her room. It's part of that old cassette player she has.'

'With an aerial?'

'Yes.'

'Snap it off when she's out. Say the cleaner left a note to say she knocked it over an' the aerial snapped right off.'

'Two non-functioning radios? I think Marianne would smell a rat. And I'd feel awful maligning Mrs MacGillivray. She's always very careful and has never broken anything. Supposing Marianne mentioned it to her?'

'Then we've got to come clean. We can't risk Marianne findin' out by chance. The press are bound to make a meal of it.'

We looked at each other for a long moment, then I said, 'All right, I'll tell her. But when?'

'You could leave it till the BBC breaks the news. I think we can take whatever they say as gospel. An' for all Marianne knows, that's the first we 'eard of it.'

'So we've probably got a day's grace?'

'Maybe,' he said, looking at the screen again. 'Uh-oh, what's this just dropped into your inbox? Don't tell me ... Too late. The

Beeb is quotin' Reuters now, namin' Keir as "one of three men kidnapped by the somethin'-unpronounceable environmental group of Kazakhstan".'

'Does it say where they're being held?'

He scrolled down. 'At sea. On a boat on the Caspian Sea. Oh, shit ...'

'What? Is it bad?' I peered at the PC, fumbling with the reading glasses on a chain round my neck.

'They say, if any attempt is made to rescue the men or scupper the boat, they'll kill one of the hostages.'

'Oh my God!'

'They're bluffin', take no notice. It's just big talk. They say they'll release two men when the oil companies agree to meet with representatives of their organisation an' they'll release the last man when they're 'appy with what's been agreed.'

'But that could take weeks!'

'Well, let's 'ope Keir is one of the first two to be released. That bit could be over pretty quick.'

'So now we really do have to tell her.'

'Yeah, reckon so. But at least we've got the facts now.'

'But we can't tell her about the death threat.'

'Nah, better leave that bit out.'

'And after we've told her? Then what?'

'Then we wait ... An' 'ope that Keir's good at talkin' 'is way out of trouble. D'you think 'e speaks any Kazakh? Or Russian maybe?'

'He makes audio-recordings of the Northern Lights and shows stars to blind people. Nothing would surprise me about that man.'

Marianne

I suppose I hadn't known until then quite how much I felt for Keir. I took the news calmly – more calmly, at any rate, than Louisa delivered it – then I went to my room and lay down on the bed, listening to the traffic.

It all came back to me ... The waiting. The praying. The weighing up of risk and probability. The calculations you made with regard to your husband's returning home a) alive and b) whole. As I lay

213

there a helicopter passed overhead. Not a Sikorsky – I'd know that sound anywhere, even after all these years – but just the thought was enough to trigger panic and despair.

I placed my hands on my swelling abdomen and prayed to a God I hadn't believed in since 1988, that I would lose this baby but that I wouldn't – dear God in Heaven, please, if you *do* exist – that I wouldn't lose Keir.

At least, not to death.

The days dragged by and life became surreal. I continued to walk in the Botanics and attend antenatal appointments. The latest ordeal was amniocentesis, which I fully expected to give me grounds for termination. I listened to news bulletins on Radio Scotland who predictably ran the story in more detail than Radio 4. We contacted Keir's employers who were cagey and referred us to his family without giving any contact details. Louisa suggested we should try to contact Keir's sister in Edinburgh, in case he'd been able to phone her, but I pointed out that we had neither her name nor her address. In any case, desperate as we were for information, I wasn't prepared to explain my connection with Keir, particularly in view of my now obvious condition. (Although, as Louisa cheerfully pointed out, given my age, people would assume I was overweight, not pregnant.)

But I thought the poor woman would have enough to cope with, worrying about her brother and her own pregnancy, so I decided to spare her an enquiry from an ex-lover. For all I knew, she might already be dealing with a few of those. I wasn't prepared to get in line.

Louisa bore up well to begin with and Garth was a tower of strength, a rock, all those clichés for which there really is no substitute. He managed to maintain a sense of proportion and a sense of humour, amid mounting female hysteria. His behaviour was blessedly normal, yet he managed to keep us quietly informed of any developments, putting tea, coffee or gin in front of us.

As the days wore on, the gins got stronger.

Marianne is on her way to the kitchen when she thinks she hears the sound of Louisa crying in her bedroom. She pauses in the hall, listens at the door, then knocks tentatively. 'Lou? What's the matter? Can I come in?'

There is a muffled reply followed by a loud sniff. As Marianne opens the door her nostrils are assailed by clouds of Opium, her sister's perfume with which she's inclined to be lavish. Louisa calls out, 'I'm on the bed, darling. Don't worry – there's no news. No *bad* news, anyway.'

Marianne makes her way towards the bed and sits. 'So why are you crying?'

'Oh, God, I don't know! The strain, I suppose. Worrying about you and the baby ... Worrying about Keir ... These wretched negotiations are dragging on.'

'It's only a week. Garth says it's early days yet. We have to be patient. But is something else bothering you? You said there was no *bad* news. Do you have some *good* news?'

'Well, yes, I suppose so.'

'You don't sound very happy about it.'

'No, I know. The trouble is, I think it's precipitated a bit of a mid-life crisis. I'm having to face up to things.'

'What sort of things?'

'My career. My future. Old age ... All the big stuff.'

'Goodness, what's brought this on? Garth hasn't dumped you, has he?'

'No.'

'Do you think he's about to?'

'No, he seems happy enough. Well, thrilled, actually. In his quiet way.'

'Thrilled? What about?'

Louisa sits up, reaches for a tissue and wipes her eyes. 'Darling, it's all so *trivial* compared with what you're going through. That's why I haven't talked about it.' She sighs, leans back on a mountain of lace-trimmed pillows and says wearily, 'They want to make a film of my books. Two films, actually. Possibly three. It all depends how the first one fares at the box office, but they're already planning a sequel to the first. Anyway, they've optioned half my books and the first film is going into production now.'

'Lou, how wonderful! You can go to a film première! You've always wanted to do that. Is this your agent's doing?'

'No, that's the funny part. It's all thanks to Garth. His brother Rhodri is a film cameraman and they were talking about my books, apparently. Garth has a much higher opinion of them than *you* do, I'm happy to say. He was telling Rhodri what an ideal subject they'd be for a film – sort of *Buffy* for the big screen, set in Victorian Edinburgh. Anyway, Rhodri happened to be making a film with Johnny Depp and told him about my books. Johnny Depp apparently took a look at one of them and mentioned it to his agent and one thing led to another. One of the Hollywood studios picked it up and now the first film is in production.'

'With Johnny Depp as one of your vampires?'

'That's unconfirmed. They're undecided just how Scottish to make it. The money's American, you see. Apparently every Scots actor would kill to be in it, but the studio naturally wants a Hollywood star in the lead. They might compromise on Ewan McGregor, but Garth thinks it unlikely he'll commit to another series after *Star Wars*. They're considering David Tennant – who'd be totally wrong in my opinion, far too boy-next-door – and another Scot, Gerard Butler. He played the *Phantom of the Opera*. I think *he'd* be rather good, but of course nobody cares what I think, I'm only the author. Anyway, *whoever* they cast,' she finishes gloomily, 'it's going to make me pots and pots of money.'

'So why are you crying, for heaven's sake?'

'Because,' Louisa wails, 'I've got nobody to spend it on! What use is half a million dollars to *me*? You can only drink so much gin! I wanted to give some to Garth, but he won't take it. I offered to buy him a car. He said, thanks, but he wasn't interested because parking in Edinburgh's such a nightmare. He says if I insist, I can take him away for a dirty weekend at Gleneagles and teach him to play golf. He's always wanted to learn, he says. Oh, and he wouldn't mind having another new suit. I thought he meant Saville Row but he said, no, from Next. Honestly, as a gigolo he's just *hopeless*.'

Marianne is thoughtful and sits for a moment, her hands folded in her lap, her arms encircling her growing bump. 'You know, you could use the money to buy yourself some time.'

'What do you mean?'

'Stop writing the vampire books. Get off the commercial treadmill and think about what you really want to write. You're a historian at heart, Lou, not a fiction writer. You've always said biography and social history were your first loves. Why don't you change direction? You've been writing about Edinburgh and vampires for nearly twenty years now. Do you actually have anything left to say?'

'No, of course not! It's just variations on a theme now. And keeping my publishers happy. I know the books are tosh, but I do love the actual *writing*. And what on earth would I do with myself if I didn't write?'

'So why don't you write something else? Write the book of your heart. Is there one?'

'Well, yes, actually, now you come to mention it, there is. I've always wanted to write a biography of Isobel Gowdie.'

'The witch?'

'Well, she was *said* to be a witch.'

'Seventeenth century, I seem to remember?'

'Yes. Not really my period, but an interesting one. Isobel was unhappily married and turned to witchcraft for consolation. They put her on trial and got these amazing poetic confessions out of her – apparently without recourse to torture – all about being transformed into various animals and having sex with the devil. *Riveting* stuff. And really quite disturbing. She was probably psychotic, of course. I thought about turning it into a historical novel years ago, but my publishers just wanted the next vampire book. But I've always kept my notes about Isobel. Just in case.'

'Why don't you kill off your main character? Bring the series to a triumphant and bloody end.'

'You can't do that with vampires, darling, they're immortal. Or rather, they're already dead, so you can't kill them off. I'd already thought of that.'

'So take a sabbatical. Tell your editor you're taking a year off to do some research. You don't have to tell them what you're researching.'

'No, I suppose not. But they'll give me a hard time if I don't come up with another vampire book.'

'How many have you done for them?'

'Fifteen. Well, sixteen if you count the one due out next year.'

'Lou, I think you've paid your dues. Anyway, they'll be happily reprinting the old books with film tie-in covers. For that matter, they could re-issue the early books with new titles. I'm sure no one would notice.'

'My fans would! They'd be down on me like a ton of bricks.'

'Just say *no*, Lou. You're a grown woman. Act your age, not your shoe size, as Garth would say. What *does* Garth have to say about all this?'

'Much the same as you. That I should try something new. He says the film deal is a golden opportunity for me to spread my wings.'

'You should make that man your manager. I don't think the world really needs another PhD on the history of witchcraft in Scotland, but you could certainly do with a manager, especially now Hollywood's come calling. You'll have to upgrade your website too. Think of all the traffic you're going to get.'

'I know. I thought I'd increase Garth's salary and let him take over all that side of things. It's quite beyond my capabilities. But I do worry ...'

'What about?'

'Well, that when we split up – which, of course, we inevitably *will*, when he comes to his senses and finds someone his own age – well, it could all be rather messy. I could be left dangling, professionally. I wonder if it would be better to keep business and pleasure separate?'

'Isn't it a bit late for that?'

Louisa's lip quivers and she reaches for the box of tissues. 'Oh, it's all such a muddle! And what with poor Keir and the baby, I just feel overwhelmed. I'm sorry, Marianne, I'm being utterly pathetic, I know. It's all *so* much worse for you. I didn't mean to burden you with my problems.'

'Not at all. I'm glad of the distraction. It makes a change from dwelling on heartburn and varicose veins, not to mention birth defects. And thinking about *any* of those is preferable to thinking about what Keir might be going through.'

Louisa leans forward and puts an arm round her sister. 'You know, he struck me as very tough. Resourceful. He'd cope well in a tight spot, I'm sure. And the kidnappers are conservationists. They love nature. And their country. If they've managed to communicate with Keir at all, they'll have discovered he's just like them. I expect by now they've all *bonded* and are getting on like a house on fire, discussing the flora and fauna of Kazakhstan. And football! I bet they've heard of the Tartan Army, even in Kazakhstan.'

'I suppose you might be right. Let's hope so.' Marianne stands and rubs her aching back. 'Is it too early for a gin, do you think?'

'Darling, it's *never* too early for a gin,' Louisa says, scrambling off the bed. 'Go and put your feet up and I'll bring you one.'

Marianne

It's always a mistake to assume things can't get any worse. They did, in a thorough-going sort of way. Two of the men were released – the ones with wives and children – and I started to bleed.

Louisa called the doctor and insisted I retire to bed, even though I pointed out it had always been my intention to let nature take its course. But she was so upset about Keir remaining in captivity that I took to my bed to spare her and perhaps to spare myself. I felt pretty ill and if I was going to miscarry, this seemed like a really bad time to do it.

The bleeding stopped within twenty-four hours. I got up again and resumed my normal activities. After the first two men were released, a meeting was scheduled for the tenth of June, to take place on a yacht owned by a Kazakh government minister, since the green campaigners refused to come ashore. The oil company demanded that Keir be produced as a gesture of good faith, so he too was to be transported to the yacht in the dilapidated cruiser that had housed the men during their captivity.

This much we learned afterwards. After the explosion.

Reports said that as soon as the cruiser's engine started up, there was an explosion and the craft burst into flames. Burning debris and fuel were scattered over a wide area. An eyewitness said, 'It looked like the sea was on fire.' Two of the kidnappers survived, although one wasn't expected to live. One of them died and his body was recovered. Keir's body wasn't.

As we listened to the news, Louisa and Garth had the sense not to say anything, not to touch me. She started to cry quietly and I got to my feet, unsteady, dry-eyed, and switched off the radio. I left the sitting room and, closing the door behind me, went to my room. I kicked off my slippers and climbed into bed, fully clothed.

I lay quite still for some time, listening to the hum of evening traffic, the swish of tyres on wet tarmac, then I reached out towards my bedside table. My unerring fingers found the CD buttons and I pressed 'Play'. A solo flute meandered, sounding like a bird, then a real bird began to sing, a bird I would never hear in Edinburgh, perhaps never in Scotland. This was a bird – followed by another, then another – from the Arctic marshes of Finland, birds whose stark, cold song formed a bleak requiem for a man I had loved but never known and now would never know. I'd always meant to ask Keir the names of these birds. I'd known that he would know, that he would have made it his business to know, that he would rejoice in their names, their song, their habitat.

So much *life* ...

There were so many things I'd wanted to ask Keir, but there hadn't been time. Now I couldn't remember what I'd wanted to know about him, apart from everything. But I remembered one question and I remembered his answer. He'd sat on the edge of the bed and I'd laid my hand on his broad, naked back, felt the vibration of his ribcage as he'd told me of his vision ...

'I never knew what it meant, just that it was bad. Very bad. By the time I was in my teens, I sensed it was something that would happen, but I didn't know what, or where, or when.'

And I had asked, *'What did you see?'*

He said, *'I saw the sea ... and it was on fire.'*

220

There was fire now behind my eyes as tears refused to come; ice in my heart as the blood seemed to slow to a standstill in my veins. Then, with ludicrously inappropriate timing, Keir's baby kicked, then for good measure, kicked again.

And – as it always does – life went on.

Summer 2007

Chapter Nineteen

Louisa

Marianne's anger was terrible to behold. She seemed to solidify, to become a pillar of fury. I'd never seen anything like it, not even in the aftermath of Harvey's death. It was like having an unexploded bomb in the house. As she moved quietly around the flat, you could almost hear her ticking. I dreaded Garth or I would say something to set her off, but at the same time I knew this was what needed to happen. The poor girl was clearly in a bad way, in a state of suspended grief: cold, calm, at times almost inanimate, except that one sensed a raging torrent of emotion, arrested temporarily, like a frozen waterfall.

She took to sitting on our little balcony, apparently listening to the birds. Sometimes she would turn her face up to the summer sun. At her request Garth fixed up a bird-table and I bought some seed and hanging feeders. She asked particularly for some dried mealworms. I thought she'd taken leave of her senses. I hadn't the faintest idea where to look for such a thing, nor had she, but as usual, Garth came to the rescue. He looked them up on the internet and found you could buy them in garden centres.

Marianne would sit on the balcony, perfectly still, her arm extended and resting on a small wrought-iron table, her flat hand offering a small pile of mealworms. She sat patiently waiting for birds to come and feed. Eventually, after she'd sat like this for over an hour, one did. I happened to be looking out through the open French windows, keeping an eye on her, when I saw a robin descend and inspect the trail of worms she'd scattered on the table near her hand. Marianne's head was cocked on one side, just like the bird's. It looked as if they were listening to each other. I watched the robin eat up the scattered worms, then fly away. Marianne didn't move. The robin returned almost immediately, inspected the table for more worms and then her hand. He turned his head this way and that, then pecked briefly at the worms in her palm and flew away again.

Marianne had her back to me, so I couldn't see her face. I was uncertain whether to approach her or not. I thought she might be waiting for the robin to return again. Then I saw her shoulders start to shake. They were moving up and down, heaving, as she sobbed silently.

She didn't know I was there and I decided – I don't know why, call it instinct or sisterly feeling – that I wouldn't make my presence known to her, I would just stand guard while she finally gave vent to her grief. But as I stood there, witness to her pain, I heard a sort of clicking sound. I thought it might be the bird returned for more food. I took one careful, silent step towards the open window.

The noise came from Marianne. She was saying his name, or trying to, over and over again, in between convulsive, almost silent sobs: 'K-Keir … K-K-Keir … ' I clapped my hand to my mouth and, making no noise, fled before my grief could intrude on hers.

Marianne

Keir had taken my arm and led me out into the garden. 'I thought we'd try to get the robin to eat from your hand. Would you like that?'

'Oh, yes! Do you think he will?'

'Aye, he might. But a certain amount of subterfuge will be necessary. The bench is behind you. Sit down in the corner, by the armrest. Now hold out your hand.' He took my hand and sprinkled something into my palm.

'Is that bird seed?'

'Och, I was hoping you wouldn't ask. I'm afraid it's dried mealworms. But they're very dead. And robins love them. Close your hand up now. I'm going to sit beside you and put my arm round

226

you like this ... I'm going to extend my arm along the bench and I'll put yours on top ... like that. Relax. Lean on me. We're trying to look like one person. Comfortable? We could have a long wait, but it's a fine day for it. Now open your hand carefully. Keep it flat and sit very still.'

There was a sudden turbulent whistle at my ear and I jumped. 'Is that him already?' I whispered, barely moving my lips.

'No, that was me. Telling him lunch is served.' Keir's voice dropped to a whisper. 'Here he comes. He's checking us out. He knows something's up. Wheesht, now ...'

And Keir was silent. I sat quite still, feeling the slight rise and fall of his ribs at my back, otherwise he didn't move a muscle. After a minute or so he whispered into my ear, 'He's on my fingers ... Looking at yours ... Don't flinch when he lands.'

I felt a touch, no weight at all, just a pricking that jumped across my fingers, then my palm was tapped repeatedly by something sharp. The pecking wasn't painful, just unfamiliar. Instinctively I wanted to recoil, but steeled myself not to move. The robin fed from my hand for perhaps half a minute (in which I doubt I breathed), then he took off in a flurry of feathers. I felt a faint current of air move over my hand, disturbing the remaining mealworms.

After the robin had gone I sat leaning against Keir, my arm still resting on his, ensconced in my human armchair. It was several moments before I could speak. Eventually I said, 'He weighed *nothing*!'

'About eighteen grammes. The skeleton is very light. Has to be, to fly. Have you never held a bird before?'

'Never. Not even a budgie. Our mother didn't approve of pets. She thought they were unhygienic.'

'Och, he's back! And giving you the eye. Sit still now.'

I sat still, so very still, and time congealed, solidified into a moment I will never forget. If I'd been turned to stone then, I wouldn't have minded – frozen for ever in that instant, with Keir's breath in my ear, his scent in my nostrils, his limbs lying along the length of mine, and a robin dancing in the palm of my hand.

When we'd said goodbye in Edinburgh, on the doorstep where we first met, he said, 'Do you know the Gaelic blessing?'

'No, I don't think I do. Something about a road, I think?'

'Aye.' He took my hand and recited:

'May the road rise up to meet you.
May the wind be always at your back.
May the sun shine warm upon your face, the rains fall soft
upon your fields,
And until we meet again,
May God hold you in the palm of His hand.'

I felt the press of his lips on my palm, then he was gone.

The results of the amniocentesis came through the day after Keir died. It appeared that, as far as anyone could tell, I was going to give birth to a normal baby. My navel was fast disappearing, as was my waist. Bending had become difficult and I now felt most comfortable standing or walking. It was no longer possible for me to ignore my pregnancy, nor the baby himself. He made his presence felt by prodding me whenever I was horizontal.

I felt physically well and strong. Mentally and emotionally, I was in pieces.

At the end of a broken night, disturbed by vivid dreams of the Piper Alpha explosion and making love with Keir, I rose early, wrecked but resolved. In my hours of wakefulness I'd come to a decision, perhaps the most foolish yet, but I felt as certain as if a judgement had been handed to me on tablets of stone. (Perhaps I should say in letters of fire.) Nothing – but *nothing* – was going to dissuade me now and it would have been a brave man or woman who tried.

Fortunately, Louisa was a complete pushover.

'Lou, are you busy? Can I disturb you for a moment?'

'Please do. I'm just staring at the screen. Come in and sit down. How are you feeling?'

'I've been thinking about my future. And the baby's. And I've come to a decision. One which entails a drastic change of plan.'

'Oh?' Her voice quailed with hope but she said nothing more and waited for me to continue.

I sat in the armchair beside her desk and launched into the speech I'd prepared. 'I've decided to keep the baby. If by any chance you've changed your mind about your generous offer of support, I'm perfectly happy to go it alone. I realise Garth has become something of a fixture now and we've all moved on. But you needn't worry, I've thought it all through. I'll manage. I'd have to move, of course, but you can buy me out of the flat and I can rent or buy something small with the proceeds. And if you cared to spend some of your surplus film money on your nephew, hiring a part-time nanny for him would certainly make life easier for me. But I just wanted you to know ... that I've had a change of heart. Nothing and no one is going to part me from this child. Not now.'

I paused for breath and heard the sound of tissues being snatched by the handful from a box on the desk. There were spluttering sounds, then Louisa finally managed to speak. 'Marianne, I don't know what to say! I'm ... I'm overjoyed! And I won't hear of you going it alone! We're in this *together*. Let's get out of this pokey old flat and ... and spread our wings!'

She laughed and, perching on the arm of the chair, flung her arms round me. I let her hold me for a moment then, my voice surprisingly steady, I said, 'There's a gap in my life where Harvey should have been. And now there's a gap in my life where Keir should have been. I'm damned if there's going to be a gap in my life where a child should have been. So I'm keeping him. I'm going to keep Keir's son.'

'Good for you, darling!'

'I'm going to call him James. James Stewart.'

'Wonderful! James Stuart ... After the Kings?'

'No, after the actor. James Stewart played the man who saw a six-foot rabbit called Harvey. Keir bought you the DVD – don't you remember?'

'Oh! *Jimmy* Stewart! Yes, of course! Even better! And will he be James Stewart Fraser? Or James Stewart Harvey? Both sound equally splendid.'

'Harvey. I'd like him to have one of his father's names. But I can't bear to give him both.'

'No, of course not. Very understandable.' She squeezed me again and said, 'I'm so thrilled, you cannot *possibly* imagine! You know, I'd already been looking at larger properties, in a half-hearted sort of way. I thought it might be nice for us to have a big garden. After all, you get so much pleasure from trees and birds. Now we have the perfect excuse to go house-hunting! When you feel up to it,' she added hurriedly. 'I know it's much too soon to be thinking about things like that. But when you feel ready, we'll make a start. Oh, I can't wait to tell Garth! He'll be so thrilled! You can count on him being a *doting* surrogate uncle.'

'I'll be counting on you both. I'm so pleased the baby will have someone other than me to welcome him into the world.'

'Oh, you wait – we'll be quite the happy family! It will be just like an episode of *The Waltons*. Nauseating.'

'Lou, you *are* a dear. I'm so grateful. It won't be easy, I know, but I'm determined to make it work.'

'I'm sure you will, darling. Sheer bloody-mindedness can move mountains. And I've no doubt you'll be a *wonderful* mother.'

I got to my feet and rubbed my aching back. 'Being blind does have some advantages. I'll never have to see a resemblance between father and son.'

'No. You'll be spared that ... I suppose you might *hear* it one day.'

'Not for many years. Possibly never. My son won't grow up on Skye, so he'll never have his father's accent.'

'Would you have liked him to grow up on Skye?'

'I hadn't ever thought about it ... It's what Keir would have wanted, I suppose. He was always trying to think of a way he could go back there, for good. I think his heart never left the island, even when the rest of him did. He said he felt homesick as soon as he got to the other side of the bridge. Perhaps that's where he is now. In spirit. On Skye. At least, I like to think so ... '

'I'm taking you somewhere special now. Well, special to me. Can you guess where you are?'

'We've moved out of the wind ... and it's suddenly much warmer.'

'Aye.'

'The smells are different too. It reminds me of something ... Something quite familiar. A fuggy sort of smell. Earthy ... Oh, it's the glasshouses at the Botanics!'

There's a sudden gust of wind, followed by the flap and slap of plastic. Keir says, 'That was a big clue. And here's another.' He takes her hand and directs her fingertips.

'Oh! ... A forest of seedlings ... No, they're too sturdy. And too tall. These are saplings, aren't they?'

'Aye.'

'So this is your tree nursery ... Inside a polythene tunnel ... And the tunnel is open at both ends, I suspect. I didn't hear you open a door and I can feel a through-draught. It's wafting smells to me from outside ... the sea ... and wood smoke from the house. Am I right?'

'Och, you don't need seeing eyes, they'd be totally redundant! You have perfectly good eyes, they're just not in your sockets.'

'What are you growing here?'

'Native trees. Hazel. Birch. Holly. Oak.'

'How many?'

'Hundreds. A thousand maybe. At various stages of development. Outside I have stratified seed – under netting to protect them from mice. In here I've got seedlings and two year old saplings in pots, ready to go into the ground.'

'What happens when you're away? Don't they dry out?'

'I'm not usually away for more than a couple of weeks at a time and in here, out of the wind, they can fend for themselves for a while. There's a primitive self-watering system for the summer. The pots and trays stand on absorbent matting and there are wicks leading rainwater from reservoirs into the mats. It's a bit of a Heath Robinson set-up, but it works. I don't lose many. I lose more after they've gone into the ground and they get eaten. Deer love birch and holly saplings.'

'Whereabouts are you planting?'

'I'm filling in gaps and extending the woodland. And I give them away to anyone who wants them. We have remnants of old woodland round here but it needs regenerating. Hazel's not long-lived – only about sixty years. And oak propagation is a chancy, wasteful business. For every ten thousand acorns, only one will make it to a mature oak. So I'm trying to give nature a leg-up.'

Marianne fingers the tiny saplings. 'How long before these are tree-sized?'

'Those are hazel. They'll grow to about six metres in ten years.'

'So you'll be ... fifty-two before they're mature.'

He places a flower pot in her hands. 'That's an oak. When that reaches maturity, I'll have been dead for about eighty years. At least.'

'It's strange to think of doing something like that. Planting a tree, knowing you won't ever see it fully grown. Knowing it will outlive you.'

'Isn't that the point? I'm planting it *because* it will outlive me. This wee feller is my bid for immortality. Well, five hundred years maybe. That'll do me ... '

Marianne

To celebrate the results of the amniocentesis, Louisa suggested we go shopping for the baby. At first I said no, then I let her persuade me to leave the flat and go with her. I warned her we wouldn't be buying much. At twenty weeks I was now unlikely to miscarry but I wasn't prepared to tempt fate. Instead we did what Louisa referred to as 'reconnaissance', a kind and clever circumlocution for window-shopping. We did Mothercare, Marks & Spencers, Boots and Jenners, touching, stroking, exclaiming, Louisa almost squealing with delight and anticipation. She would hand me baby-gros and sleep-suits to feel, then describe them to me – not the colours, but the style of the garment or the fabric design.

'Oh, this one is just adorable! It's got a dear little pixie hood – here, can you feel? – and mittens that fold back on themselves. How clever! And it's got little teddies all over ... Oh, why don't they make these for adults? I'd wear one in winter, sitting at the PC. It would be so *cosy*.'

The thought of Louisa sitting at her computer dressed in a giant babygro with a pixie hood brought on a fit of giggles. Struggling to compose myself, I realised I was close to tears, perhaps close to the edge, and so very, very tired. But we carried on, stroking blankets, quilts, terry nappies and cuddly toys. At one point Louisa dropped a tiny pair of bootees into the palm of my hand.

232

'They feel like doll's clothes!'

'Of course they do. That's the size the baby will be. Only a lot heavier, of course. Come and smell the bath stuff.' She led me to another part of the shop, unscrewed the lid of something fragrant and held it under my nose. 'Isn't it delicious? That's baby lotion. We'll get through gallons of that. And this ...' She offered me something else to smell. 'That's bubble bath. Now let me show you this very clever contraption. It fits inside a plastic baby bath. You put the baby in *here* – there, can you feel? – and it sits up, supported, so your hands are more or less free. You can wash its hair in that position too. If it has any hair. Mostly they don't.'

'Babies have different coloured hair, don't they, like adults?'

'Oh, yes. But they're all born with blue eyes. The colour sometimes changes later.'

'Did you ever notice that Keir's eyes were different colours?'

'*Were* they? Did he tell you what colours they were?'

'He said one was blue and the other was green.'

'How extraordinary!' There was a hiatus in which I sensed Louisa's uneasiness. I worried that I'd spoiled the shopping trip for her, reminding her of what we were both trying hard to put out of our minds, at least temporarily, but she resumed cheerfully enough. 'The designs are just so clever nowadays. You won't have any trouble with a bath like this. The baby will be quite secure and once you get the hang of it, you'll be able to bath him on your own, quite confidently.'

'You really think so?'

'Oh, no question! You're by no means the first blind woman to give birth, darling. Garth and I have been researching online and there's all sorts of support groups now for parents with different disabilities – a lot of them visually impaired. We didn't tell you about them because you were so set on adoption, but I wanted to know the facts, know whether we'd be able to manage, if you *should* happen to change your mind.'

'You never gave up hoping, did you?'

'No, I didn't, because I never really believed you wanted to get rid of it, despite all the things you said.'

'And you really think we'll manage?'

She put an arm round what remained of my waist. 'Darling, we will do more than *manage*. We are going to have the time of our lives!'

I put our few baby purchases away in a cupboard, then working on the principle that the task would never get any easier, I decided to put away the few things I had that were mementoes of Keir. There was no question of getting rid of them, but I needed to put them somewhere where they wouldn't ambush me. (I'd been through all this before. I knew the score about death.)

I took the Rautavaara concerto out of the CD player and put it back in its Braille-labelled case. I filed it away on my music shelf, in between Rachmaninov and Ravel, where it would languish unplayed for a very long time, perhaps for ever.

There was the postcard Keir had sent Louisa from Skye. She'd found it weeks ago when tidying her desk and asked me if I wanted it. She told me it was a view of the Cuillin and I said I'd keep it, to show people where I'd been. I knew Louisa wasn't fooled, but she handed it over without a word.

Then there was the tape of the Northern Lights, the only recording I had of Keir's voice since I'd thrown away one of his audio-postcards and the other had been stolen along with my handbag. I couldn't imagine ever being able to listen to it again – it had reduced me to tears when he was alive – but it would be treasured and kept safe, if only so that his son might one day know what kind of man his father was. I put it away, together with the postcard, in the wooden box where I kept Harvey's audio-letters.

Finally there was the scarf. Keir's cashmere scarf that I'd stolen from Skye, then surreptitiously returned. I'd hoped he hadn't noticed its absence but, as Louisa once remarked, that man's eyes didn't miss much.

'Och, it's back! Like the swallows.'

'What's back?'

'My scarf. You needn't have bothered. You're welcome to it. You've probably more need of it in Edinburgh than I have here. It gets hellish cold there in the winter.'

'You're teasing me. I know I deserve it.'

'Why did you take it?'

'You know why. Or you can work it out.'

He takes the scarf down from the hook on the back of the door and holds it to his face. 'I can't smell anything.'

'That's because your sense of smell isn't very sensitive.'

'I'll have you know my sense of smell is *very* sensitive. I'm known for it. They used to send me below on the platforms, like a canary down the mine, to smell out leaking gas.'

'Well, maybe you can't smell anything because you're surrounded by it all the time.'

'Is it a good smell?'

'Well, *I* like it.'

'So tell me, when exactly did you ... *indulge*?'

She laughs. 'You're making it sound like a sex aid.'

'You mean it *wasn't*? Och, I'm disappointed! And here's me thinking you kept it in a bedside drawer, along with a vibrator and a copy of the *Kama Sutra*. In Braille.'

'I did keep it in a bedside drawer. And I used to take it out sometimes. When I missed you. I'd stroke it ... Inhale it. Smells are instant and total recall. It was as if you were in the room.'

'Did you sleep with it?'

'Sometimes,' she murmurs.

He folds the scarf slowly, then hands it to her. 'Keep it.'

'No, really, I shouldn't have taken it, it was very silly of me – '

'I want you to keep it.'

'Why?'

'In case of emergencies.'

Marianne

I folded the scarf, put it in a plastic bag and placed it on a shelf in my wardrobe, at the back with some things I never wore. As I sank on to the bed, exhausted, the phone rang. I waited for Louisa to answer it, then remembered she was at the hairdresser's. Hoping the caller would hang up before I got there, I got to my feet and slowly headed for the sitting room. I lifted the receiver.

'Hello?'

235

'Marianne?'

I slammed the phone down and stood shaking, willing my feet to move, to take me out of the room. Now I was hearing things, going mad. It was my hormones. Defective hearing. Just grief, bloody grief ...

The phone rang again and I jumped. I let it ring for a long time, then picked it up but didn't speak. The voice said, 'Marianne? It's me. Keir.' I swallowed a sob and clamped my hand over my mouth to stop myself screaming. The voice continued, 'Sorry I startled you. I gather I've been reported as dead. I'm not. Well, *obviously* ... So I wanted to let you know. I thought you might have seen the story. It was big news in Scotland, I gather ... Marianne, are you there?'

'*Keir?*'

'Aye.'

'You're *alive?*'

'Aye.'

'Where *are* you?'

'Still in Kazakhstan. Flying home tomorrow. I'm waiting on a new passport.'

'Keir, we thought you were dead!'

'Aye, I know. So did I at times. It's a long story.'

'But – the explosion ... How did you survive?'

'I saw it coming. Och, not like that! I mean, I had some warning. I could smell leaking fuel. Or maybe it was petrol vapour collecting in the bottom of the boat, I don't know, but it was seriously bad news. I tried to tell the guys we were in trouble but their English didn't run to leaking fuel tanks and since my hands were tied, my sign language wasn't exactly eloquent. So I hung around at the stern and threw myself overboard as they switched on the engine. I figured I'd rather drown than be blown to pieces. I kicked my way up to the surface and came up underneath an upturned dinghy – the one that had been attached to our rust-bucket.'

'You hid under the dinghy?'

'Aye. It was as good a place as any. There was air and I was protected from burning fuel and flying debris, so I stayed put. The only problem was keeping afloat with my hands tied. But if I stayed under the boat I could hold on to the seat. So I just drifted with the current. I reckon I must have drifted in and out of consciousness as well. But I came to every time I started drowning.'

'Did somebody find you?'

'Eventually. I heard a fishing boat so I ducked out from under the dinghy and started yelling. This old guy hauled me in with a boat-hook. I think he was poaching sturgeon – he had no lights – but I passed out before we could introduce ourselves. When I came round I was still tied up. I got the message he'd free me in exchange for my watch. So we put in at some godforsaken village and I shared a fish supper with his family. It was all very convivial considering we didn't have a common language. But things went downhill from there.'

'What happened?'

'Well, I was potentially in a lot of trouble because I had no ID. The kidnappers took all that, along with our phones and our money. So I had to find the nearest policeman, throw myself on his mercy and hand over the statutory bribe.'

'You had to bribe a *policeman*?'

'Oh aye, that's how the system works out here. Old Soviet habits die hard. Which is why I never travel without US dollars in a water-proof bag in my shoe.'

'Did he take you to the British embassy?'

'Did he, hell! He banged me up in a cell and that's where I stayed until I produced the rest of my dollars. *Then* I was allowed a phone call. And that was when I discovered I'd been dead for three days and was risen again, like Our Lord. It took me another day – and my signet ring – to contact someone who could go through my things and get some telephone numbers for me. Anyway, I'm thoroughly alive and coming home. Kazakhstan hasn't made a very favourable impression on me, I regret to say ... Can I see you? When I get back?'

The baby fluttered and I placed my hand instinctively on the bump. 'I'm not sure, Keir. I need time to think ... I thought you were *dead*.'

'Aye, I'm sorry. You should have heard the row my sister gave me. She said she thought she was going to lose the baby, she was that shocked.'

'Is she all right now?'

'Aye, she's fine right enough. The baby too. Can I give you her number? That's where I'll be when I get back. For a while anyway. I'll head off to Skye when I can. I'm on indefinite leave for now.' He paused, waiting, I suppose, for me to ask for the number. 'I know it's been a while but ... I'd really like to see you. I've thought about you a lot.' He paused again and the silence yawned between us.

'I need some time, Keir ... It's so much to take in. I'm so relieved you're alive, but ... a lot of water has passed under the bridge since April.'

'Aye, I know. And we said "no strings" ... Och well, no pressure. Goodbye, Marianne.'

'Keir! Don't hang up!'

'A guy's waiting to use the phone.'

'I just wanted to say ... You mean a very great deal to me, I realise that now ... But I think it's probably best we don't meet.'

'Is there someone new in your life?'

'No! ... Well, yes. Yes, there is actually ... He's called James.'

There was a long silence, so long, I wondered if we'd been cut off. Then, sounding almost jaunty, Keir said, 'OK. Thanks for being straight with me, I appreciate it. Take good care of yourself now. James is a lucky guy.' And he hung up before I could say goodbye.

Chapter Twenty

Louisa

Now don't get me wrong. I adore my sister, respect and admire her more than anyone else I know, but there are times – not many, but this was one of them – when I just want to slap her.

'You said *what*?'

'I said ... I thought it best we didn't meet.'

Louisa regards her sister, lying on the bed, her face pale; registers the damp contents of the waste paper bin and a screwed-up tissue on the floor where Marianne must have missed. Suppressing apoplexy, Louisa tries to sound calm. 'But, I don't understand. *Why* did you say that?'

'Because I don't want him to know I'm pregnant. The last time we saw each other we agreed we should both be free to pursue other relationships.'

'And has he?'

'I don't know, I didn't ask. It's really none of my business.'

'Oh, for goodness' sake, Marianne – the poor man nearly *died* and one of the first things he does is let *you* know he's alive. I think he's made his position pretty clear!'

'That doesn't alter the fact that I'm pregnant – *noticeably* pregnant now – and that it's his child. If I were still putting the baby up for adoption then perhaps I could have seen him. But I'm not, so it's out of the question. The reason I didn't tell him before was because I didn't want him to feel he had to take responsibility – moral, emotional or financial responsibility for this child.'

239

'But supposing he *wanted* to?'

'He's not going to get the opportunity,' Marianne says firmly. 'There's no way I'm going to meet him in this state, like some de-flowered virgin in a Victorian melodrama. I feel ludicrous enough as it is, pregnant at an age when some women are playing with their grandchildren.' She gropes on the bed for the box of tissues, takes one and blows her nose. 'I cannot and will not subject myself to anyone's pity, Lou. Nor am I prepared to exploit whatever scruples he might have about my coping on my own. You and I agreed we would manage. And we *will*. So can we please drop the subject?'

'But if you'd told him –'

Marianne sits up suddenly, her fists clenched. She raises them to the level of her face and brings them thudding down onto the mattress. 'It's *my* life, *my* body and *my* baby! And he's *my* bloody lover! Don't tell me what I should have done!' Her voice breaks and her mouth twists into a grimace of pain. 'I *know* what I should have done! And I should have done it a long time ago! But it's too late now.'

Louisa puts an arm round her and says, 'Darling, I'm so sorry. I'm only trying to help, really I am.'

Marianne lays her head on Louisa's shoulder. 'I know you are. I'm sorry ... There was a time – before I decided to keep the baby – when I could have told Keir. I *meant* to. I might have found out then how he felt about it. About being a father. About me. But I missed that opportunity. And for a perfectly good reason. He told me he was going to the other side of the world for three months. And *he* suggested we be free agents. I couldn't tell him then. And I can't tell him now.'

'But why not?' Louisa asks gently. 'What's the worst thing that can happen?'

'The worst thing that can happen is he will realise I wanted him to be part of my future ... and then walk away.'

'He might not.'

'Of course he would! He's forty-two. He's never married, never even been engaged as far as I know. He said his relation-ships with women are always casual and that's the way he likes it. His job prospects are poor, he doesn't have much money, he doesn't even own a proper house. He's a drifter, one of life's bachelors. Attractive. Kind. Intelligent. And irredeemably single.'

'But – that's not what I see!'

'You've met him twice, Lou.'

'That's not what I meant. The man you describe wouldn't have taken up with a blind woman in the first place. Far too much trouble. Nobody wanting a carefree life would pursue *you*, Marianne! Let's face it – you're not for cissies. And a man as shallow as you describe wouldn't have sent a postcard from Skye, just to let me know you were enjoying yourself. It's very odd. It's as if there are two Keirs – the one I've met and heard about, who seems – well, a total *hero*, and then there's the Keir *you* appear to know – typical male scumbag, out for what he can get. It just doesn't add up! Is there something you're not telling me?'

'Being interested in me as some sort of curiosity doesn't mean he'd want to settle down and have a family. Don't you see? This isn't about Keir and me, it's about the *baby*.'

Louisa is silent for a moment then, taking a deep breath, she says, 'You could still have the baby adopted, you know.'

'Oh, Lou, what did it cost you to suggest that? ... I did think about it. For about thirty seconds. No, it's easier to give up Keir than the baby. Can you imagine how I'd feel if I gave up my only child for adoption, then Keir buggered off after six months?'

'So keep the baby but try to keep Keir as well! Talk to him. You can't possibly know what he wants now. The poor man almost *died*. God knows, that would change your outlook on life, surely?'

'No, Keir and death are old mates. He's spent all his working life dodging earthquakes, explosions, terrorists. Now he's just missed being blown up. *And* drowned.'

'Oh ... I *see*!'

'What?'

'I see why you won't tell him. Why you won't even give him a chance.'

Marianne's brows contract with irritation. 'What on earth are you talking about?'

241

'You're afraid he'll die. *Really* die. You think if you allow yourself to love him, he'll go and die on you. Like Harvey.'

Marianne sits very still, her shoulders hunched. She bows her head and her loose hair falls forward, covering her face. 'Die. Or leave ... I can't do it, Lou. I won't be that needy. That vulnerable. Never again. I've lost so much already. I can't cope with losing any more. And I can't cope with any more *uncertainty*. I don't know if my baby will be normal. I don't know if he'll survive. I don't even know if I'll love him! But I do know that, whatever happens, I've got to be strong. I've got to feel certain I can cope. And I'm not certain of Keir. Just certain that I love him.'

'Oh, darling – are you?'

'Yes, I am now. When you believe someone's dead, you can't really kid yourself about what you felt for them. Grief makes you honest. Keir being "dead" forced me to admit what I felt. Now he's alive again, I can't deny that, I can't just pretend. Not to myself anyway. Nor to you.'

'But you'll deceive him?'

'Is it deceit? He didn't me ask if I loved him, just if I wanted to meet with him again. And I didn't. So I said no.'

'But if you were to change your mind –'

'No, there's no going back. I told him there was someone else.'

'Oh, Marianne – you *didn't*!'

'And I don't have a number for him any more. His mobile was taken in Kazakhstan. I wouldn't let him give me his sister's number. And I still don't know her name or address. So you see, I've burned all my boats.'

'How could you *lie* to him? After all he's been through!'

'I didn't lie.'

'You told him you had a new man!'

'No, I didn't. I said there was somebody new in my life. And there is. My son. That's changed everything.'

'You said that to be absolutely certain of putting him off!'

'I told you, I burned my boats. I set fire to them, then blew them out of the water.'

'Oh, why do you have to be so bloody *heroic*?'

'This is cowardice, Lou, not courage! For God's sake, see me for what I am.'

'I do. And so does Keir. And *I* think he loves you.'

'Maybe ... He'll get over it. And I'll get over him.'

'*Maybe*.'

'Yes, maybe. But I don't think I'd get over him leaving. Leaving *me*, perhaps, but leaving his son? Well, it's not something I'm prepared to risk. For the child's sake. So it's just you and me now. And the baby. Honestly, it's better that way.'

Louisa leans forward, strokes her sister's hair back from her face and kisses her on the cheek. 'You must do what feels right for you, darling. All I can say is, if Keir's so easily discouraged, he's not the man I take him for.'

'No, he'll be the man *I* take him for.'

'Well, we'll see, won't we?'

Louisa

I'm not one of life's pessimists and there was much to be thankful for. Keir was alive; Marianne was healthy and so, as far as we knew, was the baby; I was soon to become an aunt; I was Hollywood's darling (or rather my blood-sucking boys were) and I had the personal and professional support of Garth, on whose bony shoulder I could cry when things got too much for me.

You might say, life doesn't get a lot better than that. I had it all, all I could possibly have hoped for, for myself. But I wanted more. For Marianne. I did understand her scruples. Her arguments were morally and intellectually unassailable, apart from one thing. Well, two things. She loved Keir. And – I was convinced of it – Keir loved her.

My heart bled for them both but I couldn't see any way round it, so I buried myself in glossy estate agents' brochures for country houses and indulged in an orgy of book-buying: eighteenth century history and biographies, gardening manuals, books about childcare and children's fiction. When he saw my purchases, Garth pointed out that it would be quite a while before baby James was able to tackle Treasure Island *on his own and asked if there wasn't a board-book version? I took no notice and said I was going to have a library, a proper library with floor-to-*

ceiling shelves. No more stacking books in teetering piles on the floor of my study.

I didn't tell him or Marianne that I had even bigger plans. My mind was set on a kitchen garden – walled, ideally – and an orchard. And if the house we bought didn't come with one, I was going to plant one.

For James. For Marianne. For me.

For our little family.

I hadn't discussed the move with Garth but he must have known it was on the cards. The flat was overcrowded with the three of us and couldn't possibly accommodate a baby and all its para-phernalia. He had never moved in and still maintained his tiny bed-sit in a notorious part of Edinburgh, made famous by the novels of Ian Rankin, an area nothing would induce me to visit after dark, even though Garth assured me there were posters proclaiming, 'You are now entering Ian Rankin country' and that enterprising junkies now sold autographs to tourists and posed for photos.

Garth and I never discussed our relationship. (I tried to once. He just laughed and said, 'If it ain't broke, don't fix it.') We enjoyed ourselves in bed and there was never a cross word between us, so I didn't ask myself Where All This Was Leading. Nowhere, probably, but I'd been content to take it one day at a time until, that is, Marianne decided to keep the baby. As she said herself, that changed everything.

Garth must have thought so too. He asked me out to lunch and said he was buying. I knew this would mean Starbucks. As I felt in need of a quiet word with him, I suggested we go some-where quieter, my treat. I was a little disconcerted by his invitation but thought it unlikely Garth would have chosen Starbucks as a venue in which to dump me. I assumed he wanted to talk money – mine, his or Hollywood's. We'd ordered food and were settling into our gins when he announced, 'I'm chuckin' me PhD.'

'Oh, Garth! Why?'

'Lost interest. Seems pretty pointless, anyway. I don't want to be an academic an' what else could I 'ave done with it? Me supervisor's been on at me to come up with the goods an' I can't be arsed, frankly. I told 'er there'd been too many distractions lately. Big ones an' all. Babies ... Kidnaps ... Film deals. I told 'er my academic interests 'ad been superseded by real life.'

'I bet that didn't go down well.'

'You're right, it didn't. She told me to think carefully about me future an' I told 'er I already 'ad. I pointed out that thinkin' about the future was a very good way of not livin' in the present.'

'Very true. So do you have any alternative plans?'

'Well, I'm 'appy to continue workin' as your webmaster and researcher, if you want me to. But I've got meself a part-time job in Starbucks. As a barista.'

'A barrister? Don't you need a law degree for that?'

'Nah, a barista. I've got to learn 'ow to make fifty-seven varieties of coffee and serve it with a superior smile. It'll pay me rent – well, nearly – an' give me lots of thinkin' time.'

The waiter brought our starters and Garth tucked in. I eyed the bread basket, decided to be strong and pushed it towards Garth, saying, 'Whatever you're paying for that dreadful room, it's daylight robbery.'

'Daylight robbery's the speciality of the neighbour'ood.'

'Seriously, Garth, I do wish you'd move. When we say goodbye I never feel entirely confident I'll see you again. I dread opening the Scotsman one morning and reading about your premature and violent demise.'

'Sweet of you to worry, but there's no need. Anyone can see I'm not worth muggin'.'

'But we were mugged!'

'That was on your account. You shouldn't walk around rattlin' your jewellery.'

'Oh, don't remind me! I still have nightmares about it. That's one of the reasons I want to move.'

'Another bein' the baby?'

'Yes. Marianne and I have to move to something bigger, obviously. And we want a garden. I'd like a big garden, in fact. I'd like to grow vegetables. I think that would be very satisfying, don't you?'

'So you'd abandon Auld Reekie then?'

'Yes. I'm not prepared to spend a million acquiring six

245

bedrooms and a garden in Edinburgh, only to lie awake at night worrying about being burgled. I've always thought I needed the buzz of the city, the networking, the gossip, but actually I think what I'd really like to do is become a recluse.'

Garth nodded sagely and helped himself to another bread roll. 'You know, in terms of career development, that could be a smart move, especially if you're goin' to write a serious book. There's a lot of distractions in the city.'

'I know. And I'm just too accessible here. Fans know where to find me now. Some of them are very sweet but others are pretty cranky ... And it's not just my needs we have to consider. There's the baby to think of.'

'So where are you movin' to?'

'No idea. Before Keir came back from the dead I'd thought of heading for the west coast. Wester Ross perhaps. It's mild and property is so much cheaper than Edinburgh. You get a lot for your money. But now Keir's back on the scene – or rather, now he's not – I don't think that's an area Marianne will consider. Too close to Skye. But a milder climate does appeal. And somewhere safe to bring up a child. That's definitely a priority.'

'Well, I can still run your website from 'ere, obviously. You can go anywhere and still count on my services.'

I fixed him with a meaningful look. 'All of them?'

He arched auburn brows and grinned again. 'Well, I dunno what me Starbucks shifts will be, but I must get some weekends off. Providin' you don't move to Shetland, we should be able to carry on ... carryin' on.'

'And would that be what you wanted?'

'Yeah, it would. If that suits you.'

'Yes, it does. Although,' I said, leaning forward, 'what I would actually prefer would be for you to move in. With me and Marianne. I'd pay you a salary – a good one – for running my website, dealing with my correspondence and helping Marianne with the baby. She doesn't need a nanny really, she just needs practical help. Another pair of hands. Or rather eyes. I think a nanny might be wrong. She could undermine Marianne's confidence in herself as a mother. But if she had you and me to help out, well, it would be more like a family.' Garth laid down his *cutlery and went very silent. I chased some food around my plate, my appetite suddenly gone. 'Don't misunderstand me, I'm not trying to set up anything permanent. You'd have your own room and plenty of free time to pursue your own interests. Though if that included other women our arrangement would have to revert to business only. You could leave whenever you wanted, though a month's notice would obviously be useful, to give us time to find someone else to help Marianne.'*

'An' you'd want me to live in?'

'Yes. You see, I'll still have to go away for work now and again and even if Marianne could manage on her own, I'd feel happier if someone else was around, for the sake of the baby. Preferably a car-driver.' The waiter cleared away our plates and as soon as he was out of earshot, I continued, 'I know it's a big decision and you'll need some time to think about it. And no hard feelings if you decide it's not for you. Or I'm not for you. I'm fifty-one, Garth, and not quite the bird-brain I appear. I've had a wonderful time with you and would love it to continue, but if I thought about the future – your future – I'd have to say, leave me, get a life, find a woman your own age.'

Garth took a sip of his mineral water, then looked me in the eye. 'You know, I don't 'ave a lot of time for the future. I mean, I don't think that's 'ow anyone should run their life. Look at it this way: I could be dead next week. So could you. A muggin'. A coronary. A terrorist bomb. Look what nearly 'appened to Keir! That's why I'm 'appy just to take it one day at a time. Live in the moment, as the Buddhists say. So if it's all right with you – an' Marianne, of course – I think I'll tell Starbucks they need to find themselves another barista.'

I was so pleased, I'd helped myself to a piece of bread, buttered it and wolfed it down before I knew what I was doing. As the waiter deposited our main courses, Garth said to him, 'Would you bring us a bottle of champagne, please? Your best.' He looked back at me and said, 'This is on me. I insist.' He sat back and beamed. 'I've always wanted to do that! Order bubbly on the spur of the moment, just like that! Never 'ad much worth celebratin', though. It's been a Buck's Fizz sort of life up till now. Not much call for the Bollinger.'

247

'Oh, I think all that might be about to change. Hollywood calls. Who knows what doors might open for us?'

The wine waiter brought champagne and filled our glasses. Garth raised his with a flourish and said, 'To Marianne and the baby!'

I raised mine. 'To pastures new! And a big house in the country.'

'With an orchard.'

'And a secret garden!'

'An' 'ere's to us.'

'Yes, here's to us. Thank you, Garth. For everything. There's no doubt about it, you are an absolutely diamond geezer.'

Chapter Twenty-One

Louisa

The summer wore on and wore Marianne out. She took fewer walks and slept more. She was subdued, though someone who didn't know her recent history might have mistaken her for serene. Serene or resigned, it was hard to tell. She showed little animation except for matters concerning the baby. Her interest in house brochures was dutiful, though she seemed pleased Garth was to become part of the fixtures and fittings and agreed it would be good to have a man around the house. She liked the idea of a garden but showed more interest in flowers and vegetables than trees. I couldn't engage her on the subject of planting orchards or woodland and it was Garth who guessed why. I hastily dropped the subject.

Marianne drifted around the flat in flowing ethnic gowns, silent, like a ghost. She'd turned her nose up at the maternity-wear we'd found in the shops. She couldn't see what she looked like but could tell it didn't suit her – too short, too girlish, too many synthetic fibres. Nor was Marianne the type to slop around in over-sized T-shirts and tracksuit bottoms. She wanted cotton and linen, nothing that clung. Once she'd found a source of loose-fitting Indian dresses and kaftans, she seemed more at ease with her rapidly changing body.

She was nearing the end of her middle trimester now and blooming. Her hair was thick and lustrous and her flawless skin now lightly tanned. She'd filled out, but the extra flesh suited her. In her straw hat and a pretty cotton dress – full-length, gathered

Empire-line under her now opulent bust – she looked like some-thing out of Jane Austen. I thought she looked quite, quite beau-tiful and found myself wishing Keir could see her.

June became July, the month when Marianne paid her yearly visit to the Piper Alpha Memorial in Aberdeen. I thought she might give it a miss this year, what with the pregnancy, but no, every-thing was to be as usual, she wouldn't spare herself. So I booked bed and breakfast in the place we usually stayed and on the morning of the sixth I escorted her to Hazlehead Park, to the North Sea Rose Garden, where she would pay her respects to Harvey and his dead comrades. As was usually the case on that date, it was a fine, sunny morning and the air was full of the scent of roses. But death was on Marianne's mind. On Marianne's, and many others' in Aberdeen.

Marianne and Louisa stop at the entrance to the Rose Garden and, as is their custom, Louisa reads aloud the words on the plaque that describe the memorial to be found in the centre of the garden.

Piper Alpha Memorial

This commemorates the 167 men killed in the prime of life, on the 6th July 1988, at the Occidental oil platform, Piper Alpha, 120 miles offshore in the North Sea. Only 61 men were rescued from the platform.

On the south face of the Memorial plinth above the Celtic Cross the names of the 30 men with no resting place on shore are inscribed. A casket of unknown ashes is interred behind the Cross. On the east face of the plinth are inscribed the names of the 2 heroic crewmen of the Sandhaven *who made the supreme sacrifice for their fellow men.*

The tragedy was the World's worst off-shore disaster and led to a 188 day public enquiry and detailed report by Lord Cullen. Improvement in safety provisions for off-shore personnel was strongly recommended.

The families of those lost commissioned the Memorial which was designed and sculpted by Sue Jane Taylor at the Scottish Sculpture Workshop Lumsden, cast at High Wycombe and funded by private and public subscribers listed in the Memorial Book displayed in Aberdeen Art Gallery.

On 6th July 1991 the Memorial was unveiled by Her Majesty Queen Elizabeth the Queen Mother.

After a suitable pause Louisa turns to Marianne and says, 'Usual arrangements?'

'Yes. Come back in an hour and we'll go for coffee. Is that all right?'

'Of course. I'll have a stroll around the park and find a bench in the shade. I've got a book to read.'

'Before you go, would you take a look for me and see if any of the benches are already occupied.'

As Marianne shakes out her cane, Louisa pops her head round the hedge and surveys the almost empty garden. Her spirits are simultaneously uplifted and cast down by what she sees but, turning back to Marianne, her voice remains calm and matter-of-fact. 'There's an elderly woman standing beside the memorial. She has a stick too, so watch out for that. And there's a man sitting in the far left corner. Otherwise you have the place to yourself.'

'Thanks. I'll be all right now.'

'It's ten o' clock. I'll be back in an hour. Any problems, just give me a ring.'

Marianne

I have a set routine which I've followed since 1991, the year the Piper Alpha memorial was unveiled. The North Sea Rose Garden is square and laid out in a grid pattern. It's quite straightforward to follow a broad brick path from the entrance up to the memorial in the centre. That is what I do, have always done and did that day. I approached the memorial with my hand extended and found the smooth granite face of the plinth on which 167 names are engraved. (The lettering is gold, apparently.) I know exactly where to find Harvey's name. Next to each man's name is the age he was when he died. I ran my fingers over the incised words and numbers:

HARVEY FRASER 33

As I get older the shock of the relative youth of the dead men seems to increase. Talk to anyone in Aberdeen about Piper Alpha and eventually someone will say, 'They were so *young*.' Most of them were. Some were in their twenties. If you talk to women who lived through it, even women who weren't personally bereaved, you'll hear voices become choked with emotion, then fall silent and, twenty years on, they start to weep. I'm glad of it. It's fitting that people should. It shows the men are not forgotten.

The memorial has never been vandalised. Aberdonians are proud of that and cite this as yet another indication of how deeply people were affected. The scar on the city's psyche has scarcely faded and I doubt it will, not until everyone who was there on the night of 6 July, 1988 is dead.

I ran my fingertips over some of the other names, reading them. (I don't know if I read them or whether, after all these years, I simply remember what they say.) If I raise my arm above my head I can just reach the foot of one of the three figures representing oil workers. I touch a booted toe, as I always do and wish, as I always do, that I could run my hands over the bronze figures to read them, to get a sense of what I'm told is a striking group. But I have to content myself with touching a booted toe. At that point, I always think of Bill Barron, one of the survivors, who posed as a model for the sculptor and I wonder, as I always do, if, with the passing of the years, it gets easier or harder to live with the burden of having survived.

At that moment I thought of Keir. I tried to banish him from my mind but the baby chose that moment to do one of his slow cartwheels. I braced myself, one hand on the granite plinth, another on my bump, and waited for the discomfort to pass. I walked all the way round the four sides of the memorial and then headed back the way I'd come, pausing to smell some of the many roses in bloom. I ran my hand gently over the petals and felt some cascade through my fingers and fall to the ground. Repeating the movement, I caught a handful of petals this time. I opened my handbag and withdrew an envelope, placed the petals inside and put it back in my bag. These would be dried and added to a new bowl of pot-pourri in my bedroom, a ritual I performed every year.

I continued along the path, back towards the entrance to the garden, then turned sharp left. Moving on to the grass, I located a bench with my cane. To be certain I wasn't intruding, I said softly, 'Is this bench free?' There was no answer and so I sat down and collapsed my cane. I knew I was now facing the memorial. I hadn't heard anyone else enter the garden and I thought the elderly woman had left. Earlier I'd been aware of the tap of her shoes and stick as she walked along the path, but I thought I was probably alone now.

The garden has an open feel to it, yet paradoxically, with its walls and hedges, it feels something like a room. You are surrounded on four sides (and *I* sense that because I hear sounds from all four sides: birds in the hedge, leaves rifled by a breeze or tapped by raindrops) but there's also a sense of the garden-room being roofless, open to the sky, open to noises overhead, particularly helicopters, a sound no oil wife ever hears without a frisson of dread. There were no helicopters this morning, just the distant shrieks of peacocks and children happily lost in the maze.

I laid my hand on my bump in a gesture that had become habitual. I used to think I did it to calm the baby. Now I realised I did it to calm myself. I never felt alone now. Even when the baby wasn't moving, it was impossible for me to forget his existence since he impaired most of my movements and had brought about such changes in my body that I could honestly say I didn't recognise myself, didn't recognise my new shape or weight. There was so much *more* of me now. I extended further and I would literally bump into myself as my hand or arm collided with the baby or my enlarged breasts. Even my feet seemed to have got bigger. But I was used now to the baby's company, used to the idea of a watcher within. So it was relatively easy for me to distinguish that sensation from the one I was aware of now: being watched from *without*.

I sensed I wasn't alone. I sensed that not only was I not alone, I was being watched. With sensory hindsight, I registered that I'd felt watched for some time but had dismissed it as Harvey's presence in the garden. Sentimental nonsense, as he'd been suffocated, burned or blown to pieces – perhaps all three – out in the North Sea and his body never recovered. No part of Harvey was here, only his name.

I sat still, straining every sense, but heard nothing I could ascribe to a human being. But still I felt watched. I pressed my watch and it announced the time. Louisa wouldn't be back for another half-hour but someone else would enter the garden soon. Telling myself I was being foolish and jumpy, I settled back on my bench, turned my face up to the sun and inhaled the scent of roses.

I must have been thinking about Keir. That's why I could smell hawthorn blossom. There can't have been any in the garden, nor outside it. Hawthorn had finished flowering weeks ago, at the end of May. Dismissing this olfactory *déja vu*, I tried also to dismiss thoughts of Keir. I'd come to this place to remember my dead husband, not a discarded lover. But my rebellious thoughts were not so easily marshalled. When a robin started to sing from a high branch behind me, I felt myself plunge, as if from a great height, into despair. I was overwhelmed by a sense of loss so acute, it was like a physical pain. I fought back tears and took a deep breath. Hawthorn blossom again ... I stood up and snapped open my cane. I would leave the garden, which was making me morbid, ring Louisa and ask her to come and meet me outside.

As I walked away from the bench I knew with absolute certainty that the person who had been watching me was now at my back. I wheeled round and stood, sweeping the ground in front of me with my cane, straining to hear any sound. There was none. Then a voice – *his* voice – said, 'Well, is it mine? Or Jimmy's?'

'*Keir*?'

'Aye.'

I thought if I didn't try to move, my legs would probably continue to support me. Drawing myself up to my full height, I said, with all the dignity I could muster, 'It's yours.'

254

'You're sure now?'

'Perfectly. You're the only man I've slept with in three years.'

'Poor old Jim. What's he doing wrong?'

'Why are you here?'

'I wanted to see you. And I knew you'd be here. Today of all days.'

'But I made it clear I didn't want to see *you*.'

'You can't see me.'

'How long have you been here?'

'Since they opened the gates.'

'So you saw me arrive? You've been watching me all this time?'

'Not watching. Waiting. I wanted to give you time. I didn't want to intrude. You came to pay your respects to Harvey.'

'Not just Harvey. All of them. I come every year.'

'Aye, so do I, if I can.'

'I go through the same rituals every year. I feel Harvey's name and some of the others. And their ages.'

'Aye ... They were so bloody young.'

'Did you know any of them?'

'Aye. Some ... Marianne, why didn't you tell me about the baby?'

'Because I was going to get rid of it. It was just ... a *mistake*. And I was convinced I would miscarry anyway. Or the tests would show it was abnormal and I'd have to terminate the pregnancy. So I didn't tell you.'

'You didn't think I had a right to know?'

'No, I didn't. Louisa did, but I didn't. I came to Skye the second time intending to tell you I was pregnant and that I was going to have a termination. But then you said you were off to Kazakhstan ... And we agreed there were to be no strings ... So I didn't mention it.'

'But you didn't terminate the pregnancy.'

'No. As you see ... Would you mind if we sat down? This is proving to be rather a trying morning for me.'

I dreaded he would touch me, guide me back to the bench with his hand, but he didn't. I retraced my steps, found the bench with my cane and sat down at one end. Keir sat beside me, not touching, and I continued, 'I changed my mind. I couldn't bring

255

myself to get rid of it. I decided, if I didn't miscarry, I would have the baby adopted.'

'And is that what you're going to do?'

'No. I'm keeping it now.'

'Why?'

'Because you died. You died, Keir, and I thought I was damned if I was going to lose you *and* your baby.'

'Is that why you didn't want to see me? Because of the baby?'

'Yes. And because we'd more or less agreed there was no future in our relationship. You said you didn't do the future.'

'I said that?'

'Yes, you did.'

'*Shit* ...'

'Oh, don't worry about it. I knew what you meant. But it did make it very hard for me to come clean.'

'I'm sorry, Marianne.'

'Don't be. Louisa and Garth have been the most wonderful support. Lou is beside herself with excitement. Far more excited than me, in fact.'

'Aye, I can imagine.'

'I realise, now you know about the baby, you might want access of some kind. I think it would be nice if there was some sort of father-figure in the background, so I'm sure we can come to some arrangement. But I don't expect – or *want* – any financial support from you. Louisa is in a position to support us quite adequately and is deliriously happy to do so. Do you think you might want access to the child?'

After a long moment's silence, Keir said, 'No, I don't want access.'

'That's fine. Much simpler all round.'

'I want to marry you. I want us to be a family.'

I felt as if I'd been struck, as if all the air had been squeezed from my lungs. Gasping, I said, 'I *knew* you'd do that!'

'Do what?'

'That's why I didn't tell you!'

'What the hell are you talking about?'

'I knew you'd do the decent thing! Offer to marry me and give the baby a name – all that crappy romantic hero stuff!'

'It's not crappy, romantic hero stuff, it's what I bloody *want*! Jesus, Marianne – I'm currently unemployed, my job prospects not exactly rosy and my assets are negligible. D'you think I'd saddle myself with a blind wife – and for all I know a blind baby – if I wasn't heart and soul *in love* with you?'

'What?'

'You heard.'

The robin started to sing again, impossibly loud. I felt in my handbag for a handkerchief and, taking several deep breaths to calm myself, said, 'The baby won't be blind.'

'How d'you know?'

'Well, I don't, not for certain. But it's extremely unlikely. You'd have to be a carrier for LCA and that's a one in two hundred chance. I assume there's no incidence of blindness in your family?'

'No. Rather the reverse.'

'Sorry. That was rather tactless of me.'

'Hell, I don't think we have too many behavioural precedents here.' I heard him get up off the bench and make some sort of movement I couldn't place. 'Marianne, will you please marry me?'

'Keir, are you kneeling down?'

'Aye.'

'Don't be ridiculous. Get up!'

'Will you marry me, Marianne, and let me be a father to our child?'

'Get up! Romantic gestures are wasted on me. I can't see them.'

'You can hear them. Marry me.'

'*No.*'

'Why the hell not?'

'Because it would be a shotgun wedding! Because I'm blind and pregnant and you feel *obligated*.'

'I do not! I came here to ask you to marry me anyway.'

'You're lying.'

'I didn't know you were pregnant. But I came to Hazlehead Park hoping you would be here. *Knowing* you would. I wanted to ask you – beneath the memorial that commemorates your

257

husband's death – if you would do me the honour of becoming my wife.'

'I don't believe you.'

'O ye of little faith! Or in your case, none at all ... Hold out your hand. Your left.' I extended my hand and felt him slide a ring on to my third finger. 'The stone's an opal. It matches your eyes. Cloudy blue with fiery depths. Sparks leap from it. It's beautiful. And it's yours to keep, whatever. But I was hoping you'd accept it as an engagement ring.'

I examined the ring with my fingers and exclaimed, 'It fits.'

'Aye. Louisa measured another ring of yours and told me the size.'

'So *she* told you I was pregnant!'

'*No*! Christ, does pregnancy cause a rapid degeneration of brain cells? If Louisa had thought there was *any* chance I'd marry you, d'you think she'd have told me you were pregnant?' I heard him get up off the ground and the bench shuddered as he sat down again. 'Can you not see that a lot of guys would just do a runner and leave no forwarding address?'

'Lou knows you're not like that.'

'Maybe she does. But she wasn't taking any chances. She *didn't* tell me.'

'But ... you'll surely want to reconsider now. I mean, it's one thing taking on a blind wife – '

'Aye, and a crabbit one.'

'But to take on a baby as well –'

'This isn't just *any* baby. It's mine.'

'But where would we live? What would you *do*?'

'Details! Marry me.'

'You don't have to marry me. You can offer support without our being legally bound to each other.'

'Mrs Fraser, are you proposing we live in sin?'

'Yes, I suppose I was. Why, do you have a moral objection?'

I heard him whistle between his teeth. 'Och, I think my granny might have something to say about that. Especially if we did it on Skye. If word got round that Keir Harvey had a bidie-in, the shame of it would kill her. And that would be on my conscience.'

'You have a *granny*? On Skye?'

'Aye. She's a sprightly ninety-four. Sharp as a tack still, but she doesn't like company, otherwise I'd have taken you to meet her.'

'You don't have to tell her you're living in sin.'

'With a fallen woman. A fallen *English* woman ... She'd find out. She may be housebound but her spies are everywhere. Och, there'd be hell to pay.'

'So we have to get married to appease your ninety-four year old granny?'

'Aye, I think it best. Otherwise I'd have been pleased to take up your very generous offer.'

There was a long silence during which I heard some people enter the garden. They spoke in hushed voices and walked along the brick path, towards the memorial. As their footsteps receded, I said to Keir, 'I'll marry you on one condition.'

'Which is?'

'That you get married in full Highland dress.'

'But you won't be able to see me!'

'No, but Louisa will. And she would just adore to see you in full Highland rig. So would Granny, I imagine.'

'So if I meet this *bizarre* condition, you'll marry me?'

'If you insist.'

'I do. I insist on kissing you too, if you think the ghost of Harvey wouldn't object.'

I raised my hand to his face and touched the bones I knew and loved. 'He might. But my priorities are the living now, not the dead.' I ran my fingertips over his temple and across his short, sleek hair. Resting my hand on the back of his neck, I pulled his face down towards mine and kissed him. He put his arms around me and I suddenly felt small again. Keir held me, crushing me against his body till I feared for the baby. At length, resting my head on his chest, feeling his breath ruffle the hair on top of my head, I said, 'I won't be able to do all the things that sighted mothers do. I'll be able to do a lot – more than you'd think perhaps – but once the baby's toddling about ... Well, there will be problems.'

'Aye, I know. That's why I reckon it has to be a team effort.'

'And I may yet lose it. I'm very elderly in childbearing terms. And there could be some abnormality. I've had lots of tests and

259

they've all been negative, but there are still plenty of things they can't actually test for.'

'Marianne, when you walked into this garden, I could see straight away you were pregnant. I could have cut and run then. I'm here because I want to marry you, for better or worse. And because I want – I *need* – to be a father to that child. May I lay a hand on the baby?'

'Of course.'

He rested his enormous hand on the bump and I felt the warmth of his skin penetrate the thin fabric of my dress. 'Has it moved yet?' he asked, sounding awestruck.

'Oh, Lord, yes. I'm twenty-three weeks. It moves all the time ... There! Did you feel that?' He didn't answer, but I heard him swallow and, as I leaned against him, felt his chest rise and fall once, in a great sigh. I laid my hand on top of his. 'There's one thing I *do* know about this baby.'

'Something bad?'

'No. Its gender. It's a boy, Keir. If he makes it, you'll have a son. I'd decided to call him ... James.'

He laughed then, loud and delighted, and I felt the baby kick again. I sat up and laid my fingers on Keir's lips. 'Are you *really* in love with me? "Heart and soul"?'

'Aye, and blood and bone. And I've never said that to a woman before.'

'You called me crabbit earlier.'

'Aye, and so you are! You could pick a fight in an empty room. You'll make the poor wee bairn's life a misery if I don't look out for it.'

'Him.'

'*Him* ... James is a good name. My grandfather's name. Granny will approve.'

'Well, that's a load off my mind. Will she come to the wedding, do you think?'

'Not unless we have it on her doorstep.'

'Well, that would be quite appropriate. After all, we met on a doorstep. But even if we got married straight away, you'd still be for the high jump. She'd see I was six months gone.'

'We'll go and visit her seven months after the wedding and tell her you had an *enormous* premature baby.'

260

'Don't joke – with your genes, maybe I will.'

'Jimmy'll do just fine. He comes from good breeding stock – fire-proof, bomb-proof, water-proof. Indestructible, in fact ... Och, here comes my future sister-in-law now. My, but *she* looks happy!'

'That makes two of us.'

'*Three* of us ... No, make that four.'

'Four?'

'Wee Jimmy. D'you not think he's pleased?'

'Oh, yes. He's turning cartwheels. *Feel* ...'